CW00761894

THE TROPHY WIFE

VALERIE KEOGH

Boldwood

First published in Great Britain in 2023 by Boldwood Books Ltd.

Copyright © Valerie Keogh, 2023

Cover Design by Head Design Ltd

Cover Photography: Shutterstock

The moral right of Valerie Keogh to be identified as the author of this work has been asserted in accordance with the Copyright, Designs and Patents Act 1988.

All rights reserved. No part of this book may be reproduced in any form or by any electronic or mechanical means, including information storage and retrieval systems, without written permission from the author, except for the use of brief quotations in a book review.

This book is a work of fiction and, except in the case of historical fact, any resemblance to actual persons, living or dead, is purely coincidental.

Every effort has been made to obtain the necessary permissions with reference to copyright material, both illustrative and quoted. We apologise for any omissions in this respect and will be pleased to make the appropriate acknowledgements in any future edition.

A CIP catalogue record for this book is available from the British Library.

Paperback ISBN 978-1-80483-556-2

Large Print ISBN 978-1-80483-555-5

Hardback ISBN 978-1-80483-557-9

Ebook ISBN 978-1-80483-554-8

Kindle ISBN 978-1-80483-553-1

Audio CD ISBN 978-1-80483-562-3

MP3 CD ISBN 978-1-80483-561-6

Digital audio download ISBN 978-1-80483-558-6

Boldwood Books Ltd
23 Bowerdean Street
London SW6 3TN
www.boldwoodbooks.com

For Karen, Donnchadh and Maria, with love

PROLOGUE

If... it's such a big word. You hang your dreams, aspirations, hopes on it, then it topples over and pins you down, leaving you squirming like a worm. A sad word, full of regret for what might have been. A melancholic word hinting at missed opportunities, at wonderful lives almost lived.

A life like mine.

Day after day, hour after hour, I sit in my small hospital room going over the life I've led, the things I've done, the lies I've told and the one I've lived.

Desperately trying to understand exactly where it went wrong, to pinpoint the very moment: was it when I left home? When I met Adam? Or Jane?

Perhaps it was when I discovered the truth about my parents.

Maybe it was... not when I met the stunningly beautiful Ann... but the moment I decided she'd be the ideal wife. The cherry on top of a life that had seemed so perfect.

Maybe I'll never understand and will simply have to live with the truth – that thanks to me, three people died.

Lies, secrets, regrets, and loss... this life of mine.

1

I grew up in a dreary town filled with small minds and tiny expectations, where our grey terraced house blended in seamlessly with rows of the same. But worse than having tiny expectations was my parents' pride in the fact.

'We've got no pretensions to be anything other than what you see,' my father would tell people if they enquired about plans for the future. Some people escaped, moved to bigger homes in better towns. Others stayed and extended, building out into the long back garden or up into the attic. They prettified the drab post-war build and gave their home some character, some expression. 'Ideas above their station,' my father would remark, and my mother would nod silently.

I'd applied for a scholarship to the University of Oxford without consulting them, forging their names where needed without compunction, never really believing there was a chance. But then my A-level results surpassed my expectations and I thought, *maybe*.

When the letter came, my mother handed it to me with raised eyebrows but no questions. I stuck it in my jeans pocket and waited an interminable few minutes before leaving the kitchen and heading to my room. My heart thumping, almost painfully, I prayed to any god who would listen and pulled the letter out. Held tightly in my none-too-clean hands, I stood there, staring at it, my grubby thumb brushing over the letters of my name, leaving a smear of dirt over the *Mr Jake Mitchell* printed in bold typescript. Finally, with clumsy fingers, I tore it open and pulled out the thick creamy paper that lay inside. I read it slowly, stunned to learn I had been awarded a full scholarship. Unbelievable, life-giving words of hope and promise.

I held the letter to my chest, pressing it there, wrapping my arms around it, as if it were a child I needed to protect. Holding it out now and then, ever so carefully, to read again. And with each reading, long-held dreams suddenly became attainable, my future filling with countless unimaginable possibilities. Because now I truly felt that anything could happen.

It was two days before I told my parents. Two days, while I read and reread and shivered with innocent pleasurable anticipation, putting off the telling because I knew it would result in derision, even ridicule, knew my father would see it as *an idea way above my station*. And in those two days of reading and rereading, I suppose there was a little part of me, festering deep inside, which agreed with him, and when that part came to the surface, I took out the letter and was tempted to tear it up, to settle for what I was supposed to, to stop my stupid dreaming. Then I would read the letter again, and think... why not?

Mealtimes in our house were generally the best times to broach anything contentious. We sat around a small table in the kitchen, my parents' necks craning to watch the television that sat on a shelf slightly too high for comfort.

My father would watch anything, but he especially loved programmes where he could show off his moral superiority. That night it was *Escape to the Country*, a favourite of his; he'd sneer at the couple who were trying to find a country home, pass comment on their accents, their clothes, their aspirations, would thump his hand on the table and wave his fork at the television when presented with the presenter's choice of country house. This episode, the house in question was a beautiful, thatched cottage overlooking a river near the Cornish city of Truro.

'Rats,' he said, startling my mother, who was in the middle of dishing up the cottage pie she had cooked at least twice a week, every week, for as long as I could remember.

She spun around, spoon-hand wavering, globs of watery potatoes dropping onto the floor. 'Where?'

My father chucked his head toward the television. 'Cornwall. Rats in the thatch, rats in the river. Wouldn't buy that bloody house!'

'I'm going to Oxford.' My bald statement interrupted my father's diatribe on Cornwall and rats. It drew a glare from one set of eyes, and a blank look from the other.

'What are you on about? It's Cornwall, that, not Oxford.'

What? I looked at my father, momentarily confused, but his eyes had already returned to the television. 'No,' I said, my voice loud, drawing their eyes, their faces, their giraffe-like necks toward me.

'IappliedforascholarshiptoOxford.I'vebeenaccepted.I'mgoing-toreadbusinessstudiesandeconomics.' It all came on a whoosh of breath, incomprehensible even to my ears. I looked down at the congealing mess on my plate, focused on it, afraid to look up and see what would be written clearly across their faces.

'What?' My mother's voice, puzzled.

Looking up, I caught her frown, met her eyes. 'I applied for a scholarship to Oxford. I've been accepted. I'm going to read business studies and economics.'

She looked blankly at me, swallowed. 'Oxford?'

'Nonsense,' my father said, shoving a forkful of food into his mouth, continuing to speak around it. 'I've talked to the boss. There is a place coming up at the factory, now that that fat, lazy bastard Sam has been given his marching orders. He told me any son of mine would be sure to get the job.'

Yes. Of course, they would say that. My father was fourteen when he started in the factory, working up from sweeping floors to a mind-numbingly boring job on the assembly line where he still worked. He suffered from a total drought of desire. Had never gone on strike, never made demands. Had no ambition, in fact, to be anything more than he was, and no ambition for *me* but to be what *he* was. An endless cycle of boredom. A perpetuation of a species that shouldn't. Survival of the grimmest.

A place in the factory… a life like theirs, every spark crushed by dull grinding monotony. I wanted more and was determined to get it. No matter what I had to do.

2

My mother, her mouth full, mangled cottage pie on view with each word, had little to contribute. 'Stop staring into space and eat your dinner.' Only after several minutes did she shake her head and mutter 'Oxford' under her breath as if I'd said I wanted to go to the moon.

'We should go to Cornwall,' my father said, as if I had never spoken.

She nodded. 'That'd be nice.'

I knew they'd never go. *They* knew they'd never go. The aspiration was as far as they got. Sometimes they got as far as going into a travel agent and having a look at brochures, having a chat with the friendly agent who would try to steer them towards the better parts of wherever they were enquiring about. A fool's game. They were never interested in anywhere but the cheapest bed and breakfast, in the cheapest part of the cheapest place. And when they had all the information and brochures, they would stand up, say they'd have to think about it, and head off. The brochures would sit on a shelf and gather dust for months before eventually being used as paper to light the fire.

Had my mother always been this way? I looked closely at this woman who had borne only one child, who had accepted the future mapped out for that child without question or comment. Had there been a time when she felt the stir of a breeze through an open door and wanted to run, get away from the dull plodding of her life? Had marriage to my father numbed her brain? I desperately wanted to believe that, at some time, one of my parents had had a dream, wanted to believe that in the genes, in the DNA I inherited from them, the seed of that dream existed, and all I had to do was get to Oxford and it would grow and my life would begin.

My mother cleared her throat. 'There's grey mould on the begonia outside the front door.' She spoke as if my father's words on Oxford were final and the subject was a closed chapter.

'Botrytis,' my father said knowledgeably. 'That's what that is. You'd better pull it up, get rid of it before it spreads and covers the lot.' He scraped the last of his dinner with the flat of his knife and licked it clean. 'It might already be too late; the whole lot might be grey by the morning.'

I wanted to talk about Oxford, the opportunities it would give me, instead I was forced to listen to my father's monologue on mould, while my mother strained to listen to an episode of *Coronation Street* flickering on the TV above our heads. The sheer mundanity of it all chilled me. This was the life they wished for me?

My father's voice echoed in my ears as I escaped to my room. *There's a place coming up in the factory.*

I sat on my bed in the dark until I heard the usual muttered goodnight as my parents passed on their way to the room they had shared all their married life. I pictured them, he in his worn pyjamas, she in her flannelette nightdress, climbing into bed, falling, without choice, into the hollow that years together had made.

And I thought, with horror, of the begonia lurking outside the front door. Would the grey mould creep over us during the night? Spores shooting into our bodies, infesting us, turning us all into a sea of grey slime. Would I wake in the morning and fall in line with my father's wishes, take the job in the factory, marry a local girl, make our own hollow in which to curl up every night?

And on and on it would go. Grey, endless. Sitting on my bed in the cold darkness, I shivered.

Their choice, their future. It wasn't going to be mine.

Faint mutterings drifting from next door faded quickly, and then there was silence and darkness and all my thoughts raced around. Oxford, and factory jobs, and creeping grey mould. They grew more worrisome, prodded my poor brain. I parried but it was no good, they multiplied, jumped around, the cut and thrust making my head spin. Amongst all the thoughts, all the ideas that spun, only one stood out. Escape. It shouted through the turmoil, fighting to be heard. At last, I did hear, and there was no further consideration. An old holdall, stuffed untidily in the bottom of the wardrobe, was dragged into service, crammed full of things I might need in the future, paperwork, clothes, stuff, all squashed into the too-small bag with little care, and even less selectiveness, unpacking later to find I'd brought seven pairs of socks but no underpants.

Finally, it was done. There was no moment of hesitation, no lingering last look at the room that had been mine all my short life, no regretful glance at my parents' bedroom door as I closed mine quietly and moved carefully down the stairs that told their age with a squeaky fifth and seventh step. I'd learned to avoid these on the rare times hunger drove me to raid the poorly stocked kitchen cupboards, raids my mother never acknowledged and my father probably wasn't aware of, not being a man who would have let such a thing go without comment.

The memory of my mother's consideration should have caused a twinge of regret but if it did, the twinge was buried way below the one word that still shrieked loud and shrilly in my brain. Escape. I was moving on instinct, pumping with adrenaline. Determined to get away from the creeping greyness that was waiting, slyly but equally determined, just out of sight.

The front door closed behind me with a soft but solid clunk. It was a cell door. But I was on the right side of it, freedom, escape was mine. Giving the mouldy begonias a wide berth, I stepped over the low garden gate, and headed down the street without a backward glance.

3

Nervous anger kept me walking for hours, no destination in mind, just a desperate need to get as far away as possible from a greyness that had become a big ravenous animal, teeth snapping at my heels, long hands reaching for my shirttails, almost catching hold, forcing me to walk faster and faster so that I was soon out of breath. And then it happened. The hand of fate? Destiny? Whatever? The late-night Bristol bus stopped to let someone off and its open door beckoned to me like a saviour. On I got, still with no plan in mind, but happy to be speeding away from all I was leaving behind, drifting along wherever the wind, or in this case the bus, took me.

Bristol was an almost unknown entity. Only ten miles from the small town where I grew up, it might as well have been a hundred for all the interest my parents, or my small circle of friends, ever showed. They were happily provincial, I was too busy studying, planning, waiting, to be interested. Even if I had been, there was no money. The couple of pounds I was reluctantly given each week didn't stretch far.

'Get yourself a job,' my father had shouted at me, the one time I had asked for extra.

But jobs were scarce, and those that were available demanded more hours than it was possible for me to give, focused as I was on the scholarship I had heard about in a first-year careers lecture.

'There is very stiff competition,' the careers adviser had warned me when I asked about the possibility. 'You will need to apply yourself one hundred per cent.'

And from then on, that's exactly what I did.

So, Bristol was virtually an unknown. There'd been a school visit years before to some barely remembered museum. And we'd changed trains once in Temple Meads on the way to a football game. That was it. But I was too jazzed with adrenaline to be concerned. It wasn't late, so the city was still busy, lights, people, traffic. No idea where to go, I wandered around for what seemed like hours but probably wasn't, before deciding it would be wise to find somewhere to bed down for the night. What little cash I'd taken with me was needed for food. There was probably a hostel or maybe a homeless shelter, but neither appealed, so I searched for a likely doorway to settle into.

My jeans and light jacket wouldn't give me much protection from the cold, hard pavement but, luckily for me, it was July and temperatures had been in the early twenties for days. Still, the night would be cool, and the pavement definitely hard. I found a sheltered doorway that wasn't already occupied and snuggled around my possessions for the night, disturbed only by another homeless man with bad teeth and foul breath who asked if I had anything to cheer him up.

I had a fairly clear idea he didn't mean a joke or funny anecdote, and was wise enough not to attempt either. 'I've only some clothes,' I said truthfully, patting my bag, my money safely tucked into my jeans pocket. He looked as if he didn't believe me, eyed me and my bag suspiciously, moving closer, hovering over me, noxious breath coming hot and heavy. The door behind blocked my escape. Adrenaline pumped, my heart raced but there was no time to wonder who would win in a punch-up, the fit young man or the street-savvy drunk, because, just then, he was hailed by another Bristol reprobate. With a growl of something completely unintelligible, he staggered off.

My eyes followed them till they were out of sight. 'I'd have taken him,' I muttered bravely under my breath, refusing to acknowledge the truth that street-savvy will win out every time.

4

Morning brought grey skies that threatened rain. I unrolled painfully, wincing as I stood, pins and needles making movement slow. I'd slept longer than I had expected to and already the streets were busy with people who had somewhere to go.

Somewhere to go.

Looking down at my recently vacated lodging, I decided another night on a doorstep mightn't be so much fun. Anyway, there wasn't much point in hanging around Bristol. I didn't know anybody, and it was a bit too close to home. For a moment, thinking of the safety of home, the comfort of the known, I wondered if this was all a colossal mistake. Then I remembered that creeping grey mould and my backbone straightened.

A gnawing hunger wasn't conducive to deep thought or big plans. Looking around, a familiar logo caught my eye, and feeling more cheerful, I crossed the street and pushed open the door into warmth and the glorious smell of food. A Big Mac and Coke later, things looked rosier. And felt so much warmer.

It came to me then; it was simple, really. Hadn't I been accepted at Oxford? Shouldn't I head there? Months too early, of course. And I didn't know anybody there. But what I'd do when I got there was a problem that could wait until I did.

It wasn't far to Temple Meads train station. I joined a quickly moving queue at the ticket desk, and then it was my turn. 'A single to Oxford,' I said with unnecessary emphasis on the single.

The teller tapped a few keys. 'Twenty-one pound fifty.'

'Isn't there a cheaper ticket?' I asked, my fingers feeling the small amount of cash in my pocket.

'You want to go today?'

I nodded.

'Then that's the cheapest.' He looked pointedly at the queue that was building behind me. 'You want it or not?'

A moment's hesitation, then I shrugged and counted out the coins, unfolded the notes and handed over the money, returning the meagre remaining funds to my pocket.

I managed to get a seat beside a window and sank into it with a sigh of relief-laced happiness that lasted until the earlier Coke started sloshing around, pleading for release. Too afraid to move, I sat uncomfortably until the train stopped in Oxford an hour and forty-five minutes later. So it was that my first act in Oxford was to have a piss. It could only get better, I thought, washing my hands like a well-brought-up young man, only to discover that the hand-dryers were out of order, leaving me standing there, feeling foolish, hands dripping into little puddles at my feet. What could I do but laugh? Things *would* get better.

And they did. It would be more dramatic if I had a story to tell of hardships endured and challenges overcome, but truth was I landed on my feet.

5

Not knowing where else to go, and curious to see *my* college, I made my way down George Street onto Broad Street, and there it was. Balliol College. Stretching as far as I could see. Huge and daunting. And glorious. Breath I didn't know I was holding came out in a long sigh. My God! *I* was going to study *here*?

Wandering around, mouth once more agape, eyes on stalks, I happened upon the admissions office. It was two months before my lectures began but... well, they might have some idea what I should do... freedom and excitement were all very well and might fill my soul but not my belly. It was growling painfully.

I stood at the partially open doorway of the admissions office, my hand raised to knock, when I was stopped by a voice from within.

'Australia!' the deep voice announced loudly, loathing in each drawn-out syllable.

I stood, my hand raised, not sure whether to knock or run, looking over my shoulder to see if my exit was clear.

Somebody else inside the office was obviously as puzzled as I by the one-word condemnation; I heard a soft murmur before the deep voice continued.

'The damn gardener! Gone off to Australia. Left me in the lurch. Grass a foot high. Wife shouting at me to cut it. Me!'

Whatever the soft murmur replied didn't gather favour.

'Absolutely not. He'd charge me a fortune. I don't need a horti-culturist, just someone to cut the damn grass, do a bit of weeding, plant a few blasted bulbs.'

It couldn't be that easy, could it? I rapped my knuckles smartly on the door, pushed it ahead of me, and peered around its edge into the room.

Deep voice was pacing up and down, muttering about the iniquities of gardeners, so I turned to the owner of the soft murmur, a middle-aged blonde seated with fingers poised on a keyboard. How long she had been this way, I have no idea, but the computer screen before her had shut down.

She raised an eyebrow at me as I approached her desk. It wasn't a particularly friendly eyebrow, but neither was it dismissive, and the hunger pangs were such that I took heart from little.

'I'm sorry to bother you,' I said, having decided humility was the best approach. 'I've just arrived in Oxford. I don't know the area or the college and wondered if there was, maybe, somewhere where jobs were advertised.'

She looked me up and down, gave a small shrug and then, raising her voice slightly, she addressed deep voice. 'You might want to listen to this young man, Professor James.'

Deep voice thus identified, I turned to him. He looked at me with the reluctance of a man who has to deal with my type all year and doesn't see why he should have to do so out of term-time.

'I have some gardening experience, and I'm looking for a job.' If my eavesdropping bothered him, so be it, but hunger was bothering me more. I pushed back my shoulders, increased my stance, tried to look reliable and outdoorsy.

Professor James was a small man, neatly dressed in a tweed jacket, check shirt and an incongruously floppy bow tie, a mix of dapper and flamboyant that was, I discovered later, his trademark. 'One must have one,' he explained, 'especially if, like me, one is short and uninteresting to look at.'

'Define *some*?' he said then, moving to stand in front of me.

A moment's panic... then I remembered helping my mother in the garden, of conversations she and my father had had, endless boring conversations about this plant or that. All the accidentally absorbed knowledge that I didn't know I had and never thought I would need... it all came back, and I spat it out. 'I know how to use a lawnmower, know about feeding lawns with high-nitrogen feed. Know how to weed out daisies, dandelions, buttercup and bindweed, and what to do if I see botrytis and mildew. I can dig a border and keep the edges clean.' I threw in a few more remembered words, but I think I had him on the high-nitrogen feed.

'You a student here?'

'I start in October.' I then added, with a great deal of pride, 'I'm reading business studies and economics.'

'Where are you staying?'

I shrugged.

'You don't have accommodation yet?' His eyebrows rose and joined, the unibrow a giant hairy caterpillar that bobbed up and down as if to condemn the irresponsibility of students.

'I've only just arrived,' I muttered defensively.

He took a step backward, then another, the better to see the full height of me. He looked me up and down, shook his head from side to side, considering, then nodded as if to a decision made.

'There is a room over what used to be a stable. It's nothing fancy but you can have that, if you want, as part of your wages. The gardener has left it in a bit of a state, but I daresay you can tidy it up enough.'

And that was that.

I went with him there and then, sat in the back of an incredibly dirty four-by-four that bore a strong smell of horse with a hint of dog. It was a smell that stayed with me for hours after he had left me at the stable until I pulled off my trousers that night and realised I had sat on what looked like horseshit but might have been dog shit and could have been shit from any animal under the sun, including human. I just knew, without a doubt, it was shit. And then it dawned on me. It didn't matter. I could stink all day, every day, and no one would criticise, no one would care. The euphoric freedom lasted long after the realisation that if I wanted the shit washed off, I would have to do it myself. I could have descended into squalor. Let myself go completely. But the indefinable air of Oxford had already filled my pores. I had found my milieu. This was where I wanted to be.

It was a good start. I had fallen on my feet, and I knew it. The professor's house, an early twentieth-century monstrosity surrounded by tall trees and high hedges, was less than two miles from the university. It was set on a couple of acres of land but much of that was given over to a paddock where the Jameses kept horses. The gardens were small in comparison, deep flower beds which bloomed despite my inadequate ministrations, and a rolling lawn that stayed green thanks to a generous sprinkling of lawn-feed twice a year. Neither the professor nor his wife were at all fussy; verdant grass and some form of colour in the beds were all they asked of me. I tried to give them what they wanted, and when the flowers didn't perform, I raided charity shops for artificial blooms and stuck them here and there among the greenery. I don't know that the Jameses ever noticed.

For my whole time in Oxford, I lived in that not-too-shabby-at-all room over the stable and kept the professor's garden in fairly good order. Only when the bindweed flowered, those virginal white trumpets that declared my failure at weed control, did he remonstrate, and even then it was a mild, 'Do attend to the weeds, dear boy!'

And I would go and grab the blasted stuff and pull it off the plants it had wound itself around. I'd dig it up and think I had it all, then see another white bloom and follow its sinuous body to the ground and dig some more.

You see, my knowledge was limited then. I wasn't aware how insidious bindweed was and that the worst thing to do was to dig and try to pull it up. I didn't know that its roots broke into little pieces and from every little piece another plant grew, each one sturdier and more vigorous than the last.

I didn't know, in my enthusiastic youth, that every little action, choice and deed could have significance, that decisions we made could stay with us and we rarely had the opportunity to go back and undo the poor ones we made.

Nor did I realise that one of my actions had already had consequences, ones I wouldn't discover for many years.

6

By the time lectures started, I had come to think of myself as having always lived in Oxford, choosing to forget a past not, in my estimation, worth remembering. In those two months, I had changed considerably. Physical exercise, the daily digging and mowing, built muscle where there had been none; the sun and wind lightened my hair and tanned my skin. I had always been considered a good-looking boy, but I knew, looking into the cracked mirror over the wash-handbasin in the tiny bathroom, that I was turning into a handsome man.

My parents were dim shadowy figures who became more insubstantial with every month that passed. I had written to tell them I was safe, a brief note saying I would be in contact again in the future – but I never gave them my address, never phoned, never visited. They might have guessed I had come to Oxford but if they had, they made no inquiries about me, never tried to look me up. The feeling of abandonment was verging on dog-in-the-mangerish and I shrugged it off, told myself I didn't care, that they obviously didn't either, were probably better off without me, as I was without them.

* * *

I met Adam at a party in somebody's house. No idea whose. It was like that, you'd be in the pub for a pint, someone would mention a party and you'd follow someone, or someone who knew someone, and end up somewhere. It never mattered, and usually it was fun.

But the night I met Adam, it was dire.

'It's a byob job.' The whisper came back down the line from the front door of the house we had landed at, and the group dispersed faster than freebie food from a sponsored event, apart from the uninitiated who had no idea what *byob* meant. I looked at the backs of those in the know, watched them scuttle away, resisting the temptation to grab one of them and shout *what, what is it, tell me*! Afraid I would sound as pathetic as I felt. Within seconds, there was me and one other standing on that seedy doorstep. I looked at him and he shrugged and said, 'Come on, let's go in. It can't be that bad, can it?' He pushed the door open and went in. I followed.

It was worse than bad. A dingy room, filled with smoke where the initiated held fast to their bottles of beer, standing with legs akimbo over the remainder of their supply, guarding it against all and any takers. There were a few girls drinking wine, passing a bottle from one to the other, wine trickling down their necks and staining their clothes. I tried to look nonchalant, knew I looked anything but, my eyes opening wide at the cigarette that was being passed from hand to hand, mouth to mouth, the sweet smell filling the room. I was green, but not stupid, but it was my first encounter with drugs of any kind, and I was simultaneously fascinated and shocked. My ribs were nudged, none too gently, by the guy who'd come in with me.

'Do you think we should just, maybe, run away?' I said to him out of the corner of my mouth, hoping to look movie-cool rather than cartoon-silly.

He chuckled, drawing suspicious looks from drug-glazed eyes. 'Well, maybe not run, precisely!'

We backed out in tandem, trying to look as if we had accidentally wandered into the wrong place, giving a careless wave before almost falling out the door. And then we did run, up the street, around the corner, kept running until we were both out of breath, and then we collapsed, laughing, panting.

'Okay,' I said, trying to catch my breath, 'first thing tomorrow, I am going to find out what the hell byob means.'

'Bring your own bottle,' the guy panting beside me squeezed out at last.

'You knew? Why did you go in then?'

'Sometimes there's spare booze anyway, they just say it's byob to put people off.'

'Not tonight. They had a tight hold on their beers.'

'Tight-fisted gits,' he said without any rancour. 'Come on, let's go find a pub.'

I shook my head. 'No, thanks, I have to get back. Early lectures tomorrow.'

He shrugged. 'Me too. Let's just have one. I'm Adam, by the way, Adam Brett.'

We'd little in common, Adam and I, but in the way these things often go, we liked each other, gelled in some way that defied explanation. He was posh public school with the accent to go with it, I was local comprehensive, rough and ignorant about so many things he took for granted.

He was lazy, did the minimum to get by, with the least amount of expended energy possible. Me, I was like a sponge. Everything possible to learn, I learned. Within weeks of our meeting, I had mastered his way of pronouncing certain words, so that by the end of our time in Balliol, if I didn't sound *public school*, I certainly fooled most people.

I don't know if Adam ever realised I was modelling myself on him, that I wanted everything he was. Everything he had.

7

Adam and I hung around together most days after lectures, generally meeting up in the junior common room, sometimes staying there the rest of the evening, sometimes drifting to a pub or to a party. Then, about three weeks after meeting at that fateful party, Adam came out to the stable to spend the night. He thought it was a cool place to live, far superior to his residence on Jowett Walk with its restrictions and rules.

'You can do what you like here, you lucky beggar.' He looked around, taking in my narrow cot-bed, and the makeshift bed on the floor I'd fashioned for him with straw taken from the stable below – straw from which I had to remove the dead bodies of several mice before bringing it up, but he didn't need to know that. Over several cans of cheap supermarket beer, conversation drifted to our lives before college. Adam told me stories of his parents, the family dogs, the cook who had been with them since he was a child, the land he rambled around when home from boarding school. He spoke of hunting and shooting, of fox hunts and parties. And I listened to him enthralled, awestruck that there were lives like that, full of colour and promise.

He told me about his family home in the Cotswolds, joked about the draughty old house and summers spent helping on the family estate. 'My parents,' he said finally, 'are convinced universities are dens of iniquity. No way would they let me live away from residence. Yours don't mind you living here, away from campus?'

It was my turn to talk about my family and my life... chalk to his very expensive epicurean cheese.

It was a pivotal moment, and I had a choice to make. Adam's life sounded so great, his parents so supportive, telling him the truth about mine or any version of it seemed such an admission of failure. I couldn't do it. I'd come to Oxford to find the endless possibilities it offered. I wasn't saddling myself with my past. I could reinvent myself, couldn't I? What harm could it do?

Truth or lie?

Perhaps I should have stuck with a version of the truth – I wanted to come to Oxford, my parents didn't approve. I left. End of.

Or maybe a colourful lie – my mother really wanted me to come to Oxford, was proud of me, supported me in every way she could, but was afraid of my father, a vicious bully who browbeat her, and was occasionally violent toward her.

Instead, I took the metaphorical knife and sliced my past away. 'My parents died a few years ago, in a car crash. Both were killed instantly.'

'Shit,' Adam said, his eyes filling with sympathy I refused to feel embarrassed by, accepting it with a small smile and shrug.

'It was a difficult time. They were brilliant, you know, great parents. Dad was a scientist, and my mother worked in the diplomatic corps. She travelled all over the world before she met my father. They travelled a lot with his work too. He was really clever and worked as a consultant. They lived in Brazil and Mongolia, among other places, but gave up travelling when I came along.'

The lies spilled easily, inventing my parents, reinventing me. As I spun story after story, they became real to me, took on form and substance, a solidity that in turn affected how I felt about myself. A child of such brave, intelligent people was destined to go far.

I didn't realise, then, that my life would become intertwined with Adam's, and I would be forced to live the lie forever. What eighteen-year-old thinks of the consequences of his actions? Anyway, after a while, I began to believe the story myself.

8

I was delighted to be invited for a weekend to Adam's home. The beautiful Grade II listed property was a charming house that sprawled, higgledy-piggledy, over three floors with stairways in strange places and corridors that ended suddenly, as if a room had vanished into another dimension. Visitors, like me, were always getting lost, searching for the bathroom but ending up in the kitchen, and then unable to find their way back.

The family treated it as a spectator sport, frequently taking bets on how long it would take a guest to find their way to the dining room after the dinner gong had reverberated through the house. The unfortunate visitor, already intimidated by being in a house where dinner was announced by a gong, arrived dishevelled and embarrassed, to be greeted by the sight of the host with a stopwatch in his hand, and shouts of laughter or groans of frustration from the various winners and losers as money passed from hand to hand.

It was impossible to be offended, their warm bonhomie was inclusive, sincere and hard to resist. In their home – where the wind howled under ill-fitting doors and heavy curtains swayed in the breeze from the windows, so that, apart from a few months in the summer, and despite fires that burned in almost every room, it was always cold – I always felt warm and cared for.

Adam's parents, Giles and Clara, were the solid, decent sort, old money and no pretensions, who wore frayed tweed and Barbour jackets worn soft with age. I liked them immediately, and I think they liked me. They were certainly kind to me, and if that was coloured by their belief that my parents were dead, because of course Adam had told them, I refused to feel guilt.

Adam had only one sibling, a sister, Ann, who was a year older. I met her that first weekend when she was making what was, according to Adam, a rare visit from university in Cambridge.

'She must need money,' he said. 'She hates it here.'

I couldn't understand how anyone could hate the place, until I met her. A stunningly beautiful woman, porcelain skin, full lips and bright, knowing eyes, she sashayed around the house in ridiculously high heels and figure-hugging dresses looking totally out of place. A fox in a henhouse.

And like a fox, she regarded everyone as prey. Or maybe it was only me.

Adam and I spent most of our time outdoors, so it was only in the evening that we were all together. Then I could feel Ann's eyes assessing me as if she couldn't quite make up her mind about me. I wasn't vain but I'd had enough compliments to know women liked my looks, so it wasn't that. It was something more... almost as if she was pushing aside the fragile layers I'd managed to acquire and was seeing what lay underneath and it amused her.

And her amusement angered me. Worse, it made me nervous and tongue-tied when she was around, which amused her even more. A frustrating destructive cycle which nobody but the two players seemed to notice.

On the second night, we found ourselves temporarily alone

when Adam and his father went to have a private chat. Ann had kicked her shoes off and was stretched out on the sofa. Her dress, already short, had ridden up to show an expanse of thigh. She caught me looking... of course she did... but instead of pulling her dress down, she shuffled on the seat so it moved up even further and I could see the frilled edge of her underwear. I suppose I should be grateful she was wearing any.

It was too late for me to back out of the room, so I moved to stand by the fireplace. I picked up a poker and shoved it uselessly into the glowing coals while I searched for a topic of conversation. 'Are you heading back to Cambridge tomorrow?' I asked, turning back to her. Sadly, it was the best I could think to ask, not having yet acquired the skills of witty repartee.

'Yes, thank goodness.' She stretched her arms out. 'Adam loves it here, for me it's tediously dull. I miss the city.'

'It's only my first visit, but I think I'm going to have to side with Adam. I love it here.'

She tilted her head, all the better to see through me. 'Do you know your accent drops sometimes? You sound less public schoolboy and more—' She stopped and held a hand over her mouth, feigning embarrassment.

Perhaps she would have continued, filled in the missing words, using *local comprehensive* as an insult, if Adam and his father hadn't walked into the room. She shot me a smile and ignored me for the rest of the evening.

It was many years before we met again, and by then, everything had changed and our stories had merged.

9

——————

Multiple invitations to visit the Cotswolds were extended to me over the years. Weekends during the college term when Adam and I would arrive ravenous on Friday evening to be met with laden tables and orders to help ourselves to more, which we obeyed with alacrity. We left as late as possible on Sunday, stuffed full of food and kindliness that made me yearn to return.

Ann never visited again while I was there. Her dutiful-daughter visits reduced quickly from seldom to rare. When Adam's parents spoke of her, it was with an air of longing, and I knew they missed her, and despite their pride that she was doing well, I don't think they ever really understood why she stayed away.

Too far from London, even further from the social circuit Ann buzzed around, they never heard the stories about her. Adam heard but never told, careful of their feelings, knowing they would be puzzled at some of the stories. Absolutely horrified at others.

Ann stayed away but I couldn't get enough of the Cotswolds. One glorious summer, I spent a full week there with Adam. We walked for miles and miles over open countryside, stopping now and then to exchange pleasantries with people Adam or his family, or his family's family, had known since who knew when. We would return home in the evening, exhausted, ravenous, and Adam would tell Giles and Clara who we had met, and each mention would lead into a hundred stories that rambled and intertwined, one onto another, each full of colour and people and told with warm wit and kindliness. And I listened, mesmerised by this strange unfathomable world to which I desperately wanted to belong; fascinated by the Bretts, whom I'd come to love.

Adam taught me to shoot, and we trudged across the fields searching for rabbits, Adam blowing the poor furry bundles to smithereens with every shot, me doing more damage to the trees and undergrowth, unable to confess to liking the cheeky cotton-wool-bottomed creatures too much to reduce them to blood and gore.

'Bloody hell, Jake,' Adam shouted on a laugh, as I missed yet again. 'I'll have to ask them to come closer and stand still.' And then he lifted his rifle and shot, catching the fleeing bunny just before it got to cover, cotton and blood colouring the green. 'That's the way it's done.'

His criticism was always gentle. He had infinite patience, the consummate teacher way before he had decided that was his calling. He just didn't see, and probably would never have understood, my reluctant distaste. Reluctant, because I really did want to take to this most English and gentlemanly of sports. But it wasn't me. And try as I might, want it as I did, it just seemed unnecessarily cruel, stupidly pointless. It wasn't as if we ever ate the poor things, we just left their slaughtered bodies littering the countryside. Asking Adam once why we didn't bring them back to be eaten, he laughed. 'Not the way we blow them to pieces, Jake. There's not much left to eat. If you want, we can trap some, but we usually get our rabbit from the butchers. Mum doesn't like having to clean things out.'

'No, no, that's okay,' I hastily reassured him, not fancying trapping the poor creatures, imagining them caught and suffering and giving a shiver that had Adam raise his eyebrows.

'You getting cold, shall we head back?' he asked, with the quick concern I had learned to expect from him, a kindness and concern that just didn't sit with the slaughter of defenceless animals, guessing it was something beyond my understanding, something to do with the land and owning it since time began.

Each visit, I had the same big square room overlooking parkland to the front of the house. A huge mahogany bed, with a mattress so old I was convinced it was stuffed with horsehair, faced two floor-to-ceiling bay windows. A colossal ornate mahogany wardrobe spanned the far wall and on either side of the bed stood huge bedside tables. At almost six foot, I wasn't used to feeling small, but in this room I was Alice in Wonderland, reduced in size and awed by all I saw.

The first time I stayed, I drank way too much and woke, early dawn, with a bladder a camel would have been proud of. I felt the usual disorientation of waking in a strange place and almost fell, climbing out of a bed that was at least a foot higher than I was used to. I had left the bedroom curtains pulled back, and through the tall windows the moon, full, fat and grinning, watched me. I moved closer and gasped at the view, quickly clenching every muscle I knew to avoid the embarrassment of voiding all over the old worn carpet. An early-morning mist lay low on the ground. From it, the lime trees I had passed on the long driveway to the house emerged as if disconnected from the earth, their full green canopy floating on the mist. It was all so bloody unworldly that I gasped again. Hedges bordering the grounds were rimmed with darkness giving shelter to who-knew-what. Whatever it was, whatever was there, it caused a trickle of fear to run down my back, and the hairs on my neck and everywhere else sprang to panicked attention.

I stood, pain intensifying as my bladder stretched, unable to move, unable to take my eyes off that strange sight and thought, not for the first time, that things weren't the way they were supposed to be. Not until the first glimmer of dawn did I move away, and then backwards, afraid to turn my back on the view, moving slowly, painfully to the doorway, opening the door and darting through it with a sigh of relief, rushing to the bathroom with a different fear now, reaching it, feeling the sweet relief as urine cascaded noisily on and on for so long I wondered if I had done damage by the delay, and then forgot all about it in the relief and scurried back to bed, ignoring the windows, climbing in, dragging the duvet over my head and falling asleep within seconds.

Hung-over and trepidatious next morning, it was a relief to look out the window and see rolling fields and normal if strikingly beautiful lime trees. Later, showing a courteous interest in my surroundings, I asked pertinent questions and discovered the early mist was a common occurrence in the area. Nothing unworldly about it at all. But, from then on, I made sure to draw my bedroom curtains before climbing into that huge bed. And that night I drank a little less, in the hope that my bladder would cope until morning.

It did, and a solid night's sleep restored my equilibrium. For the rest of my stay, I matched Adam drink for drink, but couldn't quite shake off the inexplicable fear I'd experienced that one night. Every afternoon, I made a point of returning to my room, shutting the curtains while the sun still shone, as if by doing so I could shut out whatever malevolence lurked in the darkness. And, if I woke during the night, I coughed loudly to scare off whatever might be hiding in the shadows, before throwing back the blankets with an air of bravado.

It was a feeling that never left me – the feeling that things weren't quite what they seemed, that under the surface or just out of sight, inexplicable things were happening. And if, in a whisper of a moment, I ever linked that feeling to the choice I made when I first got to know Adam, in a fraction of that whisper I dismissed the thought. Dismissed too the guilt that lashed me for lying to these people.

By then, it was too late to tell the truth. I had too much to lose. They would never, ever have understood the choice I made. Or the lie I lived.

I'm not always sure I did.

10

Over the years, Adam and I moved from nightly drinking sessions after lectures, to weekly drinks after work, to monthly lunches to catch up. He'd read history and geography and drifted into teaching, landing a permanent, pensionable post in an upmarket Catholic boys' college where, he said, all the boys were over-indulged brats. He should have gained experience elsewhere but didn't, digging in and staying put, calling it loyalty, but nobody was fooled and they saw his extreme laziness for what it was, shaking their heads at his narrow-minded reluctance to reach out and grasp the opportunities that were there for the taking. Five years before, he was certain he would be offered the assistant headmaster's post when the previous incumbent moved up, the headmaster having retired following twenty years in the post. But the new headmaster, determined to dust away the cobwebs of the former twenty years' stagnation, offered the post to a new, dynamic, experienced *younger* man. Adam didn't bother trying to hide his bitterness and became a barbed thorn in the side of the new establishment, sneering at every change that was made, resisting every new development, stirring up bad feeling with a word here, a complaint there. It had, instead of teaching, become his raison d'être.

I, on the other hand, qualifying with a first in business studies and economics, went from bank to bank, each position a step upward until I had soared to the pinnacle that was Sebastian et Sebastian, a small discreet investment bank where only the seriously wealthy were entertained. They head-hunted me, their approach tactfully tempting; a heavily embossed invitation to meet Francois Sebastian for lunch in Scott's, where we dined on Beluga caviar followed by a plateau de fruits de mer, the cracking of lobster a gentle accompaniment to the job offer of my dreams. By the time we finished the bottle of Le Montrachet Grand Cru 2001, a wine so good I had difficulty containing my groan of pleasure, I had accepted the job offer, and didn't so much as consider a downside to being a consultant rather than an actual employee.

Francois – call me Francois, he'd said as I stuttered over the correct pronunciation of Sebastian, his accent just French enough to be charming – mentioned a retainer, commission, a superb six-monthly bonus scheme, and an office in the centre of London. As he held his glass of wine up to the light, what he left unsaid was – you too can afford to eat here and pay over £400 for a bottle of wine.

Of course, I accepted. So, there I was, not yet thirty, a consultant fund manager for one of *the* London investment banks, making more money than I had ever thought possible. Serious money, I mean *really* serious money.

If I wasn't precisely happy, I was rich. For a while, I convinced myself that was enough. And then I met Jane.

11

Adam and his sister, Ann, weren't close, but when he started working in London, he would meet her for lunch or a drink after work. Despite his frequent invitations to join them, I was too busy hanging on to the quickly moving steps of my career ladder to have time even if I'd wanted to. It had been several years since I'd met Ann, I could happily wait several more.

Friday night was the only time I managed to meet Adam in those days. I was rarely there before ten, my working day frequently ending long after that, but he always waited. He'd choose a place with a late licence so we'd get through a couple of pints and catch up. Or sometimes, when my week had been particularly hard and I was all talked out and weary beyond anything but listening, I would drink, and Adam would tell me stories about the children he tried to teach.

He'd mention his sister now and then. She was working in public relations, but it was never her work he spoke about. Instead, he told me highly salacious, even libellous stories of the men she met, and occasionally slept with. Thus, I knew all about Tony French-Jones's very small cock, way before I met the man, and when I did meet him and shook his hand, I was really hard pushed not to tell him I'd heard about him. It is true what they say, too. He had very small hands.

Adam also recounted, in more detail than I wanted to hear, all about Peter Pendleton's penchant for sadomasochism that bordered on the bizarre, if not downright criminal. Adam was so genuinely naïve that I don't think he realised the stories told me as much about Ann as they did about the men they ridiculed.

I remembered her stretched out on the sofa in front of the fire all those years before, her dress riding up, the languorous sexiness that had so tongue-tied me. I'd like to think that being older, wiser, even a little more worldly-wise, I'd be better able for her now... but I wasn't rushing to face that challenge.

Occasionally, I would arrive on a Friday night to find Adam deep in conversation with a woman. Sometimes one he had brought with him, sometimes one he had met while he waited patiently for me. I never minded. I was always so exhausted by Fridays that it was nice just to be able to stand there, beer in hand, and listen to him doing his thing. He made me laugh, and mostly that was all I wanted.

The women we met there tended to be of a type... glamorous women out for a good time. High heels, skimpy dresses, expensively highlighted blonde hair, fake eyelashes, fake breasts, fake smile.

The woman who stood beside me at the bar that night, desperately trying to catch the bartender's attention, was an exception. She looked out of place in jeans and a T-shirt, her dull brown hair tied back in a casual knot.

Adam was chatting to a blonde with an equine face and matching laugh. I knew he wouldn't be with her long and I was looking to pass the time in a convivial way. The woman beside me was attractive enough but not my type, so I moved away. Minutes later, I was deep in conversation about share prices with a man I'd met at a conference who looked as pale and weary as I felt.

When he left and I turned in search of Adam, he'd moved on from the horse-faced woman. I couldn't see him for a few minutes... and then I did. He was talking to a woman, one of his hands waving in the air the way it did when he was talking about something that excited him.

When the crowd moved, I saw the woman, her head thrown back as she laughed at whatever tale Adam was telling him. I recognised her then. The woman from the bar, the one I'd dismissed so carelessly.

I moved through the crush of people to get a better look. Her smile was captivating and when I switched my gaze to Adam's face, I could see he was mesmerised by it. By her.

Had he seen something in her that I'd missed?

I knew, in that second, I'd made a terrible mistake.

12

I stood watching Adam and the woman for a few minutes before making my way through the crush of people to their side. It took a punch on his arm... a none too gentle one... to get his attention.

'I'm heading off,' I said.

'Already?' He glanced at his watch, then frowned at me. 'It's still early, you sure?'

'It's been a long day.'

'Okay. Before you vanish' – he turned his attention back to the woman, who waited patiently – 'this is Jane.'

I stuck my hand towards her, felt hers warm and delicate in mine. A childish thought flitted through my head. I saw her first. But it had taken Adam, the well-brought-up public schoolboy, to see her worth. 'Nice to meet you,' I said and released her hand. 'Catch you later in the week, Adam.' And I left before I could make a fool of myself.

It crossed my mind to ring Adam during the week to see if he was going to see her again, to make a casual note of interest, as it were, in seeing her myself. But, as was often the way, the week sped by in the mess of deals, transactions, actions and inactions that was my life then, and it went out of my head. It wouldn't have mattered anyway. Jane was different. When Friday came around again, there she was leaning casually against the bar, a smile lighting her face, and her eyes only for Adam, a look on both their faces telling me, as clearly as if it had been written in neon over their heads, they had come straight from bed.

In the chaos that was the norm for a Friday night, they had eyes only for one another, and I had eyes only for her. I watched the signs, the involuntary touches, the casual caresses that were anything but casual, the meaningful, lingering smiles, the mirroring of their movements. I wanted to move between them, tell her stories of Adam's infidelities, his indiscretions, his inability to commit. But, of course, I didn't. I smiled and laughed, and told her gently teasing stories about him, and then left early saying I had work to do, watching them move closer, a subtle entwining of ankles, a draping of arms, before I had even left the room. And I felt a pang of loss for something that was never mine but that would haunt me all the same.

Of course, I was happy for Adam. He was my best, my oldest friend. A good friend... our Friday night get-togethers continued, although now with Jane tagging along. And with every meeting, it became clearer to me, she was perfect... for me.

I searched for the negatives... her nose was too big, she was quite opinionated, and her idea of dressing glamorously was to wear a shirt with her jeans instead of a T-shirt... but these minor distractions were lost in her genuine kindness, her sparkling humour, her sincere interest in all that was going on around her.

Like most happy couples, they couldn't bear to see me single – or unhappy, as they translated it, despite my telling them every time we met that I was happy. And I was, really. Because, even with Adam there, being with Jane was a delight. We did a couple of double dates; women I knew or friends of Jane's, and I did try to make it work, believe me. But, for one reason or another, nothing ever came of them. And if Adam ever noticed that my eyes sparkled, my face lit up and my smile took on a softer edge when Jane was around, he never mentioned it.

And if I harboured a hope that it wouldn't work out between them – well, I never mentioned that.

Three months later, I walked into the bar on Friday night, and Jane wasn't there. Adam looked a bit grim, his face pale, and I thought *yes! She's dumped him*, and I wondered how long it was necessary to wait before I could make a move on her.

It wasn't that I wanted him to be miserable, he was my best friend, after all. But he'd had everything so easily all his life... why should he have Jane as well?

13

I tried not to sound too cheerful, as I slapped a hand on his back. 'Hi, Adam, you're looking a bit miserable.' He did, but right then, I didn't care. He'd had his chance and had blown it. My mind was flying ahead to when Jane and I would be climbing out of bed to come and meet *him* on a Friday night, maybe we would laugh and say, *let's not bother, let's just stay here. Adam won't mind.*

He sank the remainder of his pint before putting the glass down. 'Hi, Jake.'

'You okay?' I asked, prepared to be supportive, trying to keep satisfaction from my voice.

He nodded, then put his hand in his pocket and took out a small box. He didn't say a word as he opened it. I watched, my heart beginning to feel like a weight in my chest. 'What do you think?' he asked, and I looked at the tiny diamond engagement ring and wanted to scream, laugh or cry but couldn't for the life of me figure out the correct response, stunned as I was.

So, I just nodded, took the small box, looked closer at the ring and nodded again. It gave me enough time to get a grip on myself, to find a voice that had died. 'She will love it.' He could have chosen bigger, more ostentatious, but, for the first time, I realised he knew her well and had chosen perfectly. But that didn't stop me, at that moment, hating him with every fibre of my being, didn't stop me wanting to take the damn ring and throw it across the crowded pub, didn't stop me wanting to sneer at him and his tiny little diamond and his tiny little expectations.

'Thanks, Jake.' He pocketed the ring. 'I'm meeting her in an hour, back at her place. I'm going to ask her then.' He hesitated, lifted his glass, surprised to find it empty.

'Another?' I asked, lifting my finger to attract the bartender's attention. I needed a drink, planned to have several and get absolutely smashed.

He shook his head and tapped his pocket as if in explanation of his unusual restraint. 'I never thought I would meet someone like her, you know. She's too good for me, really. Maybe she'll say no.'

Maybe she would, but I had my doubts. I had seen the way she looked at him. Seen how they were together. I had to face the truth; Adam was going to marry Jane. That was that. There was no point in feeding hope, better to let it die, and face reality.

'Of course she won't, idiot. She's crazy about you.'

He smiled, his lips curving in the way they did when he was with her, or thinking of her, and I felt sick with envy, felt the green tinge of it gurgling and devouring, and I knew I had to get away, so I made vague excuses to leave early, apologising even when I knew he didn't give a monkey's. Why would he, when he was going to propose to the woman I loved?

There... I said it... the woman I loved. I'd add it to the list of secrets I kept because if I let it out, if Adam knew, I'd lose his friendship. And if I lost that, I'd lose Jane completely and forever.

Her saying yes to his proposal seemed such a fait accompli that I didn't realise I harboured a shred of hope until my phone rang later that night, and I heard first his excited voice and then hers, and I heard the crack as that last shred split into a million tiny pieces of pain that stung and hurt and caused tears to spring, to run uncontrollably down my face while my voice said all the right things, managing the right tone of voice so I was crying and saying, *Fantastic, so pleased for you both, congratulations.*

Luckily for me, they decided not to have an engagement party. I really don't think I could have gone. Not then.

It was, in fact, several weeks before I met Adam again, pleading pressure of work every time he tried to arrange our usual weekly meeting. I wasn't lying; I had agreed to take on far more than I should have in an attempt to bury myself in work, and the resultant avalanche nearly killed me as I worked till midnight most nights, had power-breakfasts and worked through lunch. I lost half a stone before I met him again, and I knew I looked dreadful.

'You look like shit, Jake,' Adam said worriedly as I walked into the restaurant where I'd agreed to meet him, a tiny Chinese he liked and always chose if the choice was his. I never minded, although Chinese food wasn't my favourite.

'Thanks,' I replied with a wry smile. 'I did tell you I was manic at work, didn't I? It's been a crazy few weeks. Anyway' – I gave him a friendly punch – 'what's it like being half shackled?'

He grinned happily. 'It's great. Jane says hi, by the way, she was sorry not to be able to come tonight.'

'It was unfortunate this was the only night I could make,' I said, lying through my teeth without compunction. Jane being busy was the reason I had agreed to meet Adam, otherwise I would have stuck to my pressure of work excuse. I wasn't ready to meet them as an engaged couple. I needed more time. But it was good to see Adam.

'Never mind,' he said. 'Jane wants you to come to dinner, made me promise I'd get a date from you.' He nodded to my jacket pocket. 'So just you pull out that BlackBerry thing and give me a date.'

I took it out and spent a few seconds spinning through my diary, humming and hawing, wagging my head, making all those *I'm such a busy man* noises everyone knows so well. I had to choose a day and I did, one about five weeks away. For God's sake, I should have my act together by then, shouldn't I?

'Did I tell you I've given up my flat and moved in with her?' Adam said, with a twist of the knife he didn't know he was wielding.

I shook my head, a smile plastered firmly in place.

He nodded happily. 'Her place isn't much bigger than mine was, but it's nicer and there's an en suite bathroom as well as a main one so we won't be fighting over the shower in the morning. The kitchen is bigger too. She's a really good cook, you know.' He laughed. 'Well, you don't, but you'll find out when you come.'

His happiness should have pleased me, but it didn't. I hated him for it, wanted to sneer at the picture of domestic bliss he painted, but couldn't because it sounded so absolutely perfect. And I wanted to destroy it and knew I wouldn't even if I could. He was my best friend, and she was the woman I loved.

Over the next five weeks, I looked at that date every day, several times putting a call through to Adam to make my excuses, hanging up before I did, only to reconnect hours later and go through the whole rigmarole again.

I was being ridiculous. It was one evening. How hard could it be?

14

There is a lot of nonsense talked about ambience, but Jane's poky little apartment had it in spades. The inexpensive furniture was well-worn and faded. But an old oak table glowed, the patina rich and begging to be touched, and when you did, when your hand moved despite itself to caress it, the wood was warm and smooth with years of warm hands doing exactly the same, and you felt connected to it. The rug on the floor, faded and worn thin in parts, hinted at the hundreds of feet that had walked across it. I felt instantly at home and choked back unbidden tears that it was Adam who would be sharing this space with Jane, and not me.

I had had five weeks to prepare for this, had prepared conversational topics to discuss, afraid that once in their nest I would clam up, choke up with emotion, and be unable to think of something to say. In fact, it was easier than I expected.

They greeted me with hugs. Adam's manly back-slapping followed by Jane's sweetly scented body meeting mine, her lips brushing my cheek – one side and then, oh torture, the other. My hands rested for an infinitesimal moment of pleasure on her small waist before she pulled away with a smile and a quip about returning to the kitchen sink, leaving Adam and me to catch-up over a couple of beers.

We chatted about this and that, sipping ice-cold beer, and in the background the convivial music of domestic bliss.

'Okay,' Jane called a short while later. 'It's ready.'

And we rose from the comfortable sofa and moved to the other end of the room where flickering candles made the oak table glow.

'This smells great,' I said, as Jane placed a plate of food in front of me, steam rising in curls carrying aromas that tantalised my taste buds. It was roast lamb, cooked just the way I liked it. I was impressed and told her so. 'This is delicious. It's my favourite meal.'

Adam laughed. 'Of course she knows. She quizzed me up and down... does he like this, does he like that... honestly.'

I turned to her and smiled. 'Really?'

'Nothing as bad as cooking a meal and discovering one of your guests doesn't eat this or that,' she shrugged, then smiled. 'It's bribery. I hope you will come more often. I know Adam has missed meeting up with you.'

'Rubbish,' Adam said through a mouthful of food. 'I was getting bored with him; I've known him far too long.'

I heard the touch of hurt behind the words and felt a quick dart of remorse. I had to stop blaming Adam for something he couldn't change. 'It's just been so busy.' The lie came easily.

'Adam explained. But you need to look after yourself, you need to eat properly. You've lost weight since I saw you last. It's not good for you.'

Her concern pleased me. In fact, I had put on a few pounds since I had seen Adam last and didn't look quite as bad as I had done, my belt only one hole tighter than it used to be.

Adam put an arm loosely around her shoulders. 'He needs a woman in his life.'

'I thought you and Amy would hit it off,' Jane said, referring to one of the friends she had tried to set me up with.

We'd had dinner, but I found her conversation boring, her smile ingratiating and irritating, and her whole demeanour designed to annoy. I shook my head. 'I'm just too caught up in work at the moment; don't have time for all this nauseating billing and cooing stuff.'

Adam looked horrified. 'We don't do billing and cooing, do we?'

Jane laughed. 'He's pulling your leg. Honestly, Jake' – she put a warm hand on my arm – 'he is so gullible.'

None of the conversational gambits I had prepared were needed after all. I have no idea what we talked about, or laughed about, but we didn't stop doing either and time flew by, the way it always does when you don't want it to.

'I like this place,' I said, sipping good coffee, more relaxed than I had felt in a while. 'You should be happy here.'

'Oh, we're not planning to stay here,' Adam said, with a smile at Jane. 'We're going to hang on here for a few months until we get a house. We've started looking but haven't found anywhere suitable yet.'

'He means we haven't found one we can afford yet.'

'But this flat is so nice,' I said. 'You wouldn't think of staying here?'

Jane blushed and Adam, seeing it, hugged her and laughed. 'We're planning our future, Jake, we want a gang of kids. Hundreds.'

Jane laughed and punched him. 'Funny!'

Of course, I should have guessed Jane would want children. I imagined her swelling with Adam's child. His glowing pride. I pictured the two of them, surrounded by children, deliriously happy. Giles and Clara would be wonderful grandparents, and the house in the Cotswolds would echo with laughter and children's cries. Such a gloriously perfect life with me looking in from the outside, getting more bitter and green as the years passed by.

'We have to get a house in a good catchment area,' Adam said.

'So grown up,' Jane said, her expression serious for a second before it creased in laughter at the thought of Adam being so sensible when he was generally anything but. He looked affronted for a moment before chuckling along with her and I joined in from desperation.

Then it was time to go, a taxi arriving far too quickly, goodbyes said, promises to return soon made, and I was out in the street, a misty rain wetting me within a few footsteps, chilling my skin to match the chill inside, the sense of cold loss.

I climbed into the taxi, gave him my address, changed my mind and told him to drive to Waterloo Bridge.

It had been my mother's favourite movie, *Waterloo Bridge*, the 1940s movie with Vivien Leigh and Robert Taylor. I had seen it too many times to mention, sitting at her knee, listening to her cry when the end came.

I got out, walked across, and stood looking out over the river, the rain coming down heavily now, soaking me, making me feel just the way I wanted to, wet and bloody miserable. Sometimes it is good to wallow, and wallow I did.

It didn't matter that I only had myself to blame... I *had* seen Jane first, had the opportunity, but let it pass. I didn't have that innate good breeding that made everything, including knowing quality when he saw it, come so damn easily to Adam.

The happiness he'd found with her, it should have been mine.

I felt the rain soak through my clothes with a kind of pleasure. 'I'll die of pneumonia, then she'll be sorry.' I heard the words falling in the raindrops that dripped off my nose and chin, and started to laugh. How sad and pathetic was I? How damn childish? The lights of the city twisted and danced in the river. I was so wet by then that if I had jumped in, it wouldn't have made a difference. But suicide wasn't my style.

Anyway, then I remembered Vivien Leigh's character Myra had walked in front of a truck, not jumped off the bridge, and I wondered what the hell I was doing, soaking wet and feeling so very sorry for myself. I hailed another taxi and headed home.

15

Adam's voice came down the line, excited, exultant. 'It's August!'

I didn't have to ask him to explain. They'd set the date for the wedding. It would have been churlish of me to have said, *what are you on about?* So, I just listened to him babble about hotels and churches and ceremonies.

If I had hoped for a small discreet registry office wedding, I was to be disappointed. It was going to be a big affair. Jane's family, it seemed, was very well-to-do indeed, and insisted on splurging for their only daughter's wedding. So, it wasn't just the wedding day itself to get through. Oh, no! There was a succession of pre-wedding dinners to mark this and bloody that... dinner to meet her family, dinner to meet his family, dinner the night of the rehearsal... and on and on.

And of course, I was best man, and so was involved in the lot. Best man. Such a stupid title. If I were the best man, surely Jane should have been marrying me, not someone else.

There was so much damn smiling involved, my face ached from the effort while at the same time envy gnawed away at me.

An Incredible Hulk waiting to burst forth and rip the smile of genuine happiness from Adam's smug, self-satisfied face.

My best man speech took weeks to write. I tore up the first draft, the one where I told Jane she'd made a mistake, she should have married me. I was half serious and totally drunk when I wrote it and fell asleep with it clutched in my hand. When I woke, completely disorientated, and read it, I was embarrassed to have written such maudlin rubbish. I tore it into tiny little pieces, paranoid in case, by some weird quirk of fate, a line of it might escape and land in the wrong hands. Perhaps I wouldn't have been so paranoid if my alcohol-damaged brain weren't beating a loud tattoo inside my skull.

Over the next few days, I managed to cobble together a not-too-bad-at-all speech, settling, finally, for the traditional, conservative sentiments with the requisite amusing anecdotes about Adam's past. I spoke of what a good guy he was... I didn't have to lie there... and I promised to look after Jane if ever anything happened to him... I didn't have to lie there either. As speeches went, it was passable, if a bit dull. But at least I didn't lose a friend or ruin the wedding.

We had the wedding rehearsal dinner at the Ivy, where I renewed my acquaintance with Adam's sister, Ann. She arrived late and strolled into the restaurant like a movie-star, stopping here and there as she crossed the room as if to check her bearings, but really to give everyone a chance to admire her as she gracefully arched her neck to peer around. Without a doubt, an appreciative silence fell. And why wouldn't it; my memory hadn't lied, she was stunningly beautiful. Her dress was designed to reveal a hint of flesh as she moved so that once she caught your eye, you didn't want to look away. I swear there wasn't a man in the room whose eyes weren't following her as she sashayed over to our table.

As coffee was being served, I decided to go and have a word with her. After all, I was the best man, there were obligations. She stood up when I touched her arm. She was tall, maybe five ten, but wearing such high heels, her piercing blue eyes were almost the same level as mine.

'The infamous Jake,' she said, as if she hadn't met me all those years before. Perhaps she'd forgotten. Or she was playing a game. When she leaned forward to kiss my cheek, her dress shifting, the silk clinging to tantalise and reveal a curve of breast, the faint hint of nipple, I guessed it was the latter. *Infamous* was a bit rich coming from her. I hadn't forgotten the stories of sadomasochism and small cocks, but I nodded and smiled because that was what you did, you played the game, even when you were weary of pretending.

I took the hand she held out to me. It was small, slim and incredibly soft, but even as that thought was skipping through my mind, I felt her index finger trace a circle in the palm of my hand. It was incredibly erotic. Suddenly, I was neither weary nor pretending as a lick of lust swept over me, and my grip on her hand tightened.

She smiled then as if she had proved something to herself, and withdrew her hand with a small, almost unheard *humph*. With a smile curving her lips, and her eyes fixed on mine, she moved her fingers along the neckline of her dress, the red painted nails leaving a fine white line in their wake. They travelled up her neck to her mouth. I watched, fascinated, as her lips parted just a little and the tip of a pink tongue darted out to lick her index finger. And all the time she held my gaze. I was only human. Despite myself, and what I knew of her, I was fascinated.

Then she laughed. 'You're quite cute,' she said, and with a dismissive wave, she turned and sat down again, giving her attention to the man seated beside her. I wasn't sure whether to be amused or offended. Returning to my seat, I watched her across the table for a moment until some uncle of Jane's came to talk to me. I didn't get a chance to speak to Ann again and, at the end of the night, when everyone was saying their goodbyes, I noticed she had already left. She intrigued me... maybe because, for the first time in a long while, I was thinking of a woman other than Jane.

16

Depending on your point of view, the wedding could be viewed as a resounding success or absolute nightmare... my view tended toward the latter. Adam and I arrived, too early, at the beautiful fifteenth-century church they had chosen for their wedding. We were forced to stand around like two dopey penguins until the first of the guests arrived. Then it was small talk and good humour, back-slapping and kissy-kissy, tears from both Adam's mother, Clara, and Jane's mother, Susan, each careful not to smudge their make-up, pulling tissue upon tissue from miniscule bags I decided held nothing else.

Adam turned to me and grabbed my arm. 'This is it.'

I resisted the temptation to take his hand and break it, to punch him and keep punching till he fell bleeding at my feet. Our roles should be reversed, I should be marrying Jane, he should be *my* best man. It seemed I had spent the better part of my life so far envying him, and now I would spend the rest of it doing the same. Hate was a stronger emotion than envy, it dampened down the green monster, then it too faded and I managed to drag a smile into place. 'Yes. If you want to change your mind, this is your last chance.'

Adam laughed. 'Some best man. Don't be giving me ideas.' He turned towards me, hand still gripping my arm, and pulled me into a bear-hug. 'I'm the luckiest man alive, aren't I? I don't deserve all this. It's going to be a fantastic day!'

All I could do was nod. Keep smiling and nod. A gormless, nodding penguin.

And then it was time to head inside and walk up the aisle, acknowledging the smiles thrown our way with more smiles.

The minister, an old friend of Adam's father, Giles, met us at the altar, shook my hand perfunctorily, then took Adam's in both of his and held it. 'It gives me such great pleasure to be here,' he said, smiling warmly. 'Jane is a lovely girl. I wish you every happiness.'

He stepped back to the altar, and we moved to the front pew. We waited silently, Adam occasionally shuffling from foot to foot, taking surreptitious glances at his watch.

Moments later, a side door opened and four men entered. They moved to a corner of the church, sat and began to unpack their instruments. Three violinists and a cellist. Curiosity flitted across some watching faces, dawning knowledge on others.

'What are they going to play?' I whispered to Adam.

He shrugged. 'Not a clue. Jane organised it all. Wanted it to be a secret.'

Just then, the musicians started tuning their instruments, discordant notes shattering the quiet.

'Bloody hell,' Adam said, 'I hope that's not it.'

Giles, sitting just behind, leaned forward. 'It's going to be Pachelbel's Canon in D, I think. Three violins and a cello. Can't be anything else. Don't worry, it's a lovely piece of music. Very traditional.'

Adam turned to him with a smile. 'Never was much for classical music, you know. Kind of thought she'd go with the *here comes the bride* music.'

Giles sighed. 'You do know that *is* a piece of classical music, don't you, Adam? It's Wagner. The "Bridal Chorus".'

'Really? Did you know that, Jake?' he said, turning to me, glancing at his watch as he did, determinedly making conversation, trying to appear calm, failing miserably.

'Relax, Adam,' I reassured him. 'She'll be here.'

Unless she got sense, realised she had it wrong, that it was me she loved, me she should be marrying. Me she should be spending the rest of her life with in that clichéd happy ever after. But then, the minister, in response to some unknown and unseen signal, stepped forward and raised his hands, palms upward, and as if under his spell, we all stood and the music started and I knew she was coming.

My plan was to stare straight ahead but Adam's indrawn breath broke that resolve in a second, and I swivelled automatically, looking back to where Jane stood with her father, biting my lip so hard a sudden metallic taste filled my mouth.

I have no idea whether she floated down the aisle to Pachelbel's Canon in D or not. They could have been playing 'The Teddy-Bear's Picnic', for all I knew. All I could think was how stunningly beautiful she looked; all I could hear was my heart breaking.

Adam stepped into the aisle to meet her, Jane's father gave him her hand, and they stood there, like wedding cake decorations, Adam in his morning coat, Jane in an ivory lace gown, something sparkling in her hair, lace falling from it to frame her face.

All so damn perfect. Except it should have been me standing there, saying the vows.

17

The reception was held at Broadfield Castle, a historic pile with gothic windows and mullioned glass, opened by owners who had compromised between the financial need to open the house to the public and their desire for privacy, by opening only for weddings. And they did it with expert flair. From the red carpet that led into the big stone entrance hall, where even on this late summer's day a fire blazed in the enormous fireplace, to containers of old roses everywhere you looked, the blooms fat and blousy, the scent intoxicating.

People hustled and bustled about, laughing, talking, shouting greetings, being merry. There was champagne, of course. I grabbed a glass from a passing tray, swallowed it in two quick mouthfuls, reached for another, hesitated then took my hand away. Much later, I could get hammered. Not now. I was the best man. I had a part to play and I was good at that. Hadn't I been doing it most of my life?

It was easy, really. I just said the same things, the same lies, over and over again. It didn't matter. Yes, it was lovely... she looks beautiful... he is very lucky... she is very lucky... it's a fabulous place. Very nice to meet you, of course, I remember. Yes...

After dinner, which I'm sure must have been superb, although I don't remember eating it, came the bane of every wedding. The speeches. Mine was well received. I think. Well, nobody booed. Adam's was better but then, to my surprise, Jane made one, and hers was the best. Unlike me and Adam, she'd nothing written down. She just thanked everyone for coming, thanked both sets of parents, spoke about how wonderful it was to be part of Adam's family, of how very lucky she was.

Of course she was. Clara and Giles would make the perfect parents-in-law. Had Jane married me... as she should have... she'd have been landed with my parents. The thought hit me a blow... I couldn't have married her without telling her my secret, the lie I'd been living with. I wasn't sure how she'd have taken it.

I felt a dart of bitter resentment towards Adam. It was his fault I'd told that stupid lie in the first place. He really had a lot to answer for... then he steals Jane right from under my nose.

Revisionist history. I'd already proven myself adept at reinventing my past when it suited. And it suited me just then to make Adam the villain of the piece.

18

Following the speeches, we were asked to return to the entrance hall while they cleared the tables and moved furniture around for the entertainment. Drinks were served while we waited and I thought it was safe enough to indulge. My duties were nearly over, a few obligatory dances I could do just as well drunk as sober... better, probably. I wasn't a great dancer.

I'd barely had time, however, to down one drink before we were called back to the transformed room. On each table, candles had been lit, and they cast a romantic pool of light. The carpet had been removed, and wooden floorboards gleamed. At the far end of the room, on a raised dais, a band was tuning an array of instruments, discordant notes gradually achieving harmony.

'Jake, come and sit with us,' Adam called, as we all drifted back in. I smiled and nodded but slowed down to allow others to get ahead of me, seeing with some relief that the table he sat at was soon full.

He was too busy to notice I hadn't joined them... busy with his wife, his parents, her parents. One big happy family. I'd fooled myself into thinking I was part of Adam's family, that Clara and Giles regarded me almost as a second son. Fooling myself. I didn't belong. Never did, never would. Self-pity was added to the party of negative emotions that had made themselves at home in my head, each fighting for superiority. Taking turns. Giving me a fucking headache.

I made my way to an empty seat at another table, started chatting to an aunt of Jane's I had met previously, saying the same stuff again, desperately wanting another drink, keeping my eye out for the waiter, trying not to look frantic.

I still hadn't managed to get one when the lead singer announced the start of the dancing by inviting the bride and groom to take their places on the dance floor, so I was stone-cold bloody sober as I watched Adam and Jane waltzing around the floor, their eyes only for each other.

Then, of course, as tradition dictated, I had to join in with Jane's bridesmaid, the lovely Amy whom I had blind-dated, and never bothered to ring. Jane had said Amy didn't hold it against me... but oh, I think she did. As we moved on the floor, her left hand barely touched my shoulder, and only the tips of the fingers of her right hand rested in my left. Despite that and my lack of expertise, we managed a pretty decent one-two-three, one-two-three around the floor. Maybe we didn't precisely glide, but it wasn't *Strictly Come Dancing*, nobody was keeping score.

Adam and Jane did glide, her dress swaying, and sparkling in the lights from the chandelier overhead. They had eyes only for each other as if Amy and I, and every other person there, had vanished. And it was just the two of them.

Trying to keep my eyes off them, I risked trying to melt the ice that crackled between Amy and me, using the same banal comment I had used so many bloody times already, to so many people.

'Lovely wedding, isn't it?' I said, bringing my lips closer to her ear.

'Lovely,' she replied, pulling her head further away from me, her voice arctic cool.

How did they do that? Women? Manage to get so many layers of meaning into one totally unconnected word. I heard, stuff you for not ringing me, you bastard, and if you think I am going to play nice because you're Adam's friend, think again, arsehole!

And her expression never changed a whit.

I didn't bother trying again. More guests got to the floor, taking the spotlight off us, hiding Adam and Jane from our view. Before the final note of the music faded, we pulled apart and Amy tottered off the floor, leaving me standing there, alone, watching as Adam and Jane held on to each other as the waltz faded, and the band leader announced the next number and invited all the guests to take to the floor.

Of course, I couldn't just sit down. The curse of being best man. The duty dances. Actually, the dancing was okay, at least I didn't make anyone limp from the floor. No, the dancing wasn't the problem. It was the damn conversation. Jane's mother wasn't too bad, I didn't know her so well, so she stopped at, 'What about you, Jake? Is there a woman in your life?'

I'd had a couple of glasses of wine by that stage and I could feel my tongue dancing around words that were begging for escape. I wondered what Jane's pleasant, quiet mother would say if I told her I was obsessed with her daughter. I stumbled over my feet at the word I'd used... *obsessed*... no, that wasn't right, I was in love with Jane. I got back into the rhythm of the dance and apologised for stepping on Susan's toes. She didn't repeat her question.

Clara was different. She'd known me too long. Took liberties. 'Now, Jake,' she said firmly, as I tried to manoeuvre her around the room without stepping on her feet. 'It's important to make some time for yourself. Adam tells me you work far too hard. There is more to life than work. You need to meet a nice girl. Settle down and have a family. There'll always be work.'

It had to be the longest dance ever. And she just kept going on and on. If she only knew, if I could just tell her, then she'd shut up. But of course I didn't. For one thing, it wouldn't have changed anything. For another, I really liked Clara.

Then, thankfully, the most pressing of my best man duties were over. Ordering another drink from a passing waiter, I sat and waited for it to arrive, letting my eyes drift over the party, not deliberately searching for anyone in particular, trying to stop my gaze settling on where Jane and Adam sat chatting to her parents.

Just then, Ann caught my eye. She was, once again, wearing an exquisite dress, a sapphire-blue silk that seemed to shimmer as she moved, showing just enough flesh to be sexy without being risqué. I don't know if she was looking for me or if it was just coincidence that when I looked around, I immediately caught her eye. She held my gaze, lifted her chin and smiled; her eyes locked on mine. Then she looked away, and within seconds back again to see if I was still looking. I wasn't too flattered. The only other single man in the room was a distant cousin of Jane's. A fifty-year-old balding obese man with tufts of hair sprouting from every cranial aperture, who constantly blew his nose into a disreputable handkerchief kept, oblivious or uncaring of its germ potential, on the table before him.

But so what if the frisson of attraction between us was nothing more than convenience. She was charming, intelligent and sexy. A little flirtation could be just what I needed.

19

When the band played a waltz, I sauntered over and asked her to dance, enjoying the feel of her body as it relaxed into mine, feeling the warmth of her skin through the soft silk. She was a good dancer and managed to follow my inexpert lead without tripping over my size elevens. Her elegance was contagious, and I reckoned we cut a good figure on the floor.

After the waltz, the music picked up tempo with an Abba number and she, with gratifying if assumed reluctance, stepped back from my arms. Her dance style was surprisingly restrained, a twitch of her body to the right, followed by a similar twitch to the left, with a double twitch if the tempo warranted it. Each twitch was accompanied by a slight dip of her knees, and I'd imagine the view from the rear would have been gratifying, each dip jiggling her curvaceous backside.

'Good band,' I said.

She looked at me blankly, then held her hand cupped to her ear in invitation. I moved closer, trying to synchronise my approach to her twitch to the right, but just then the tempo changed, and she did a double twitch and caught me out, my mouth brushing her ear in an inadvertent kiss.

I stepped back, did an open-hand gesture of apology, wriggled my fingers before my mouth, beside my ear, trying to make it quite clear nothing untoward had been intended.

I must have made a good job of it because she leaned close to me, stretched her elegant neck to bring her mouth close to my ear – managing far better than I had – and whispered huskily, 'Shame!'

The music ended suddenly and she moved away.

Maybe she wanted me to follow, but I noticed various elderly female relatives of both Jane and Adam sitting waiting for some poor sod to ask them to dance. God forbid they would get up and bop around the floor unescorted. Sighing, I pulled my best man guise on and headed over, a smile firmly in place.

I danced with them all; various aunts and cousins, single friends, neighbours, whoever. Half the time, I hadn't a clue. It was a wedding; it didn't really matter. Ann danced past me, now and then, without a glance in my direction, partnered with some man or other. Her little twitchy dance never changed and I wondered about her, about the stories I had heard over the years, and watching more closely, tried to guess if all this restrained elegance hid a heady sensuousness. I *was* right about her backside, though; it did jiggle delightfully when she dipped her knee, but it wasn't deliberate, and if her restrained dance hid any kind of sensuousness, it was doing a bloody good job.

Still, she was stunningly beautiful, and I might have been interested in following the mild flirtation up with an invitation to dinner, but this was Ann, whose aim in life, Adam had told me, time and time again, was to meet a rich man. Preferably one with a title, but definitely one with money.

I was making good money but was a long way from what she

would consider rich. There was another issue that kept me in my seat. The story about poor Tony's small cock wasn't to be forgotten in a hurry, and whereas I had no worries on that score, I didn't want my sexual proclivities being the butt of her anecdotes for years to come.

Watching her, weighing up possibilities, I wondered if I was being foolish. Perhaps Ann was exactly what I needed, as different to Jane as chalk to cheese.

It was something to think about.

But before I had a chance, the band played a last waltz and packed up for the night, leaving a silence that was quickly filled with chatter of departing guests.

'Jake!'

I turned to find Jane standing there, her arms held out.

'Jake,' she said again, 'thank you so much for everything. You were the best best man we could have asked for. I saw you dancing with all the aunts. How kind you were.'

'All part of the service.' I smiled down at her, taking her into my embrace, holding my best friend's bride for a moment before releasing her, and taking a self-defensive step backward. 'Where's Adam? Not tired of marriage already?'

She laughed gaily. 'Hope not. Wouldn't want to go on the honeymoon alone. He's over with his parents, saying his goodbyes.'

We were laughing comfortably together when Adam joined us, slipping his hand around Jane's waist and pulling her unresistingly towards him. 'Time to go. The car is here.' He turned to me and held out his hand. 'Jake, you were brilliant. Thanks.'

'You're welcome. You can do the same for me someday.'

We were soon surrounded by others pressing their goodbyes and best wishes on them both, and I was parted and pushed to the back of the group, further and further back until only the tops of their heads were visible. Realising my duties were done, I slipped away, found my car and sped down the long driveway, determined not to see the final departure to their secretly located honeymoon hotel.

But no matter how fast I drove, I couldn't stop thinking about it.

As I did, as I was swamped with envy for the life they had before them, I thought of Ann.

20

As it happened, the pace of business in Sebastian et Sebastian notched up quite a bit in the clamour to make more and more money for my clients and I had little time for the niceties of friendship or relationships with women. Especially ones as high maintenance as I guessed Ann would be. It was several weeks after the wedding before I spoke to Adam and then it was a brief *how are things* before cutting him off to take a far more important call. Adam understood. He always did.

By then, if I hadn't quite managed to forgive him for what I would probably always think of as his stealing Jane away, I'd at least learned to accept it as a fait accompli. I had to if I wanted to retain his friendship, and I had to have that if I wanted to stay close to Jane.

'How about meeting for lunch?' he said one day, catching me in a rare quiet moment, when I was weary from exhaustion, and beginning to question if it was all worth it, and I thought, *Hell, why not?* And so a new chapter in our friendship began as we slipped from the long-lost Friday night drinking sessions into a monthly lunch routine, and it was like before, Adam would talk and I, exhausted, would listen.

They became important to me, those monthly lunches, grounding me in a normality I seem to have lost in the fever that was the financial sector in those days. And yet, it was this very normality that grated, Adam's damn delirious happiness emphasising how far apart our lives were. The same damn happiness I knew was the root cause of my failure to find any. After all, he had Jane, I didn't.

It was a year later before I finally got a grip. Adam might be deliriously happy, but I was rich, my bonuses stacking up, unspent, and the world I lived in positively glittered with opportunities just waiting for me to get up and grasp.

'I'm thinking of buying a house,' I told Adam when we met for lunch that month. I hadn't actually, not until that moment, not until I saw his smiling face coming through the pub door and felt such resentment it almost choked me.

'Really?' he said, sitting and picking up the pint I had ordered on arrival. 'I like your apartment.'

'I need something with...' I searched for a word.

'That certain *je ne sais quoi*?' Adam asked flippantly, draining his pint and nodding, first at mine, and then toward the bar in the age-old silent question, *shall I get you another*?

I shook my head. 'Too many meetings this afternoon. Can't afford to be reeking of booze.'

He shook his head and smiled, patting his shirt pocket. 'Mints, Jake. Suck lots of mints.' He shrugged when I shook my head again. 'Suit yourself.' When he sat back down, an amber pint in his hand catching the dim light, he drank half and turned to me. 'So, a house, eh?'

'Yeah,' I said. I picked up my sandwich and took a bite. As I chewed, I thought, well, why not? My apartment was nice, but it didn't reflect my position, and it certainly didn't equate to Adam's happiness, nor was it a sufficient antidote to what I recognised just then, just in that one weak moment, as a gut-wrenching loneliness.

But a house? Well, it would be a start.

And it had to be the *right* house, I decided that evening as I drove around London, picking areas where I'd like to live. Next morning, I rang a reputable estate agent and told them what I wanted. When they heard my budget, I could hear the lip-smacking down the phone, and smiled. Money did make the world go around so smoothly, didn't it?

'I'm going to rent out my current apartment,' I added, hearing a sound that could have been a groan of pleasure. 'I'll want to move as soon as possible. Finance is in place. I've looked at your website. There are a few houses that interest me.'

'Excellent,' the agent said. 'We also have a couple of houses we are selling quietly, you understand. One of those, a house on Elgin Crescent, may be of interest. I don't know if you know the road?'

Did I? Elgin Crescent? I had driven along it. Lusted after a house there but seen nothing for sale.

'Yes, I do, in fact,' I said, trying to keep the tremor of excitement from my voice. A house there... it would shout success. Would invite envy. It would be... and the thought surprised me as it slipped sneakily into my head... as good, maybe even better, than the Bretts' house in the Cotswolds. 'I'd very much like to see that. Perhaps first?'

We arranged he'd pick me up the following day, to view three houses. The Elgin Crescent house, and two others that seemed to suit my needs.

The agent arrived on time, my doorbell pinging on the dot of eleven. 'Mark Curtis,' he said, holding out his hand as I opened the front door of my apartment block. I climbed into the passenger seat of his Saab and tuned out his patter as we made our way through the busy London streets he negotiated like a taxi driver, zipping up side streets and down laneways, until I had no idea where we were.

Finally, we arrived in Elgin Crescent, stopping in front of a huge, elegant nineteenth-century white semi-detached house that drew a groan of pleasure from me, my *wow* an instinctive gut reaction from a soul I didn't know I had. This was a house that screamed that the owner was someone. Someone important. A success.

For the first time in a long, long time, I thought of the house I'd grown up in, and my parents with their mind-numbing lack of ambition. I could imagine my father's voice, his critical, *ideas above his station*. I laughed, drawing a curious look from the agent.

Then I pushed my father back into the past where he belonged and climbed the steps to the front door.

21

The inside of the house lived up to the exterior. Huge rooms perfect, as the agent said, for entertaining on a grand scale.

I nodded knowingly, as if I entertained on a regular basis, and walked through the second reception room to where floor-to-ceiling glass doors overlooked the gardens, biting my lower lip to stop myself whimpering. It was stunning.

All the while, the agent was muttering dimensions and statistics, telling me about this or that feature. I wasn't really listening, but then he pressed a button and the wall of glass doors slowly opened. Luckily for my pride, my gasp of pleasure was swallowed by the swish as they all but disappeared. I walked across the threshold, feeling like Alice stepping through the looking-glass, and was mesmerised by the artfully decorated veranda where cloud-pruned box and beautiful acers in a mix of colours lent an oriental feel, the huge pots themselves works of art. I moved, as if in a daze, to the edge of the veranda, stood and looked down over the beautiful gardens, and knew I had gone to heaven.

The agent left me standing for some minutes before coughing softly and dragging me earthward. 'It is rather remarkable,' he said. 'The gardens are communal, private but communal. You can sit and admire but not actually have to do any work in them. There is a full-time gardener, of course. And,' he added, 'a yearly charge.'

A full-time gardener. For the second time that morning, I was transported back to my past, to the Oxford admissions office, and the eccentric Professor James who'd so kindly rescued me by offering me that gardening job and the room over the stable. How far I had come. The professor had died the previous year. I was sorry, I could have contacted him, told him how far his hand-up had got me.

He'd have been proud, I know. Not my parents, though. I had no intention of contacting them and hearing their sneering criticism.

I followed the agent down to what I would have called a basement but he referred to as lower-ground level, and took in the plunge pool, sauna and Jacuzzi without saying a word. In the well-equipped gym, I looked intently at some of the equipment, nodding knowledgeably, flexing a muscle, hoping to give the impression that I was a regular user.

'The vendors have indicated they might leave the equipment behind,' the agent said, as if that would be a deal breaker, as if I wouldn't buy this amazing house unless I could have the rowing machine, the treadmill and bench press.

There was also domestic accommodation on this level, two en suite bedrooms, kitchen and sitting room, with a separate front door so the 'help' could come and go. I couldn't imagine my ever having a need to use it, but I nodded as the agent showed me around as if having staff was something I was used to.

Back on the ground floor, we strolled through the kitchen but by now I was suffering from sensory overload and, apart from registering it was vast and well-equipped, thought no more of it.

Bedrooms – all six of them – were, of course, en suite, each luxuriously appointed, and far more spacious than the norm. The main bedroom had, in addition to the spacious en suite, a walk-in wardrobe so vast all my clothes would have fit in one corner.

'This is the one,' I told the agent, when we returned to the entrance hallway. 'I don't need to see any other houses. This is it.'

Mark Curtis, a man of my age, looked stunned, then disbelieving. 'They're asking ten point five,' he said. And then, just in case I was a total idiot, he added, 'Million.'

I nodded, smiled at him and said calmly, 'Tell them I'll pay ten.'

22

We settled, after multiple phone calls, on 10.255m, but as they agreed to leave all the curtains and carpets, some of the furniture and the gym equipment, I think I did okay. The bank, of course, had no problem with my £8 million mortgage, a figure I calculated I could pay off in four years – six if I didn't push it.

It was a vacant possession, the vendors having moved to Switzerland ahead of the approaching financial storm the rest of us pooh-poohed at, so the sale went through quickly and without the slightest hiccup. I kept expecting one, kept thinking I couldn't possibly be this lucky, expecting someone to turn up and offer more money for this dream of a house. But they didn't, and two months after seeing it, I had the keys in my hand. It was mine. I took a couple of days' holiday – an event that caused consternation and raised eyebrows in Sebastian et Sebastian – Francois even having the temerity to ask if I was losing interest in the company; if I had lost focus.

When I explained about my new house and name-dropped *Elgin Crescent* without compunction, I saw his eyes narrow. Buying a house like that was making a commitment... I was committed to making serious money for a long time. He knew that, so he smiled and congratulated me, told me to take all the time I wanted, knew I wouldn't because I couldn't bloody afford to. Consultants didn't get paid holidays and, anyway, there was always someone waiting to grab your clients if your focus so much as shimmied.

As it turned out, one day was enough. My apartment was being rented furnished, so there was little apart from a few personal belongings and clothes to move. I debated getting in a removal company but there was so little, really, I decided a small van would do the trick and hired one from a local company five minutes' walk from my apartment. But there's always more than you think. Two of the cardboard boxes I'd managed to find were soon filled with the contents of several drawers, paperwork I should really have gone through, read and shredded, but hadn't. Shoving it into the boxes, I made a mental note to go through it when I had a minute to spare, even as I knew I'd probably unpack it into drawers in Elgin Crescent where it would lie undisturbed until next time.

Everything else had to fit into the remaining three boxes and two suitcases. But of course, it didn't, so what was left was thrown into large refuse bags. Finally, it was all done, cupboards, drawers empty, checked and double checked. Now all I had to do was move the boxes and bags down in the lift, load it into the van, unload the other end and unpack. A removal company would have been so much easier, I thought, bending down to pick up the first box, feeling every muscle in my back groan. Of course, it was too bloody heavy. I had to empty half of the paper and books out and fill it with some of the clothes. Even then, I struggled to manage as I staggered with each to the lift I had wedged open. Finally, I had everything jammed willy-nilly in the van and was driving the short distance to Elgin Crescent, parking outside the house, and staring at it from the van with a sense of unreality. This was *mine*?

It seemed a shame to mess up the hallway, cover the lovely old tiles with all my belongings, but it was the easiest thing to do, especially since I hadn't thought to label anything and didn't know what was what.

Dropping the rental van back, I picked up my car, drove back to the house and parked outside. As I sat, tired beyond belief, it seemed to loom over me suddenly, its grandeur intimidating, making me almost afraid to go in. I thought of the small grey house I'd grown up in and my father's scathing criticism of those who reached for something better. What right had I to live in this glorious house on Elgin Crescent? I was a fraud. Shaking off the silly notion, and all memories of a life I had left way, way behind, I got out of the car and went up the steps to my front door. Inside, the sense of unreality that had swept over me might have persisted if I hadn't stupidly tripped over one of the bags that had slipped from the pile I had made. Arms flailing, I fell heavily and let out a blood-curdling yell as my right kneecap connected with the tiled floor. I grabbed my knee, convinced it was smashed and that my hand would come away red and dripping with blood. It didn't, of course, but bloody hell it hurt, so I stayed there, curled in the foetal position, groaning for a long time, wondering if this were an omen for the future. And then, my head resting on one of the bags filled with clothes, I slept.

It was dark when I woke, disorientated and still in pain. Wincing, I stood and hobbled over to the wall, feeling along it for the light switches, cursing loudly when I walked into a box, or was it a suitcase, shuffling along carefully until, eureka, my fingers found a switch and pressed it.

I checked my watch. It was only 10 p.m. The hall was a mess, and for a brief moment, I was tempted to leave it like that. My knee hurt. I had to work the next day and I was exhausted. And if I had had the sense to have labelled the various bags, boxes and cases, maybe I would have left it all. But did I know which case held my suits and shirts? Did I hell!

So, limping slightly, I hauled cases and bags upstairs, shoved some of the boxes into the kitchen and some into a downstairs room out of the way.

It didn't take long, after all, and soon my belongings were swallowed up by the vastness of the house, the few clothes I'd bothered to unpack eaten by the huge walk-in wardrobe in the main bedroom. The emptiness echoed around me, and I searched for the feeling of contentment I had expected, wandering from room to room, my sore knee forgotten. I admired the curtains that had been left behind by the previous owner, and made vague lists in my head of things that were needed to make the house into a home.

I gave up when my head-list became too long and complicated, forgot about the emptiness, and headed downstairs to the gym. I played around with some of the equipment, almost broke my neck trying to bench press above my weight, then jumped into the plunge pool before heading to the sauna to relax. But, of course, it had been turned off, as had the steam room. I stood there, naked and cold, and felt indescribably empty. I don't know how long I stood there, but realised I was going a pretty shade of blue and shook myself out of the depths in which I floundered.

I took a bottle of beer from the huge American fridge in the kitchen – beer being the only thing in it – and strolled from room to room, playing with switches, trying to see what was what. In one of the smaller rooms, a flick of a switch had a giant television screen slide quietly out of its hiding place. The room was empty, but I knew a small sofa had been left behind in the front reception room. I dragged it in, puffing and panting as I manoeuvred it through several doorways, then sat, exhausted. I switched on the TV and watched what came on without bothering to channel surf, sipping my beer, fetching a second and then a third and wondering what the hell I was going to do with such a big house.

The first thing I was going to do, I decided, getting up to fetch my fourth beer, was to buy a small fridge for this room.

Adam would enjoy that and Jane would be amused. I regretted not asking them to help me move in, but I'd wanted to wait till I had it perfect. I wanted Adam to see what I'd achieved and for him to be envious of me for a change, when I had spent so many years being envious of him.

And I suppose I wanted Jane to have a twinge of regret that she'd fallen in love with the wrong guy.

Maybe it was a combination of alcohol and exhaustion, but as I crossed the hallway to the kitchen, the slap of my leather soles on the tiled floor seemed to echo in the vast emptiness of the house. It was a strangely eerie sound, carrying memories of walking through other places... the grey home I'd been brought up in; the tiny but homely apartment that Adam and Jane lived in; the shabby ancient comfort of the Brett home in the Cotswolds. I didn't bother going for that fourth beer. I'd had enough, it was making me maudlin when I should have been brimming with excitement.

With a sigh, I kicked off my shoes and climbed the stairs in my stockinged feet. No more echoes. It was tiredness and alcohol. A good night's sleep would sort the first. But when I opened my bedroom door, I groaned.

I was letting my apartment fully furnished and planned to buy a massive new bed for this bedroom. Planned... I hadn't, though.

The carpet was soft but when I looked around the vast empty

space, I couldn't bring myself to simply curl up on the floor. Instead, I went into the dressing room, shut the door behind me, and in this small, cosy space, I tried to sleep.

23

I passed Francois as I headed to my office next morning. He looked me up and down and laughed softly.

'It was a stressful day, no?'

I grinned and nodded. 'Slightly, Francois.'

He gave a gracious smile and moved off.

Of course, *he* wouldn't bloody know how stressful it was. Probably had hundreds of minions to do all the hard work. I couldn't imagine Francois having to sleep on the floor because he didn't have a damn, blasted bed.

My eyes felt gritty from lack of sleep, my head aching from the surfeit of beer. Coffee, gallons of it, seemed to help, focused me on what to do.

A very helpful sales assistant in Harrods assured me a bed would be delivered that very day. Several questions narrowed down my requirements, and I was promised the delivery would exceed my expectations. That's the way they speak in Harrods. I was so impressed by their service, it was tempting to order a house full of furniture and be done with it; six beds, twelve bedside tables, twelve table lamps; a dining room table and chairs; a kitchen table and chairs. And a partridge in a pear tree. No, really, that wasn't the way to do it, was it?

At least I had a bed. Or I would, if I could organise someone to be there when they delivered. No way could I take more time away.

There was only one person I could call. I checked the time... nine... picked up the phone and dialled the number from memory, drumming my fingers impatiently as it rang and rang. Then, just as I was about to hang up, a sleepy voice muttered something incomprehensible.

'Adam?'

'Jake? It's the middle of the night.'

'It's nine, Adam. The rest of the world is hard at work.'

There was whispering at the other end of the line, I didn't catch the words. 'Jane says hello,' Adam's still sleepy voice said. 'Sorry, mate, we have a few days off and stayed up late watching some stupid chick-flick... oomph! Bloody hell, Jane, that hurt. Jake, she attacked me, save me, I'm married to a violent husband-beater.'

My smile was automatic, but brief. 'Adam, I'm in a bind. Would you be able to go out to Elgin Crescent for me? I'm getting a bed delivered. You'd have to call here first and pick up the keys. If you have plans, obviously I'll understand.'

'Hey, we'd love to, wouldn't we, Jane?' Jane had obviously moved closer to listen in on the conversation because her *absolutely* came through clearly. 'We've been dying to get a look at the house,' Adam added. 'You know we'll investigate every nook and cranny.'

'Knock yourselves out,' I said, relief at having the bed situation sorted swamping the tinge of regret they were seeing it before I was ready. 'I'm going to be tied up most of the day; I'll leave the keys at reception. I owe you.'

Hanging up, I leaned back in my chair and took another sip of coffee. Jane would love the house. I imagined her wandering around its lovely rooms, planning what sort of furniture she would have if it were hers. The seed of an idea came to me; ask her to choose the furniture for me. She had such good taste, and I know she would do a fantastic job. Even as that seed took root, I poured paraquat on it, let it wither and die. That way definitely lay madness.

But someone else? Wouldn't that be the solution? And I knew just who to ask.

Moments later, I was tapping gently on Francois's office door, waiting for permission to enter, waiting the requisite time to show his worth and prove my lack thereof. Sometimes, I wondered how much longer I could put up with all the crap I had to deal with. Then I thought of the money and shrugged.

Francois's office was a huge, gracious room with windows on two sides. Walking into it was like stepping back in time; if the designer, who had redecorated just two years ago, had been aiming for *Victorian gentleman's club*, he did a brilliant job because that's just what it felt like.

The big oak desk was incidental to the room and sat discreetly in the farthest corner. Francois looked up from behind it as I entered and beckoned me forward. 'What can I do for you, Jake?'

'I was wondering...' I started, then stopped, not sure how to phrase my request. 'It's just that...' I tried again. Admitting I needed help, was that the persona I wanted to show? No, it wasn't. Okay. 'I love this room, Francois. It has that certain something that I hope to achieve when I furnish Elgin Crescent. You would be doing me an immense service if you could tell me who the designer was.' That was better... strong... I know what I want, and how to get it.

Francois nodded. 'I too love this room. Of course I will give you the name. It is my friend, Marcel.' He reached into a drawer of the desk, and almost without looking, removed a card and handed it to me.

'Thank you, Francois.'

He nodded my dismissal. I stood a few seconds more, as was the accepted behaviour of a Sebastian et Sebastian underling, and then turned and left, the precious card safe in my sticky little paw.

I didn't look at it until I was safely back to my own office, and then I did as if it were the Holy Grail itself. But I didn't shout *eureka* when I looked at the rather garish purple card with the name Marcel in Copperplate Gothic font on the front, and an address and phone number on the reverse, in fact, I felt a distinct anti-climax. This was it?

I'd wanted to be grabbed, to feel as if Marcel could make my dream come true and turn Elgin Crescent into a home... like Jane's, only bigger, like the Bretts', only modern. Garish purple wasn't a good start.

Having nothing to lose, I dialled the number and got a pleasant voice asking me how she could help.

'Hi,' I replied, 'I'd like to speak to Marcel, please. My name is Jake Mitchell.' And just in case it might speed things up, I added, 'I work with Francois Sebastian.'

If I had hoped using Francois's name would open doors, I was destined to be disappointed. 'I'm afraid Marcel is out of the country at present. Is there some way I could help you?'

'I've just bought a house and wanted someone to do some interior decorating stroke designing for me. I was recommended Marcel.'

'Ah, I see,' the voice said, and I could almost hear the head nodding. I certainly could hear keys clicking. 'Marcel would be able to fit another client into his very tight schedule sometime in January.'

'January?' There was a definite tone of disbelief in my voice, I couldn't help it. For God's sake, that was six months away.

'As I said, Marcel has a very tight schedule. There may be another designer in the company with fewer demands on their time, if you would be interested in going with someone else. They will have trained with Marcel. They are not, of course, *Marcel*, but...'

'Fine,' I said, getting the picture. I could get my house done by someone who works for Marcel, but I wouldn't be able to say my home was *done* by Marcel. Who gave a monkey's? 'That would be fine. Is there anyone available immediately?'

There was an indrawn breath, as if I had asked the unthinkable, and keys clicked away for a full minute before she came back to me. 'As it happens... and this is a very rare happening... a client has had to pull out, and one of our designers has a window free. Her name is Daisy Cranford.'

Daisy? Isn't that a cow's name? 'Daisy Cranford. Great. Perfect. When can she come out and get things started?' I was already getting bored with this.

'I just need to take some information, Mr Mitchell. Then I will forward your details to Daisy, and she will contact you to arrange a preliminary meeting. She will have a contract for you to fill out, and it will list payment structure and terms.'

'Fine, fine.'

A minute later, I had had enough.

'Okay, miss, I really do have to go now, and earn some money to pay for what sounds like is going to cost a small fortune. If Daisy needs any more information, she can ask when she rings. Just tell her I need this done as soon as, okay?' And on that note, I hung up.

For the next eight hours, I didn't think about the house apart from a small smile when I read a message from Adam.

Hse mega, bed humungus, Jane droolin.

When the phone rang at 7.30, I assumed it was one of my over-seas clients, and tried to shake off the weariness as I answered. 'Jake Mitchell.'

'Hi, Mr Mitchell, this is Daisy from Marcel.'

God, did I need this now? Scraping together a modicum of enthusiasm, I answered, 'Hello. Thank you for getting back to me so quickly.'

'Well, Janet said you had emphasised the urgency of your need, Mr Mitchell.'

I laughed. 'That's a nice way of putting it.'

I thought she would laugh too, but oh no. 'We take our clients' concerns very seriously, Mr Mitchell.'

Very seriously, oh, my God. Why had I answered the damn phone? 'Listen, I'm sorry, I'm just heading to a meeting. Can we arrange a time for you to come and see the house?'

We settled on the following evening.

24

Daisy was on the doorstep when I got home the next day, a slim briefcase in one hand, the other reaching out for mine, the standard conciliatory smile curving her decidedly pretty mouth. I switched my door keys to my other hand, clasped hers in what I hoped was a manly shake, being careful not to hold for too long, I didn't want to appear to be making moves on her. Actually, I thought, as she moved ahead of me, her derriere moving with well-toned grace behind her smart pencil skirt, I wouldn't have minded making a move.

In the hallway, she stopped and admired its generous proportions before following me into the lounge.

'I'd invite you to sit,' I said with a smile, 'but as you can see...'

She nodded and looked around, her face still serious. Was it so Botoxed that she couldn't crack a smile?

Opening her briefcase, she took out a notebook, placed the briefcase gently on the floor at her feet and started scribbling, walking from one wall to the other and, I suppose, guessing dimensions in that manner. 'This is just a rough guide, obviously,' she said, without lifting pen from paper, 'but I find it helps me envisage the area better than the equivalent electronic equipment.'

From room to room we went, and after my first unsuccessful attempts to lighten the communication between us, I stopped trying, and eventually, when I opened a bathroom door and caught myself saying the blindingly bloody obvious, 'This is a bathroom,' I stopped talking altogether, and opened door after door in an increasingly uncomfortable silence. All I wanted, then, was for the whole thing to be over, and to get rid of the blasted woman. Who needed furniture anyway?

We finished the tour, back where we started. She closed her notebook, picked up her briefcase and, opening it, dropped the notebook inside. I drew a breath of relief, thinking my torture was nearly over, then her hand came out of that damn briefcase holding an A4 pad of paper. Placing the briefcase down again, she looked at me. 'There're just a few questions, Mr Mitchell, regarding your likes and dislikes, colours, styles, et cetera.'

In fact, there were so many questions I had to bite my lip to stop myself from screaming. Finally, I had had enough. 'Ms Cranford...'

'Please,' she interrupted me, 'Daisy.'

I nodded. 'Daisy. I want the house to look elegant and charming.' I thought of Adam's family home in the Cotswolds, the old inherited *stuff*, the shabby gentility, the air of having been like that for aeons... that was what I wanted. *Adam's life...* the thought made me blink... was that what I was trying to recreate?

'Elegant and charming.' Daisy didn't bother to scribble the words down. I thought she looked disappointed. Maybe elegance and charm were too yesterday.

Desperate to get finished, I tried again to get my idea across. 'Think old country house meets city mansion.' I used my forefingers to make inverted commas around the phrase. 'Give me a coherent mix of old and new. Don't fuss about colours; give me warmth, comfort, style. Do you understand?'

'Old country house meets city mansion? Hmmmm.' Then she put the pad back into her briefcase and, thank the Lord, held her hand out. 'I'll have my ideas ready in a week, Mr Mitchell.'

'Tomorrow,' I said, holding on to her hand.

She raised her eyes to the ceiling and sighed. 'The day after. That's the absolute best I can do.'

And she was true to her word. Five o'clock, two days later, she arrived at Sebastian et Sebastian, and handed me a smart folder filled with her ideas. There were scraps of material pinned to some pages, with accompanying pictures, or drawings of sofas and chairs, photos of lamps, table lamps and artwork, and on and on. I didn't read past the first page. 'Okay,' I said to her. 'How soon can this all be done?'

The silence stretched far longer than it should. 'You want me to get everything?' Her voice was bemused.

Why was she making this so difficult? 'This is all the stuff you think I need, isn't it?'

Stuff. She bridled at the word. I suppose if you call yourself a home design consultant and charge the earth for your services; a word like stuff *is* slightly dismissive. But I was the one coughing up the earth. I could call it what the hell I liked. 'Yes,' she finally admitted, probably thinking of the huge commission she would earn, 'but...'

I didn't give her a chance to finish. 'Then go and get it. How soon can it all be done?'

And that was that. Two weeks later, I arrived home and opened my front door to a different house. Lamps cast pools of light, artwork adorned the walls, chairs, some obviously old, stood in little groups huddled around modern, low occasional tables. Big sofas invited in the lounge, soft leather recliners in the den. A huge, very old oak table almost overwhelmed the dining room, only saved from doing so by the modern, very delicate chairs in a variety of hues that surrounded it. It shouldn't have worked, but it did. 'Well done, Daisy,' I said into the silence, spinning around, delighting in how well it all looked.

I rang Adam... who else? 'You have to come and see how it looks. Bring Jane, come and I'll open a bottle.'

'It's ten o'clock, Jake,' Adam said with a laugh. 'How about tomorrow?'

Mentally flitting through my schedule for the next day, I groaned. 'No can do. Maybe Thursday, but I'll have to get back to you, okay?'

I hung up and wandered around the house again. I should have been happy, shouldn't I? This was everything I wanted... proof I was doing well. But as I walked around, my footsteps echoing on the tiled floors, all I could think of were my father's words, *ideas above his station.*

25

In the way things happened in those days, it was almost two weeks later before Adam and Jane came, the doorbell chiming just as I unpacked canapés grabbed from the deli on the way home. Luckily, they came arranged on platters because just at that moment, as the last peal of the doorbell faded, I realised the one thing Daisy hadn't bought. Unable to decide on what type of dinner service I wanted, I had told her to leave it, I would get something myself eventually. Of course, I hadn't. Had, in fact, forgotten all about it. Never having eaten at home since I moved in, it had never been an issue. Now, here I was with guests and food, and no damn plates. Or cutlery.

And then, with a feeling of absolute dread, I thought of the champagne. Did I have anything to drink it from?

The doorbell pealed again.

Where had I seen glasses? I rushed from the kitchen into the hall, made a half-dart towards the lounge then swerved to the den. Yes! There they were. On top of the fridge. They were beer glasses, but at least we wouldn't have to drink from the bottle.

I grabbed them, hurried back to the kitchen and dumped

them on the counter just as the doorbell pealed again. I rushed to answer it, pulling the heavy door open, smiling, and sighing with relief at the same time. 'I'm so sorry,' I said, waving them through the door. 'I'm only just in myself and have just found out something absolutely shocking.'

'Oh, no!' Jane had closed in for a hug; she pulled back and looked at me with concern. 'What is it?'

I laughed. 'No, don't worry, I'm being a drama queen. It's plates. Well...' I elaborated with a sigh, 'plates, cutlery, proper glasses.' They followed me as I walked back to the kitchen where I picked up a beer glass with a grimace. 'We'll have to drink the champagne out of these, I'm afraid.'

'Suits me,' Adam said, picking one up. 'Fit a lot more in.'

'And we don't need plates.' Jane picked up a smoked salmon canapé and popped it into her mouth with an exaggerated *mmmm* of pleasure.

With the champagne opened, we drank to my new home, beer glasses clinking heavily. I waved my glass towards the open door to the hallway. 'Let me show you the rest.'

'Hang on.' Adam reached out and moved the remaining canapés onto one tray, then, picking it up in one hand and his glass in the other, he stood. 'Okay, ready.'

I caught Jane's eye and smiled. She smiled back and shook her head. 'He's a hopeless case, Jake.' Then she took my arm, leaving Adam to follow, and I took her... them... around my home.

'I had a few old things inherited from my family, the designer incorporated them in quite well, I think.' I'd practised the lie and it came out easily.

'It's absolutely lovely,' Jane said, letting her hand linger on fabric, paper and paint. 'She did a really good job. It's a beautiful house, of course, but she has made it even better.' Picking up a vase, she held it up to the light, admiring the delicate pattern.

'That was left to my mother by a favourite aunt,' I lied smoothly. 'I'm not sure how old it is, but I've always liked it.'

'It's lovely.' She turned it over, as people do, to read its provenance on the base and looked slightly puzzled before smiling and returning the vase to its place without further comment.

We finished the champagne, opened another, finished that. The canapés were good but totally insufficient for our alcohol-stimulated appetites, a problem easily rectified with a quick phone call to a nearby Indian takeaway who did fast delivery. We used the trays from the canapés as plates, and our fingers in lieu of cutlery, and it was one of the best meals I had ever had. I remembered the estate agent's remark about entertaining on a grand scale and laughed, then had to explain why, and Adam and Jane laughed too.

Midnight came and went. I wanted them to stay, take my new bed, but they wouldn't have it and insisted on going home. I countered their insistence by ordering a taxi on my account, and when it arrived, I walked with them, stood in my doorway and waved them away. I stood as the lights of their taxi turned the corner and were gone, stood a while longer, reluctant to turn around and face the emptiness, so much emptier now they had been and gone.

I did finally turn, then, remembering Jane's puzzled expression from earlier, I went to the vase and picked it up, admired it as she had done, turned it over as she had done, read the word written there.

As she had done.

Debenhams.

I remembered her smile. Her pitying, condescending smile, and in that second... for just that one tiny moment... felt an intense hatred for her, for Adam, for this damn house, a hatred that sent the vase flying across the room, before it dissolved, like the vase, into a million shards and splinters.

26

There had to be a party, of course. I invited everyone; people I didn't know but worked with in some capacity or other; people I had met briefly and wanted to get to know better; those who knew people I knew; those who might be interested in investing money with Sebastian et Sebastian; and, of course, Adam and Jane.

I had mentioned having a party during their visit, and they were keen to help. 'I can do some cooking for you, if you like,' Jane offered, but I shook my head.

'I'm getting a catering company. Just come and enjoy yourselves.'

It was, in fact, an event management company, not a catering company, but I didn't want to sound pretentious. Recommended by one of my party-animal clients, S'amuser offered a very comprehensive service and the manager, Horace, was extremely helpful. 'If you like, Mr Mitchell, you can leave it all to us. Just tell me what you want, a rough idea of your budget, and we can work out a plan. It will be sent to you tomorrow; you can look it over and let us know if it's acceptable. We can tweak it as you need.'

Breathing a sigh of relief, I agreed and, true to his word, next day I received a beautifully presented plan sent by courier to my office. There was nothing they had left to chance, nothing they didn't charge an astronomical amount of money to provide, but the best cost, and I wanted the best. I looked at the final page, the discreetly written figure on the bottom right-hand corner, shook my head at the cost and picked up the phone. A moment later, I was speaking to Horace.

'It's Jake Mitchell. Thank you for the proposal for my house-warming party, which appears to cover every eventuality. Explain to me the payment details.' I wasn't a fool; I wasn't paying the lot upfront.

'A fifty per cent deposit, Mr Mitchell. With the balance paid within twenty-four hours of the party. We prefer electronic transfer; I can give you the details now, if you wish.'

It was all very civilised. Is there any language as powerful as money? If you had enough, you could be whatever you wanted... make your life whatever you wanted it to be... and the past didn't matter.

It didn't matter... but sometimes, especially when I was debating the morality of spending such a ludicrous amount of money on party food, it would come barrelling back and I'd be there in that poky kitchen with my parents, steam rising from that revolting cottage pie to make my eyes water.

No matter how rich I became, that past was always going to be there. And once again, I was back to being envious of Adam.

27

The afternoon of the party, having obtained keys earlier in the week, the S'amuser staff arrived and got to work. I've no idea how many staff were involved, but when I arrived home from work, the house was transformed. Twinkling lights lined the steps to the front door and inside strands of lights draped the stairway. Dramatic floral arrangements brightened several corners of the house. Nowhere was left undone.

There was nothing for me to do except shower, change and wait for the first guests to arrive. A butler answered the door, checked the invitation, and directed the guests to where they could leave their coats. The invitation said eight. By 8.30, the house hummed, and I was meeting and greeting, smiling, nodding acknowledgement of various people's congratulations, drinking in the envious looks as my guests wandered around rooms, their oohs and aahs loud enough to be heard over the light background music chosen by S'amuser to heighten the ambience.

Uniformed waiters walked around with strange-looking edible things on trays. 'What are these?' I asked one, as a huge tray was balanced and lowered before me.

'Mini boeuf en croute, sir,' the waiter replied, holding the tray steady as I picked one and popped it into my mouth. It was delicious. I wasn't so lucky with the next, popping the offering into my mouth without enquiring what it was, biting down on something salty, slimy. I swallowed without chewing. Oysters, I guessed, taking a swig of my champagne and surreptitiously swilling it around my mouth to get rid of the taste.

I looked around for the waiter bearing the mini boeuf en croute, caught Jane's eye across the room, and smiled. I headed across the room to join her. Almost at her side, a client grabbed my arm. 'Jake! Great party. Let me introduce you to Pieter Anderson. I've told him all about Sebastian et Sebastian and he is keen to hear more.'

Wasn't this just what I had hoped for? Impress people, and they will flock to you, want to be a part of your success. I could read their minds, knew most, if not all, were thinking, *he's doing well for himself. Sebastian et Sebastian must be doing extremely well.* And, as I half expected, some of those present were on the phone to me next morning looking for investment advice which, of course, I gave... and charged for... and earned money for Sebastian et Sebastian. That was the way business went... then. Still, my eyes drifted to where Jane was chatting quietly with Adam, and I wished my client and his friend to the far corners of the globe.

Pieter wanted a cigarette, so we drifted onto the veranda, the glass doors open wide to the night. Determined not to spend too long talking business, I promised to arrange a meeting with him to discuss investment options. I gave him my card, introduced him to some other people, then left them talking and headed back into the house to mingle with other guests. I wandered from group to group, accepting the congratulations I was offered with a modest smile. Drink flowed; champagne corks popped. It was all a great success. Everyone loved the house, the men lusting after the gym and the television room, the women in raptures over the sauna, the kitchen and the dressing room attached to the master bedroom.

By two o'clock, most of the guests had left, some so drunk they could barely stand. The caterers tidied up, cleared away the mess of half-eaten food, dirty glasses, and even the vomit that pooled by the cloud-pruned box. Jane wanted to help them, but I pulled her and Adam into the den, and sat drinking wine with them until the work was done, and all the catering staff had left.

'That was fun,' Jane said.

I saw the lie in her eyes and laughed. 'Liar, you hated it!'

'No,' she demurred, then seeing my eyebrows raise, conceded, 'well, you know me, it's not really my scene. All those business types.'

'Boring buggers.' Adam's voice was slurred.

Jane thumped him on the arm. 'He's had way too much to drink. We'd better get going before he does something I will regret.'

I watched as she fished around in her handbag for car keys. 'I wish you'd taken a taxi, or you could have stayed here, then you could have had some champagne.'

'That's okay, I didn't feel like drinking tonight.'

Suddenly, it dawned on me. It was so unusual for Jane not to drink at all. Was she trying to get pregnant? Or maybe already pregnant? Her belly looked as flat as usual in the figure-hugging dress she was wearing. But then when does the bump become apparent? I had no idea. 'You sure you're okay?' I said, giving her the opening, the opportunity to tell me.

'I'm fine, honestly. Just preferred to drive tonight, that's all.'

'You'll have to come over another night, stay over and we can have a meal and a few bottles. Okay?' Another opening. Now was the time for her to say, *well, actually…*

She didn't, or maybe there was nothing to tell. 'That'd be lovely. We'll look forward to that, won't we?'

She nudged Adam, who had fallen asleep, and he jerked awake with a snort and a cry of, 'Whaat, whaat!'

'Come on, let's get you home.' She sounded exasperated, her voice sharper than I'd heard before.

Did I have a moment's hope? No. For even in that exasperation, the hand that lay on Adam's arm caressed in a reflex action of intimacy, her eyes softened as she looked at him, and the sharpness gave way quickly to a sweet, 'Come on, darling.'

'S'all over?' He looked at me, his eyes slits in his sleepy, inebriated face, then he swayed over and enveloped me in a bear-hug, his breath 100 proof. 'You're a good friend.'

I saw them out, watching from the doorway as Jane opened the passenger door and all but pushed Adam inside, before turning, waving, and climbing into the driving seat. She reversed and drove out the gate, and I stood, my hand raised in a salute nobody saw, then turned and closed the door behind me.

The house seemed suddenly big and empty, and very, very quiet. I thought of Adam and Jane's cosy apartment, and then of Jane, her belly swelling with a child that wasn't mine.

Money could buy me so much... but it couldn't buy me that.

28

Six months later, Adam and Jane finally bought a house. Way out in Hanwell. Despite saving every penny, and a generous amount of help disguised as a wedding present from Adam's parents, it was the best they could afford. They wanted a family home with a garden for the children they hoped to have. If they were trying, if Jane had been pregnant the day of my party, nothing had come of it. But I suppose that's the way it is with babies, you spend years trying not to make the little buggers, then when you want one, they go nah, nah, nah nah, nah.

Adam had phoned, told me they'd seen a house they liked. But they had seen any number over the last few months and had either been outbid or had decided against making an offer for any one of several reasons. He'd shown me the list he and Jane had made of their requirements and had been annoyed when I laughed. Why wouldn't I? This was London. With their budget, they were already going to find it difficult, and they had a list as long as a Chinese takeaway menu.

'It's got a south-westerly garden,' Adam gushed down the

phone. 'Three decent-sized bedrooms, good-sized reception rooms, an attic ripe for development, and it's on a quiet road. It's just perfect. It needs a bit of work, which is why we can afford it. Jane is afraid to get too excited. She's worried we'll be outbid again.'

'If it's what you want, I hope it works out for you this time.' I couldn't think of anything else to say. After all, it was Hanwell. Miles away.

Their offer had been accepted by the time I spoke to Adam again. He immediately insisted I come with him to see the house.

'Meet me at Paddington,' he said, his excitement buzzing down the line. 'It's not on a Tube but we can get a train from there and it's about a ten-minute walk the other end.'

We fixed on a time and, as usual, I was there on the dot and he was five minutes late. I watched him bouncing towards me, his excitement palpable and contagious. 'Jake,' he said, by way of a greeting, grabbing me in a man-hug, then pushing me away roughly. 'Can you believe it? We've bought a house.'

He gave me a brick-by-brick description of it, so my expectations were high as we walked from the station and turned into a narrow pretty road with red-bricked terraced houses and neat railed gardens.

'They're Edwardian, like yours, but on a much smaller scale. There's a lovely park nearby and' – Adam pointed to the end of the road – 'around the corner there are shops, coffee shops, a pub. Everything we need.'

I was nodding. I could see the appeal. It was a very attractive area.

We were still walking when, with a grand wave to our left, Adam stopped. 'This is it.'

My expectations high, I turned, mouth already open, congratulations sitting on the tip of my tongue waiting to be said. Wanting to say it. Really, really wanting to say, *Congratulations*, *it's lovely*. Unable to squeeze out a single word. Of any sort. Unable to do anything but stand and stare.

He'd told me they'd got it at a good price, so I should have guessed. It was a wreck. Window frames rotten, glass cracked in two of the four front windows. Even from where we stood, it was obvious the roof needed retiling. A gutter hanging perilously, waited to drip, or worse fall, on the head of anyone who dared pass through the front door.

Adam, watching me as I struggled to find something positive to say, grinned. 'It needs a bit of work.' Then he laughed. 'I'll rephrase that. It needs a *lot* of work.'

I joined in, trying desperately not to allow my laughter take on an edge of condescension, keeping my mouth shut for fear of what I might say.

Still laughing, we turned automatically in the direction of hurried footsteps on the path. 'It's the agent.' Adam waved a hand in greeting at the harried young man who approached, key in hand.

'A fine property you've purchased, Mr Brett.' The agent smiled ingratiatingly and inserted the key in the door.

Adam caught my eye and winked.

The agent struggled with the key, twisting and turning it in a lock that hadn't seen oil for a long time. The door was obviously rotten. I was tempted to say one good push would have opened it, would have sent it flying through the even more rotten door frame, but in deference to Adam's feelings, I bit my tongue. Hard. I kept biting when the key eventually did turn with an ominous click that told me he'd never lock it again, kept biting when Adam, with an air of possessiveness, invited me in.

I wanted to sneer at the tiny decrepit house, instead I felt a piercing dart of jealousy as I pictured him, some day in the future, carrying Jane over the threshold of the first home they'd bought together. Imagined them making the house into a home and filling it with children, love, and laughter.

And I'd be on the outside, looking in.

29

I tried to put my stupid jealousy to one side as I followed Adam through to a tiny hall with peeling wallpaper and the cloying smell of old dirty carpet.

'The roof needs to be retiled but the house itself is structurally sound,' Adam explained as he led the way. 'We had an extensive survey done. It just needs cosmetic work. Maybe a new kitchen.'

The stench upstairs was nauseating. I noticed the agent stayed well clear, and I could understand why. I could feel the stink pervading my clothes, my hair, my skin, knew it would stay with me for the remainder of the day. The agent would probably be going to visit other houses, other potential clients. He wouldn't want to smell like decay.

The stink was worst in the bathroom where an old suite sat, stained, cracked and reeking of effluent. The floor had been carpeted sometime in a dim and very distant past, and now, peppered as it was with stains of unknown origin, it had taken on a life of its own.

'I tell you what, Adam,' I said, closing the bathroom door in a vain attempt to be able to draw a breath, 'I still haven't bought you a wedding present. I'll give you a new bathroom.'

He looked stunned. 'No way! That's not why I brought you here. It's very generous of you but I couldn't let you do that.'

'I insist. I was thinking of a painting by that new artist you were admiring. But I think a new bathroom would be a better option. It's up to you, though, if you'd prefer...'

'Bentley Combs?' Adam interrupted me in awe.

I nodded. 'To be honest, a bathroom will be a cheaper option. But if you would prefer the painting...'

Adam grinned. 'No... well... yes, but I think maybe we need the bathroom more. Bloody hell, Jane will be thrilled.'

I followed him downstairs to the kitchen. Although compact, it was big enough to fit a small table and chairs. In the corner of the room, an old television was affixed to the wall by a bracket.

'They'd have had a right pain in their necks craning to watch that.' Adam turned away to open and close the old-fashioned cupboards, one of which lurched sideways and refused to be shut.

He was explaining what they were going to have done. I wasn't listening... or not to him... I was staring at the TV and listening to echoes from my past.

Without warning, the walls closed in on me and the ceiling pressed down. My eyes darted right and left. Where was the door? I had to get out. An unaccustomed panic hit me, beads of sweat pinging from the pores on my forehead, under my arm, in the small of my back. An acrid smell of sweat, mingling with the other odours, swirled around me.

I felt a hand on my arm.

'You okay, Jake?' Adam looked worried. He reached a hand out to hold my arm.

I could feel beads of sweat running down my face, trickling down my neck, soaking into my collar. 'Need to get some air.'

Adam kept his hand on my arm and guided me without fuss towards the door that was directly behind where I stood. He pushed it open with his foot and led me down the hallway to the front door. The agent stood there; he opened his mouth to speak but was silenced by a hand-chop from Adam. 'Not now. Jake's not well.'

I sat on the doorstep and wiped my forehead with my shirt-sleeve. 'Sorry. Don't know what came over me.'

'Just sit there for a while,' Adam said, then left me to have a word with the agent.

My eyelids fluttered closed. After a while, I felt someone brush by and heard muttering and the metallic sound of a key in a lock rattling, rattling, more muttering, more rattling.

'Lock seems to have broken,' the voice eventually said, the words floating across me to where Adam stood at the small gate to the postage stamp-sized front garden.

Adam stepped over me and tried the key.

'It broke on the way in,' I said, my voice clear, opening my eyes and looking up at the two men who were standing squashed together between me and the front door. 'I heard it snap when you opened it.'

A look of annoyance flitted across the agent's face as if, somehow, I was to blame. 'I'll have to get a locksmith to come and change the lock.' He looked at his watch, closed his eyes on a mental oath, took out his phone and quickly tapped in a number. He walked away from us, speaking rapidly.

'You feel better?' Adam asked, looking down on me.

'I feel like a right idiot, but I feel better. I think it was the smell.'

Adam opened his mouth to speak, then hesitated and hunched down beside me. 'Are you sure you're okay, Jake?' His voice was so unusually serious I wondered what he had seen in my face.

I stood abruptly, unbalancing Adam who reached out instinctively for the nearest solid surface. Unfortunately, he reached for the door, whose wood was anything but solid. Rotten and weakened by woodworm, it gave way immediately, and Adam's hand went straight through. Followed quickly by his arm.

I tried to pull him back, even as more and more of him vanished. Adam flailed around, blinking and spitting away dust and rotten wood, doing more and more damage so that within the space of seconds he had demolished the lower half of the door.

'Shit, Adam, I'm sorry,' I said, desperately trying to help. 'I didn't mean... are you all right... let me help you.' I managed to get him on his feet, and we were brushing wood, dust, and insects from his clothes and hair when the agent returned and looked at the door in disbelief.

'What the fuck!'

We tried to explain, our explanations becoming increasingly incomprehensible as we struggled not to laugh. As we stood, the three of us looking at one another, a soft creak came from the door. We swivelled to look, hurriedly stepping away as the creak became a groan. In slow motion, the upper part of the door, no longer supported by its lower half, decrepit as that was, collapsed.

We couldn't hold it in any longer. Adam and I collapsed into raucous laughter, holding on to one another, tears streaming down our faces.

'It's not funny,' the agent tried. Then a smile pushed up the corners of his severe mouth and a restrained chuckle followed. Moments later, all three of us were howling, grabbing one another, pointing at the door.

The agent was the first to recover. Shaking his head, he pulled out his phone. He took another look at the door, as if to make sure it had really happened. Then, with a final chuckle and head shake, he walked away from us with the phone to his mouth, speaking slowly this time in a bid to explain his current predicament.

Adam dried his eyes on the end of his T-shirt. 'Jane is never going to believe this.'

'She'll be sorry she missed it,' I said. 'Oh, hang on...' I pulled out my phone and took several photographs of the now empty doorway and the pile of rubble that was all that remained of the door. 'I'll send these to you; otherwise, she'll never believe it.'

The agent bustled back. 'I've someone coming to board it up. On the basis that the door was rotten, we won't be replacing it, I'm afraid.'

Adam held both hands up appeasingly. 'Don't worry, mate. We had planned to have the windows and doors replaced first thing anyway. Sorry for all the trouble. We're heading for a pint if you'd like to join us, help wash all the dry rot away.'

The agent shook his head regretfully. 'I'm going to have to stay here for the carpenter, but thanks.'

Adam nodded, and we headed off, brushing dust and debris from our clothes as we walked, an occasional chuckle still coming from Adam, who would turn and punch me on the arm.

Neither of us mentioned the earlier incident, and Adam didn't repeat his question.

If he had... perhaps I'd have told him why his kitchen had so affected me, dragging me back to my past as it had done, a past I was so desperately trying to forget but which, now and then, insisted on pushing its way into my thoughts.

And perhaps if I'd confessed my lie to him then, I wouldn't have felt obliged to keep trying to be something I wasn't, and my life might have ended differently.

30

The sale of Jane's apartment went through faster than they expected, and she and Adam found themselves temporarily homeless.

I held my breath when I heard, not believing my luck. 'You'll move in with me until everything is sorted,' I said to Adam, then laughed. 'I'll squeeze you into one of the smaller rooms in the attic.'

Initially I thought about giving them the room next to mine; it overlooked the rear garden, double doors opening onto a Juliet balcony where I envisaged Jane standing – only Jane, my imagination would never face up to reality. But then it was *my* imagination, it was allowed to dream.

I worried the room was too close. Would I hear the cosy domestic noises of running water, flushing toilets, murmuring voices? Worse, would I hear the intimate sounds of lovemaking, the grunts and groans, the moans of ecstasy? Would I lie awake, listening, taking vicarious pleasure in their cries?

Impossible. I could never sleep with them that close, with *her* that close. If I didn't hear anything, I would imagine I did. And if I did hear... no, it didn't bear thinking about.

Anyway, why on earth wouldn't I give them the unused staff quarters? They'd have their own door and could come and go as they pleased. There was plenty of storage for the furniture they were taking from the apartment. Plenty of room for their boxes and suitcases. It was ideal.

The decision was a relief. When I told Adam the next day, he was delighted. 'That's brilliant. We won't feel we are intruding or getting in your way. Thanks a million.'

I brushed his gratitude away. 'For goodness' sake, it's not like I don't have the room. Anyway, it will make up for all those wonderful weekends I spent in the Cotswolds, won't it?'

The first night they spent in Elgin Crescent, they insisted on taking me out for a meal to thank me, leaving the choice of restaurant up to me. I chose a little Italian I liked, where the food was good, the ambience great, and the prices reasonable. We chatted with the ease of old friends, jumping from topic to topic, nothing confrontational or heavy. We wandered home, arm in arm, Jane in the middle, bookended by the man she loved, and the men who loved her.

They had the keys to their house a week later, but I persuaded them to have the windows and doors done before they moved in. 'It's a filthy, dusty job. You may as well stay here; let the workmen crack on with it. It will probably get done a lot faster.'

To my surprise, they acquiesced readily. I expected to have to argue my case, but Adam just nodded. 'As long as you don't mind. I don't want you to feel we are taking advantage.'

I thumped him on the arm. 'Don't be daft.'

He smiled. 'That's okay then. Another week, at the most.'

Jane gave me a hug. 'It's really very kind of you.'

'I like having you here,' I said. I did. Even though I didn't see them every day, had, in fact only seen them twice since they'd moved in, I knew they were there, and the house felt more like a home since the first day I moved in.

Sometimes, I lay in my bed, wondering if they were down there, making love, and I imagined I could hear them through the two floors and several walls that separated us.

And then they were gone, and I couldn't hear anything except my own breath, my own heart beating.

31

What I didn't know then, didn't know until two weeks after Adam and Jane had moved into their house in Hanwell, was that she was pregnant.

I only found out when I met Adam for lunch. I arrived to find him pale and wan and unusually quiet. He was sitting in front of a glass of water in a dark dismal pub he liked, where we met if I was particularly busy and not 100 per cent sure I would be able to make it. Meeting in a pub he liked and frequented regularly meant that if I didn't turn up, he was always certain of convivial conversation.

He didn't seem too keen on conversation that day, convivial or otherwise. I sipped the pint I had treated myself to as an antidote to an intensely trying morning, and waited until the first few mouthfuls hit the spot before speaking. 'You okay?' I asked, putting the glass down on the heavily scarred and not particularly clean table.

He rocked his head from side to side without saying anything, his eyes intent on the table as if he were trying to decipher the graffiti that had been scratched there over the years. I was starting to get worried. I had never seen Adam – king of the nonchalant – like this.

I leaned closer. 'You're starting to worry me.'

He lifted his face, and I saw his eyes were red-rimmed. 'It's Jane.'

I grabbed his arm. 'What's wrong?'

His lower lip trembled. 'She's had a miscarriage, Jake.'

My first reaction was relief. She wasn't dead. My second was anger that they hadn't told me. My third was sadness that close as we were, I wouldn't ever be the second to know, only the third... who was I kidding, they'd tell their parents first, I'd be seventh.

Then I stopped thinking of myself, reached over and dragged my friend into a hug that drew stares and raised eyebrows from a couple of elderly men who propped up the bar.

'I am so sorry, Adam. Is she okay?'

He pushed away, straightened up, dug in the pocket of his jeans for a disreputable piece of tissue to wipe his face and blow his nose. 'She started to bleed last night,' his voice faltered, 'just a few drops at first. She wasn't too worried. Then... God, it was awful, Jake. The blood just kept coming, and she kept saying it was okay, even when I had to fold a bath towel to put under her to soak up the blood.' He laughed, a small sad sound. 'Even then, she refused to believe she had lost the baby, you know? She kept hoping. The paramedics who came were really good, said all the right things, ignored the blood that by that stage had soaked through the towel and was dripping onto the floor. They didn't say the blindingly obvious, just kept telling her she was okay and not to worry.

'The obstetrician came as soon as we arrived in the hospital. He didn't even examine her, he just took one look at the blood and told her bluntly.' Tears ran down Adam's face. 'Jane kept telling him she hadn't lost it, that he was wrong. She kept insisting until eventually, out of kindness, or just to shut her up, I'm not sure, he did an ultrasound and showed her. There was nothing there. Nothing.'

Adam bawled then, like a baby. He crossed his arms on the table before him, dropped his head into their care, and sobbed loudly, on and on. For the first time in years, he wasn't the man who'd stolen the woman I loved, or an object of envy... just a friend who was suffering. Words were inadequate, so I stayed quiet, let him cry and patted him on the back to let him know he wasn't alone. We stayed there most of the afternoon. I rang the office; told them I needed some personal time and was taking the rest of the day off. I rang Adam's school, told them there was a family emergency and he would be in contact when he could. I didn't tell them about the miscarriage, it wasn't my tale to tell.

I watched Adam's sobs subside to a soft snuffle that became a gentle snore as exhaustion pushed him to sleep, then I watched him as he slept, shushing the barman who came to clear the glass I emptied, then quietly asking for a refill, sipping it while I watched guardian-angel-like for two hours.

Adam woke noisily, yawning, straightening his neck and arms with a groan of discomfort. Then he looked at me, momentarily disorientated before memories clicked into place.

'I fell asleep.'

'You were exhausted. You needed it.'

He looked at his watch, raising an eyebrow when he saw the time, looked at me and nodded. 'Thanks. I feel a little better.'

'I'm really sorry, Adam... about the baby.'

He smiled sadly. 'Yeah.' Stretching, he yawned. 'I'd better go. Jane'll be awake and will be wondering where I am.'

'Tell her...' What? I shrugged. 'Tell her I'm thinking of her, will you?'

He nodded. 'Thanks.' He gave my shoulder a squeeze. 'And for being here for me.'

We left together. He hailed a passing taxi and, with a wave, headed away to comfort his wife. Another taxi slowed when it saw me, but I waved it away. I didn't feel like rushing home, to sit in my big house and think about Jane and her loss.

I walked. It was miles and took me hours, but at least when I got home, I was too tired to think much. The large brandy I poured, or was it two, well, anyway, they took the final edge off. Later, I climbed naked between the sheets, curled up into a foetal position and thought of parents and children. And loss.

And for the first time since I'd walked out that door all those years before, I wondered if my parents had missed me.

32

I sent flowers, of course, asking a very avant-garde florist to send something dynamic and vividly coloured, wanting it to be as far away from pastel baby colours as possible. Adam said it was the most terrifying floral arrangement they had ever seen. 'We had it in the hall,' he told me later, 'but we had to move it after Jane's mother stabbed herself on one of the leaves. We put it in the lounge then, put a cordon around it. It gave us a good laugh, thanks, Jake.'

We didn't meet for weeks, but I spoke to Adam regularly and learnt that Jane was doing all right. Putting on a brave face, he said. And I guessed he was too.

Several weeks later, an invitation to their housewarming party was sitting in the post-basket inside my front door when I got home from work very late one evening. It had been hand delivered, a crazy cartoon drawing where a stamp should have been, the envelope itself covered in a combination of Jane and Adam's writing, strict instructions that I was not to miss their party, that no excuse was going to be accepted. The invitation was a simple mass-produced card stating time and date, but again Jane and Adam had scribbled all over it, *you have to come, you have to come, you have to come.*

I imagined them sitting around the table, taking turns scrawling on the invitation... imagined them saying to one another *we have to get poor Jake to come...* poor, poor Jake, so alone in that big house. Poor Jake. I stood in my beautiful hallway, and an anger I didn't know I possessed ripped through me. I took the invitation and tore it into tiny pieces, took the envelope and shredded it, tore it into smaller and smaller pieces until I could tear no more, opening my hands and letting the pieces fall to litter the floor around me. Every time I opened the door, for months after, they swirled around, bits following me out and down the street. I swear I saw some blown into corners of buildings in the centre of London.

Anger directed inward drains beyond belief. They felt sorry for me. We weren't a threesome, united in everything, facing a future together. They were a couple, and I was a hanger-on. A good friend, one who would be told, eventually, about important things, who would be included, invited. But I would always be apart and there would be many things I would not be privy to. And while I would be a valued guest, I was a *guest*. Not part of the planning twosome. Not part of the two-man team. Apart. I would always be apart. And, as much as I loved Jane, as much as I loved Adam, they were the couple, and I, well, I was just Jake.

Adam rang the next day. 'You will make it, won't you?'

I had sworn several times during a sleepless night that I wouldn't go, that I'd miss the party, slowly drift out of their lives and lock them out of mine. In the small hours of the morning, it had seemed to make perfect sense. I could walk out of their lives... after all, hadn't I walked out of my parents'?

But what I'd done with casual thoughtlessness at eighteen was more difficult as a man of thirty-five.

So when I heard Adam's words, I heard myself say, 'I wouldn't miss it.'

33

___

It was, of course, a very enjoyable night, as every night in company with Adam and Jane tended to be, their relaxed conviviality ensuring success without trying. Jane had worked the same magic on the house in Hanwell that she had done on her apartment, and it was comfortable and inviting, and felt as if they had lived there for years. I recognised some of the furniture, admired the new additions. Jane showed me the bathroom I had paid for and insisted on thanking me again.

'Believe me,' I said with a smile, 'it was self-preservation. No way could I have used the old one.'

'It was very generous of you, Jake. We do appreciate it.'

I shook my head, and she laughed and said no more, her small hand resting on my arm. I could feel the heat of it through my shirt, the imprint of her delicate fingers. My own itched to grab it, hold it. Then she moved away to get me a drink and was swallowed by the crush of people, and the moment, as it always did, passed.

She didn't come back with the drink; I saw her minutes later, deep in conversation with people I didn't know. She'd forgotten. I tried not to take umbrage, looked around instead for convivial company.

Ann was at the party, of course. It was the first time I'd seen her since the wedding. She looked stunning, as usual, her dress a shimmer of silk that hugged firmly toned curves with a skill many women didn't possess – that of knowing just how much flesh to flash to be alluring rather than cheap. Sun-kissed, perfectly tousled hair and that certain unmade-up look that you knew cost a fortune, and took both time and effort, completed her look. She might as well have had *high maintenance* tattooed on her forehead.

She threw me a wave across the crowded room. I acknowledged it with a tilt of my head and a mouthed *hi* and thought about squeezing through the crowd to speak to her, but more people pushed through the front door, and she was hidden from view. The crush of people made navigation of the small house extremely difficult, people tending to find a space and stay put.

Stupidly, and still without a drink, I got myself boxed into a corner by two teacher friends of Adam's who were mildly interesting to talk to for maybe three minutes, but whose conversation quickly veered towards school matters which completely excluded me. 'Excuse me,' I said eventually, bringing their eyes, if not their attention, back to me. 'I'm not a teacher, and this conversation is intensely boring. Would you mind if I...' And I squeezed between them and escaped. They returned to their conversation without even acknowledging my rudeness, perhaps they hadn't even noticed I was gone.

Adam approached, a wine bottle in each hand. 'Jake, Jane said you were here. It's a crush, isn't it? Hey, you don't have a drink. That won't do.' He disappeared through the crowd, returning moments later with a large wine glass. 'Here you are, have some wine,' he said, filling the glass almost to the top.

'I got caught between those two,' I said to him, indicating the two men in the corner, their conversation becoming louder as it became heated.

Adam grinned. 'Don't tell me! I bet they were arguing the cognitive theories of Piaget and Vygotsky. Constructivists!' He shook his head.

I had no idea what he was talking about and didn't want to know. 'I see your sister is here.'

'So are the folks, have you seen them?'

I swallowed a mouthful of wine and grimaced. 'I hope you didn't pour Giles some of this stuff then, he'll spit it out.'

Adam grinned again. 'Three ninety-nine in Aldi. What were you expecting?'

He left me to go and pour his poison elsewhere, and I looked around for his parents. Adam's wedding was the last time I had seen them; it would be nice to catch up. Craning my neck, I looked around the room I was in and couldn't see either Giles or Clara. By dint of squeezing and pushing, I moved into the hall and from there into the small kitchen where both stood, pouring wine from a bottle I knew damn well hadn't come from Aldi.

Throwing the contents of my glass down the sink, I nudged Giles. 'I'll have some of that.'

'Jake,' he said, the pleasure in his voice pleasing to hear. 'You weren't drinking the stuff Adam was pouring, were you? Rotgut, you know, absolute rotgut. Have some of this. I brought it with me.'

Much better. I swallowed a mouthful and breathed a sigh of relief.

'We brought a case of it,' Clara said, with a wink and a grin she'd passed directly to Adam.

We settled against the kitchen counter and caught up, like old friends, emptying one bottle, opening another. They quizzed me about my work with Sebastian et Sebastian, listened intently with genuine interest, asked questions showing they understood. From there, they moved on to my new house in Elgin Crescent.

'Adam says it's very grand.'

I smiled at Clara's not very subtle hint. 'Why don't you come to lunch tomorrow and you can see for yourselves?'

'Oh, we couldn't put you to that trouble,' Giles said, then doubled over, exaggerating for effect, when Clara thumped him in the solar plexus.

I laughed. 'Honestly, I would love to have you both. After all, how many times have you fed me in the Cotswolds?'

Clara put her hand on my arm. 'We loved having you, you know that. But Giles is right. You don't want the trouble of having us to lunch.' She grinned again. 'But I would really like to see the house.'

Shaking my head, and mentally making a note to ring the caterers when I got a moment, I put my hand over hers. 'I insist. Lunch. One o'clock. I'll invite Adam and Jane too. It will be fun, honestly.'

'What will?' Ann's voice questioned softly, as she squeezed her way through the crowd in the hallway and joined us.

There was a moment's hesitation. Giles and Clara looked uncomfortable, but I couldn't read their faces to know if they wanted her to be included in the invitation or not. Adam had mentioned they had heard some rumours of the lifestyle Ann enjoyed in London, a lifestyle that was foreign to them, that separated them from their daughter far more than the miles between the capital and the Cotswolds, but he hadn't gone into detail, so I wasn't sure how bad it was. They were lovely people, but conservative, so even some of the less racy gossip must have been a shock to them.

The silence was uncomfortable, so I shrugged and said, 'Lunch. I've invited your parents to lunch tomorrow.'

'Lunch, how bourgeois.'

'Why? Don't you eat lunch, Ann?' I replied, annoyed.

She smiled, fluttered her eyelashes. 'Not usually, Jake. But for you, I'll make an exception.'

I laughed and shook my head. She really was one of a kind... what kind, I hadn't yet decided. 'Great, one o'clock, then.'

She cringed dramatically at the time and mouthed the word *one* with exaggerated horror.

'You don't have to come, Ann.' Clara's voice was unusually sharp. I guessed she must have heard some of the less than salubrious tales about her daughter.

It was water off a duck's back to Ann. 'Mother,' she replied, with an eyes-half-closed sideways glance at me, 'I wouldn't miss it for the world.'

34

Living in Elgin Crescent was easy. Everything was available for a price. A late-night phone call to S'amuser, and lunch was arranged for the next day. I had used their top-end package for my housewarming, their serving staff, butler, china, glasses, and so on, but this time I settled, simply, for food. I didn't want to seem over the top. And anyway, after the champagne out of beer glasses evening with Adam and Jane, I had bought a beautiful dinner service and some exquisite glasses.

I'd bought the damn stuff, but that was as far as I had got. It was still in the Harrods boxes that had been shoved into the utility room. Fifteen boxes. I had spent so long in deciding what to buy, had hemmed and hawed, picked first one design and then another, wondering which Jane would choose, which would best suit Elgin Crescent, if I would ever use the bloody stuff. I was so long trying to choose that the ever-so-awfully-professional sales assistant started to look really pissed off, clearly thinking her precious time was being wasted and I was going to leave without buying a thing.

Her snooty little nose rose higher and higher as she trailed around beside me. When I turned to her, pointed to the Wedgwood Cornucopia set I had seen first, almost an hour before, and said, 'This one. I'll take this one,' she looked at me blankly, as if she had forgotten why she was there. 'I'll take twelve of those, those and those,' I continued, pointing to the dinner plates, bread plates and cups. 'And saucers, of course. Twelve. And I'll take two of those vegetable tureens, four serving bowls, two sugar bowls, the ones with the lids, two milk jugs, two... no, make it four sandwich plates, two gravy boats, a teapot and a coffee pot.' She was so stunned; she hadn't taken note of what I was saying and had to ask me to repeat myself.

I went from there to glassware, buying simple classic designs that felt good in my hand, glass that sang when I flicked it gently. 'I'll take twenty-four of these, and twenty-four of those, those and those. Twelve of those and those.'

Why I picked twelve and multiples of twelve, I have no idea. The number just popped into my head, and I went with it. I don't know why. It just seemed like a good idea at the time.

When she handed the bill to me, I remember signing the credit card receipt with a flourish, as if I was in the habit, every week, of spending almost ten grand on china and glass. Almost ten grand, and I didn't even blink.

They needed to be delivered, of course, all fifteen boxes. They gave me a date and time, but when the day came, I couldn't get out of a meeting, had to excuse myself and make a quick phone call to Adam, who was on another of those endlessly recurring breaks all teachers get. He'd help me out. He always did.

'Sure,' he replied, when I asked. 'We've got keys, I'm happy to sit around in luxury for a few hours. What are you having delivered, anyway?'

'Just a dinner service and some glasses,' I said, trying to play down my purchases.

He laughed. 'Why couldn't you have carried it with you? You getting weak in your old age?'

I told him why.

'You bought how many?' he asked in amazement. 'What the hell are you going to do with it all, you rarely eat there anyway.' Then realisation hit him. 'Hey, and you needn't think I am going to unpack all that lot... forget it, mate, you can do that yourself.'

'No, no don't worry,' I reassured him, 'just get them to put the boxes in the utility room. I'll sort them out sometime when I have a minute.'

The minute never arose, and the boxes and their contents were still there, unpacked.

So, there I was, almost a year later, at one in the morning, hauling the boxes through to the kitchen. I used a knife to open them all, then unpacked each into the empty cupboards. It was only then, when I stood back to admire what I'd achieved, that I remembered what was missing. Milk jugs. They hadn't had any in stock that day, the sales assistant profusely apologetic, saying she would have them ordered for me. I'd said I would do it online myself, but it had gone out of my head until now. What the hell was I going to do for a milk jug? Stick a damn Tetra Pak on the table? Damn, damn, damn! I really wanted lunch to be perfect, elegant, sophisticated. Wanted to try, in some way, to compete with all those meals I'd had in the Cotswolds, the fine old china, often cracked and chipped, but old. Venerable. Smacking of something that can't be bought. Years of history. Of being born to it. I couldn't compete. Could I?

Certainly not with a blasted Tetra Pak in the middle of the beautiful Wedgwood. Damn!

Sometimes, and this was one of them... I was weary of pretending to be something I wasn't.

35

Next morning, I was up at cockcrow and driving like a maniac to my local supermarket where I hoped to find a jug that would pass muster. I was parked outside before remembering it was Sunday. My fingers white knuckling on the steering wheel in frustration, I turned the car in a screech of brakes and went home to wait for the S'amuser delivery. Stupidly desperate to impress, I had ordered far more than necessary, and when the delivery arrived and the platters of food were laid out on the kitchen counters, I wondered if Clara would think the excess vulgar.

Ann would probably sneer and call it bourgeois.

Luckily, the big refrigerator was empty apart from wine and champagne, so with a bit of manoeuvring, everything fit inside. The excess could be another of my well-kept secrets.

Suddenly, it was twelve, and I still had no blasted jug. Driving way too fast, I was back down at the supermarket and trawling the aisles searching for that now essential element. They had two, a heavy striped one that looked as if it was designed to hold milk straight from the cow, and a nicely shaped, floral-patterned one that would clash horrendously with the Wedgwood. I stood there, in the aisle, with a jug in each hand, feeling, and probably looking, like an idiot. Bloody hell, I thought, suddenly seeing the funny side of it all. Worrying about a damn jug.

Then a garish pink jug, a melamine one designed probably for outdoor use, caught my eye. Perfect. I picked it up and paid the £2.99 it cost, and headed home at a more reasonable speed, smiling to myself, determined to regale them all with the story of the jug over lunch, knowing it would make Clara and Giles smile. And Adam, well, he would howl. The jug would be worth the entertainment value.

Back in Elgin Crescent, I decided against using the formal dining room and instead set the table in the small, cosy eating area off the kitchen. Big floor-to-ceiling windows overlooked the pretty veranda, giving the area a continental feel when, like today, the sun was shining. There was plenty of room for six, plenty of space on the table for the large plates, a selection of wine and water glasses and the necessary cutlery. It was all set but didn't look quite right, so I moved everything around, fussed and faffed, arranged and rearranged. I was driven to distraction by my desperation to have everything perfect; by a silly childish desire to be seen to be as good as them.

I'd just moved things around again when the doorbell pealed, and I took one final frantic look around and breathed a sigh of relief. It looked good. Anyway, they were here, it would have to do.

I opened the door, and there they were, smiles, expectant eyes, open arms. Hugs all around as we mingled on the doorstep, until laughing, I said, 'Welcome, everyone. Great to see you. Come in, come in.'

'Is Ann here yet?' Adam asked, leading the way inside.

'No, not yet,' I replied, my attention on his mother, who was oohing and aahing over everything she saw.

'No, of course not. She'll arrive late. Make a grand entrance. Some things never change.'

Jane thumped him gently on the arm. 'Adam,' she said, with a note of warning in her voice.

'What?' His voice mock indignant. 'She *does* like to make an entrance.'

Jane grimaced at him; he stuck his tongue out at her. Then they both giggled.

Clara and Giles ignored them, and sailed through to the front reception room, admiring, commenting, their eyes seeking, measuring. They said little, but the murmurs were of apprecia-tion. I basked in their obvious approval, taking for myself what was directed towards the house. After all, I had chosen it.

Adam and Jane sat in the kitchen chatting while I gave the guided tour. It was done at a leisurely pace, Clara, in particular, determined to miss nothing, opening doors, peering out windows. 'It's all so lovely,' she said, and I heard, or perhaps hoped I heard, the faint wisps of envy.

Twenty minutes later, we were back in the kitchen. I half expected to find Ann sitting with Adam and Jane, but there was no sign of her.

'Let's have some wine.' I opened the fridge and removed a bottle.

'At last,' Adam said, moving out of reach as Jane tried, once more, to thump him.

'Honestly, Jake,' she said, 'I think he's getting worse.'

'I don't pay any attention to him, don't worry. I know if he had really wanted a drink, he would have helped himself.'

'True,' Adam nodded, 'but I'm trying to be on my best behaviour. Impress the folks.'

Giles shook his head sadly. 'Too late. Way too late.'

Then the conversation drifted into generalised Sunday social chit-chat that was pleasant and comfortable. Thirty minutes later, Clara looked at her watch. 'It doesn't look like she is coming. Perhaps we should ring her?'

Adam shrugged, then reached for his phone, dialled her number, waited a few seconds, closed it and put it away. 'Straight to an answering service.'

I got up and removed lids and covers from the plates and dishes I had arranged on a side table. 'I think we'll go ahead. Ann may have been caught up in something she couldn't get out of. These things happen.'

Nobody argued the unlikelihood of this. She had changed her mind. Simple as that.

We got on with lunch without further mention of her, everyone helping themselves from the array of dishes I placed in the centre of the table.

'This is an amazing spread,' Jane said, spooning some couscous onto her plate. 'I love baked salmon.'

Clara agreed. 'Absolutely delicious, you've gone to so much trouble.'

'It's no trouble. Everything was done for me, delivered this morning. The only trouble I had was about the jug.' I told them, in exaggerated detail, the story of my careering around the city that morning looking for a jug.

Even as I told the story, I realised how ridiculous I had been, and joined in their laughter, laughing at the man I had been only a few hours before.

A few hours later, they were gone, and I was left with an empty house and enough food to keep me fed for at least a week.

Ann hadn't turned up, nor did she ring to offer an explanation for her absence. Common courtesies were only maintained when they fit in with her plans and schemes, and her plans at that stage didn't involve lunch with Mummy and Daddy.

They did, as I discovered not long afterwards, involve me.

Adam had always said his sister was a manipulative, scheming woman. It wasn't long before I realised he was right.

But by then, it was way too late.

36

A week later, I answered my phone to hear a sultry, 'Hi, Jake.'

I recognised Ann's voice instantly. 'Who is this?' My voice hard and blunt.

'Ann,' she replied, less sultry, and when I said nothing, she added, 'Adam's sister,' clearly irked at having to provide the information.

'Oh.' Nothing more. Waiting for something from her. An apology, perhaps.

'You're mad at me.' Her voice came, breathy, little-girly.

What could I say? 'No.'

'Yes, you are,' she insisted. 'I missed your lunch. And I heard you went to so much trouble.'

'For your parents,' I clarified. 'They've always been good to me.'

'And I'm sure they loved it. I am sorry to have missed it. Something unexpected came up.'

If she expected me to ask what, she was deluded, I wasn't interested in playing her games. 'Well, thank you for the call,' I said, preparing to hang up, but she started telling me some trivial gossip about people I knew very vaguely, and led from that into a slightly boring anecdote about her parents, one I had already heard from Adam that wasn't particularly interesting the first time around. My replies were monosyllabic, dismissive almost, but she wasn't deterred and chatted on, her voice relentlessly cheerful. Despite myself, I became intrigued. Why was Ann so interested in spending time chatting to me? I was sitting on the veranda having a beer, the scent of magnolia drifting on a warm breeze from the garden below, my feet up on a cushioned lounger. My gaze drifted back towards the house, where the glass doors stood partially open, then it hit me, the staggering unbelievable truth. I was now what Ann would consider a catch. Not titled, not even very wealthy, but I had a house in Notting Hill. And not just any old house, but one on Elgin Crescent.

I shook my head. It couldn't be that simple, could it? 'Are you free tonight?' I asked, dangling a very small worm. If she bit, she was really interested. It was Friday evening, surely she had other plans.

Her voice switched from babbling, to low and seductive. 'Why, are you asking me out?'

I was so tempted to say *no, just wondering*. Then I thought of my big empty house, of Adam and Jane and their total contentment, and I decided *what the hell*. 'Yes,' I said quickly. 'Perhaps dinner, if I can get a reservation this late.'

'Oh, I'm sure you'll manage something.'

'We could always go to McDonald's.'

She didn't know me well enough to know if I was joking or not, so her laugh was perfunctory. 'Perhaps something a little healthier,' she suggested.

'Perhaps,' I agreed, thinking that at least she had the grace not to say expensive. 'I'll pick you up at nine.'

'Make it 9.30.' I soon discovered that was Ann all over, determined to have the last word even when it didn't really matter. Or perhaps, especially then.

Putting my beer down, I stretched and rested my hands behind my head. An acrid smell reminded me I hadn't showered after a strenuous workout in my home gym. Glancing down, eyeing the scruffy tracksuit, I wondered what she'd say if I turned up to collect her like this.

It was tempting, but it would also be insulting, and that wasn't the man I was.

Sighing loudly, I hauled myself from the comfortable lounger and headed for a shower, stopping on the way to phone a restaurant I'd heard about, fortunate to get a table for two at 9.45. Then I remembered the two beers I'd had after my workout and quickly ordered a taxi.

After my shower, standing naked in my dressing room, I reviewed my wardrobe. Ann would be dressed to kill. Should I try to match her? There was the black Armani suit. Maybe with a grey silk shirt and tie. Was that too formal? Maybe a bit too business dinner? Perhaps the suit with a white linen shirt, no tie. Yes. That would look good, relaxed but expensively casual. Minutes later, I stood in front of the mirror and knew I'd made the right choice. Damn, but I looked good.

The taxi arrived dead on time, and I climbed in, gave her address, sat back and contemplated the evening. Would we end up in bed? She had quite a reputation. But she was the sister of my best friend, and despite their quite acrimonious relationship, she *was* his sister. Perhaps we'd better take it slowly – if it was going to go anywhere past that night.

37

Whatever was going to happen, I realised quite quickly that she was a master of the game. Arriving outside her apartment on the stroke of 9.30, I buzzed her intercom and waited for an answer. When there was none, after a few minutes' impatient waiting, I put my finger on the bell and pushed again, keeping it there for a longer period of time, hearing her voice before the buzzing finished, annoyed with myself for the display of impatience.

'Hello?' Her voice still little-girl-breathy.

I smiled at the question in her voice, the implication that there could have been any one of several people ringing her doorbell at 9.30 on a Friday night. Perhaps she wasn't as tough and hard as she appeared, I thought, seeing her need to be seen to be popular as evidence of a vulnerability that appealed to me.

'It's Jake.'

'Jake!'

If I hadn't known better, I would have sworn the surprise was genuine.

'I could have sworn it was you I was speaking to an hour ago,' I said, keeping my voice light.

Her laugh gurgled down the electronics, coming out tinnier and falser than it probably was. 'Oh, you! Come on up, I'm not quite ready.'

'Wait a sec,' I said quickly, afraid she'd hang up and I'd have to buzz again and the whole night would descend into farce. 'I'll tell the taxi driver to wait, give me a minute.'

The taxi driver didn't look too impressed till I slipped a twenty into his hand. 'We'll just be a minute.'

'Okay,' I said into the intercom, and heard the buzzer unlocking the door. I pushed and made my way up the two flights to her apartment, the door opening as I approached.

My breath caught on the vision she made standing there, my brain searching for the appropriate word even as my treacherous body reacted automatically. *Deshabille*. That was the word I needed. Her hair was bed tousled, her robe carelessly tied and barely covering curves that seemed more voluptuous than I remembered.

'Jake,' she murmured, pleasure lighting sleepy eyes.

Moving into the light of her hallway, I realised that the sleepiness was the result of meticulously applied smoky grey eye shadow and the longest eyelashes I had ever seen. Like a lot about Ann, they were very good fakes.

She led the way into the lounge. 'Can I get you a drink while you wait?'

It was safer to keep my mouth shut for the moment. I was afraid my tongue would hang out or I would start to drool, so I shook my head and glanced pointedly at my watch.

She laughed and rested a finely boned hand on my arm, leaving it there while she raised those smoky eyes to mine. She held my gaze and smiled. 'Hungry, are you?' She dropped her eyes, let them sweep the length of my body, lingering where they really shouldn't, and where I would have preferred they hadn't, before bringing her eyes back up to meet mine. 'I'd better not keep you waiting then.'

With that, she turned and headed back into the hallway. Just as she got to the door, she dropped her robe as if she were rushing to remove it to dress, giving me a glimpse of her perfectly rounded derriere.

Damn!

It felt suddenly unbearably hot, and I looked around with a feeling of panic. The room was large with square bay windows to the front. I guessed they let in a lot of light during the day, but at night, they were chilly black holes. I knew Ann had lived there for a number of years, and I wondered why she had never put up curtains. I stood there seeing my reflection in the window and felt a shiver run through me. There I was, smart suit, crisp shirt, looking handsome and successful but behind my reflection a big black nothing. And, as so many times recently, it seemed to replicate the way I felt.

Turning away from the window, from my reflection, from the emptiness, I spotted a small kitchen tucked into the far corner of the room. Feeling hot and very bothered, I opened cupboards to find a glass. The first was filled with a selection and, taking one, I filled it and took a cooling, calming drink, draining the glass.

Finished, idle curiosity tempted me, and I looked into the other kitchen cupboards. Glasses. Glasses in every cupboard. No food, of any description. I opened the fridge. Wine, vodka, beer. No food.

Dropping the glass into the sink, I headed back into the lounge and sat on the sofa. It had been, as usual, one of those weeks and my eyelids felt suddenly heavy with exhaustion, drifting towards closure, impossible to stop. A snort woke me. *My* snort. Jerking awake, I looked around, hoping to be alone, wondering how long I'd slept. A quick glance at my watch told me it hadn't been long. It also told me it was nearly 9.50. The taxi driver would not be happy. I was wondering about heading down to have a word with him, when the door opened and Ann walked in.

'Sorry to have kept you waiting.'

She looked stunning and knew she did. She had that wonderful, almost smug expression women have when they know they have their man in the palm of their hand. When they know he is being led by his misbehaving dick.

And mine was misbehaving. Dammit, if it wasn't reaching for the sky, pushing in vain against wool, straining for release. I took a deep breath, regained control, and told her what she already knew.

'You look lovely.'

Her smile grew wider. 'Why, thank you, I could say I just threw on any old thing, but then you'd know I was lying, wouldn't you?'

Without a doubt. I wasn't terribly au fait with women's clothes, but I knew expensive quality when I saw it, and her dress screamed it, that understated elegance that only comes with a hefty price tag.

Unable to think of anything to say in response, I smiled at her. It must have been the right sort of smile, my face must have shown the correct response, because she gave a small nod and turned away, her derriere swaying seductively as she led the way out and down the corridor to the lift I had missed earlier. Obviously, she wasn't risking her very high heels on the stairway.

The taxi driver looked fierce when we approached the car. 'A minute,' he growled. 'This is going to cost you, mate.'

'Fine,' I said quietly, 'not a problem.'

He took off at speed, throwing us back in our seats. I opened my mouth to remonstrate but Ann reached out and laid a slim shapely hand on my thigh. 'Don't worry about it,' she said calmly.

I felt the heat of her hand through the fabric of my trousers and all thought of taking the taxi driver to task vanished. All my control was required for my errant dick. I just hoped Ann couldn't feel the movement under her hand. I glanced at her. Oh, she knew. There was that blasted smug smile again.

38

I had managed to get a table in a small, fairly new French restaurant in Kensington, and when our taxi pulled up outside, I was amused to see she showed neither approbation nor disdain, just a sublime indifference. Truth was, I suppose, she expected and only ever got the best. She sat, waiting until I came around and opened the door of the taxi before climbing out, her knees and ankles tight together, an elegant manoeuvre of beautiful legs.

I paid the fare, handing the exact amount, refusing pointedly to add a tip. After all, he'd already had a twenty out of me. 'I'll make it a point not to use your taxi service again,' I told the driver.

'Well, that's me taught a lesson then, isn't it?' He took the money, shoved it into his shirt pocket and wound up the window before I had thought of a response, leaving me standing there, my mouth half open, my brain stalled.

'Oh, forget about him,' Ann said impatiently as I stared down the street, fuming. She put her hand on my arm, tugged gently until I gave in and turned back to her.

She really was stunningly beautiful, and I felt the tension ease.

'Sorry.' I took her hand in mine and we headed towards the restaurant door.

Ann stood, regally silent, while I addressed the major-domo who led us to our table. She waited, without as much as a glance at him, while he drew her chair out. Then she folded herself onto it gracefully and elegantly, and looking at him, murmured a soft *thank you*.

I could tell he was charmed, impressed even, and I had to admit, so was I. Perhaps, it was going to be a better evening than I had expected.

'You order for me.' Ann put down the menu the major-domo had handed her. 'There isn't anything I don't like. Except snails,' she added the last hastily. This was a new experience for me, ordering for my date, and I had to be honest, I liked it.

It was a trick she had, I learned later, to make you feel so much in control when it didn't in the grand scheme of things matter a jot. Important things, things that made a difference, well, then she could get her teeth in like a damn Staffordshire bull terrier and hold on till you dropped from exhaustion.

But I didn't know that then. I sat opposite a beautiful, charming, elegant woman and I thought, *Yes, this is what I need. This is what my house needs.* And there and then, as I was reading the menu, I made the decision that I would marry her. It never struck me that I was being unfair to her. I could see what she wanted; I could give it to her. It seemed like a fair exchange, quid pro quo, if you like. As it turned out, it *was* enough for her; my mistake was thinking it would be enough for me.

The waiter bustled over to us, and I ordered our food then discussed wine choices with the sommelier and sat back, feeling quite pleased. Ann and I made small talk about nothing, dipping a toe in the water of each other's lives, the concentric circles rippling and vanishing with ease. Before our food arrived, we had the full measure of each other, and we sat back and smiled as two waiters arrived, bearing colossal domes that gleamed in the candlelight. They stood a moment beside the table, that overused and much abused irritating pause that is supposed to build tension and excitement and succeeds only in pissing people off. Then, synchronised to the millisecond, the two, with closed faces and bored eyes, set the domes before us.

They stood bent over our table, standing together like some stupid clockwork toy that has run down, a pseudo-dramatic pause that went on so long I was within aces of slapping their hands away and taking the bloody domes off the plates myself. Before I snapped and committed what would have been, I suppose, a restaurant solecism, they lifted them, and with a *bon appétit*, moved away in tandem, the domes held high above their heads.

I smiled across at Ann, then looked down at my plate and blinked. The plates were huge, elegant white china. But the portions, bloody hell, they were miniscule. Beautifully and artistically arranged, granted, but *tiny*. I had ordered a ballotine of foie gras for Ann, and a salad of roast red-leg partridge for me. Knowing partridges were pretty small, I presumed I would get a few legs, but as I moved pieces of greenery around, I decided the menu was being incredibly truthful. Roast red-leg, it had said, and one miserable red-leg is what I got.

It tasted very good – at least the two mouthfuls I managed to scrape together were, but it was definitely an appetiser. Now I was starving.

'Is yours okay?' I asked Ann, spearing a piece of tomato I had found hiding under some of the green stuff that constituted my salad, the discovery giving far more pleasure than a half-slice of tomato usually did.

'Delicious,' she replied, cutting a miniscule piece off her very tiny ballotine and putting it delicately between her lips. Definitely not a McDonald's girl. I watched the manoeuvre with growing desire, her lips closing over the fork, the tip of her pink tongue darting out to capture an errant crumb. Very sensuous, but also very slow; I probably would have enjoyed it more if I hadn't been so damn hungry. As it was, I wanted her to eat up so they would come and take the plates away and bring our main courses.

Eventually, our plates were cleared and we had to go through the whole dome arrival palaver again. I would have eaten dome and all at this stage, my salivary glands tantalised by the succulent smells coming from tables all around us. Thankfully, I had ordered a Chateaubriand of Scottish beef for me, and roast Cornish sea bass for Ann. My expectation was as high as the shiny domes that were carried with such reverence across the restaurant. They were placed before us, as offerings before deities. Had I been able to eat the build-up, I might have been happy.

But, when they finally removed the domes, my heart dropped. The Chateaubriand was tiny, possibly the smallest I have ever seen. I'd had amuse bouche that were more substantial.

The steak sat looking lonely in a small puddle of gravy. Three julienne carrots were criss-crossed to form a star, positioned dead centre on a small tower of what turned out to be mashed potato and onion. I looked up hopefully. Maybe there was more to come. Maybe I would see those damn domes floating back with more vegetables. It took a few moments before I realised this was it. No more vegetables, or, God forbid, French fries, were coming.

I caught Ann's eyes, wondering what she was making of it all.

'This is wonderful,' she said. She sounded sincere.

'Isn't it?' I hoped my voice sounded equally sincere, my mind racing to thoughts of the Big Mac and double fries I was going to indulge in on the way home.

I waited, and watched as she cut into her fish, manipulating a tiny flake onto her fork before raising it to her mouth. Her lips barely parted to accept the offering. Somehow, I didn't think fellatio would be her thing.

Hiding a smile at the thought, I picked up my cutlery and cut into the Chateaubriand. I watched as blood welled and gave myself a mental thump to the side of my head. I'd forgotten that the generally accepted norm of well done, medium and rare was translated to pink, bloody, and still mooing by a French chef. Blood oozed, its dark redness merging with the gravy, the resultant mess just that, an unappetising mess. I sat, unmoving, my knife embedded in the meat, my fork holding it captive to prevent its escape. The candle on our table flickered, attracting my attention, and I wondered, if I held the meat in front of the flame, would it cook a little more? I could do it slice by slice. It amused me to imagine the waiters' reaction. It was the only thing that amused me.

Ann, shaving another morsel from her fish, cast a questioning look at me when she noticed my untouched meal. 'I thought you were hungry.'

'Delaying my gratification,' I said quickly. To send it back, to open myself up to contemptuous dismissal by the French waiter, was never an option. I cut a sliver of meat, lifted the bloody trembling mess to my lips, closed my eyes at the last moment so my determination wouldn't waver, swallowed without chewing and took a mouthful of red wine to wash it down. I repeated the process, mentally calculating each time how many more bites it would take to finish a piece of meat, once so tiny, now seeming to fill my plate.

'Delicious.' I smacked my lips on the lie and tasted blood. Taking a mouthful of wine, I surreptitiously rinsed my mouth.

Ann nodded in agreement as she cut a splinter of carrot into three.

We chatted about this and that. People we knew. London life.

Gentle, trivial stuff, relaxing and undemanding. Easy. If the silence lasted longer than a few seconds, Ann managed to break it with some anecdote about something or other. I didn't have to do any work at all. Nice, very nice, and very easy. Definitely, I thought again, this was definitely what I needed.

Ann finally laid her cutlery down. I could see she'd barely touched her fish, and her potato tower still stood unscathed. My own, soaked with blood and gore, leaned mortally wounded to one side, I gave it a final push with my fork before surrendering and putting my cutlery down.

'Well,' I said, unable to think of a comment on the food that wasn't scatological.

Ann smiled across the table. 'What a lovely place this is, Jake. A very good choice, thank you.' Meeting and holding my gaze, she lifted her glass. 'To many more delicious meals together.'

I touched her glass with mine, then reached across and caught the hand that lay there waiting and held it in mine. 'To many more,' I said, with a smile.

But we never ate in a French restaurant again.

39

Once I had decided to marry Ann, I didn't see the point in hanging around. Two weeks later, on our third date, I brought her back to Elgin Crescent and gave her the grand tour, saw her eyes light up as I brought her from room to room. In the dressing room attached to my bedroom, she gasped with pleasure, spinning around with a laugh. Her hand reached out to a drawer, then pulled away, her face puzzled.

'There's no handles.'

I took her hand, guided it back to the drawer and pushed gently. The drawer popped open with an expensive whisper.

'Very nice,' she said, closing the empty drawer, opening it again. Moving on to another drawer, pushing it, watching as it too whispered open. She laughed. 'Are they all empty?'

I pointed to the row of drawers behind her. 'I've stuff in those drawers. To be honest, a lot of my clothes are still in boxes in the spare bedroom. I haven't had the time to unpack them.'

Her fingers brushed the fabric of the suits that were lined up, side by side but inches apart, her gentle brush making them sway lazily. My shirts, still folded from the dry cleaners, sat on several shelves.

Ann spun around again. 'This is fabulous, Jake. All this space.'

I smiled at her enthusiasm, hoped she was picturing her clothes filling the empty spaces, her belongings lining the drawers. 'It's big, all right,' I said, making my voice low, and I hoped seductive. Slipping a hand around her waist, I pulled her against me. My erection was hot and heavy. And determined. Dropping my hands, I cupped her bottom, pulled her into closer contact, knowing she could feel the heat through the fine fabric of her dress.

Without saying a word, she pushed away slightly, reached behind, unzipped her dress and let it drop to the floor. She stood there, her body decorated rather than concealed by wisps of frothy lace, stood there while I admired, knowing I would admire. And why wouldn't I? She was stunning.

'Ann,' I said, reaching for her, my hand just brushing her warm skin before she stepped back out of my reach. She picked her feet daintily out of the puddle of her dress, one elegant stiletto-shod foot at a time. With a final smouldering glance, she sashayed to the bed, her barely covered buttocks swaying with each deliberate step. She swung around, tossed her head to make her hair ripple, ran her hands up her body and around to quickly undo her brassiere, shrugging the straps so that it fell into waiting hands, a move so practised, I had a glimmer of sanity asking me how often she had done the same, and for how many men. But then those wandering hands hooked into the tiny G-string she wore, slipped it down and with a practised flick, sent the garment sailing through the air.

'Well,' she breathed, posing, breasts thrust towards me.

Well indeed. At this stage, my erection was a painful reminder of how easily manipulated by their dicks men are. I was putty in her hand. I would have done anything just then. Anything.

But, as it happened, I didn't need to do much. I reached for her, we fell back on the bed together then, suddenly... and I can't even remember unzipping my trousers... suddenly I was in her and, just as suddenly, shooting pent-up desire with a cry that was three parts exultation and one part embarrassment at a performance that could only come under the heading *Premature Ejaculation*, in anyone's book.

She lay beneath me, unmoving, unspeaking, her breath warming my shoulder. Easing my weight off her, I thought, *what a story this will be for her to tell.* Shaking off the post-coital inertia that beleaguers every male, I tried to make an effort with the supporting act and moved to kiss her gently on the lips, on her neck. 'You are so beautiful,' I whispered, running my hand down the curve of her waist, over the swell of her hips. 'It will be better next time, I promise.'

'Jake, don't be silly, it was wonderful. I haven't had an orgasm like that in a long time.'

I pulled away and looked at her. She looked sincere. 'I didn't think... I mean, I came so fast, I thought...'

'You're not the only one who can come quickly,' she said with a laugh. 'You had me so excited, I almost came before you did.' With that, she reached a hand up and pulled my head back down, kissing me deeply, her tongue dancing with mine. Encore time. This time, I was determined if she was going to tell tales, it would be a good one, and I went to it with gusto. There wasn't an inch of her body I didn't kiss, lick, guzzle. Never a fan of cunnilingus, this time I got to it like it was my raison d'être, licking and slurping. Whether it was my method, the sound effects or whether she wasn't much into it either, she pulled my head up, and to my relief and instant delight she pushed me over, climbed aboard and rode me like a rodeo rider.

Her orgasm this time, and for months to come, was accompanied by cries that would have done credit to a banshee. Then they reverted to the quietness of the first. I never knew, and never asked, if she actually ever achieved orgasm with me. When I cared, I was afraid to ask. When I didn't care, I couldn't be bothered.

40

We made love once more that night, then curled up contentedly exhausted. 'You'll stay the night?' I asked Ann sleepily, assuming the answer would be yes.

'And wear the same clothes in the morning, I don't think so.' She pushed away and looked down at me through make-up smudged eyes before giving me a gentle kiss. 'Another time?'

I nodded. 'Sure.'

Slipping from the bed, she scrabbled in the dim light for her clothes, then stood in front of the mirror and pushed her fingers through her hair. Turning, her face was serious. She looked down at me, as I lay naked, relaxed. 'Have you told Adam about us?'

I sat up. Less relaxed now. I hadn't, wasn't sure how he would take it.

'There's time enough for that, isn't there?'

'It's up to you. But if he hears from someone else, he might be surprised you hadn't told him.' She shrugged her slim shoulders. 'You know what London is like, Jake.' Her face took on a sharper look. 'I can tell him, if you prefer?'

'No,' I said quickly, the single word coming out harshly. I saw an eyebrow rise. 'Sorry... no, thank you, it would be better if I told him. Honestly.'

She nodded, leaned down to kiss me again, then left.

I lay there without moving.

Telling Adam. Adam and Jane. Jane.

I stood, suddenly restless. I had no idea what Adam was going to say. He would be surprised, without a doubt. But would he be pleased? After all, if I did ask Ann to marry me, not only would we be friends – we would be family. He would be my brother-in-law. Jane would be my sister-in-law... by marriage, anyway. Our lives would be forever linked, and I sighed, a sigh of pleasure at the upward turn my life was suddenly taking.

Next day, I rang him. 'Hey, Adam, you free for a pint?'

It was unusual for me to ring him at the weekend, and his first response was so like him.

'You okay?'

I smiled, and it sounded in my voice. 'Yeah, fine. I just have something I wanted to talk to you about... if you can't make it, don't worry.'

'No, no, I can make it, of course. Shall I bring Jane or is this a man thing?'

The last thing I wanted was Jane there. She and Ann didn't get on at all, not that she ever said anything. It was the fact she never spoke about her, and rarely spoke to her that gave it away. There couldn't have been two women more dissimilar than they. Maybe that's why Ann was the perfect woman for me. Maybe I was fooling myself.

Adam choked on his pint when I told him. Wiping his streaming eyes, he looked at me as if I had suddenly grown two heads. 'You and Ann? Are you crazy?'

This wasn't the time to tell him that I planned to marry her, so I just shrugged. 'She's beautiful, intelligent. Why not?'

'You're sleeping with her?' he asked, eyes popping out of his head. 'You and Ann! My God, I never saw that coming.' He downed the contents of his glass and headed to the bar for two more pints. It obviously gave him time to reflect, he was calmer when he returned, and his eyes had gone back into their sockets. 'Are you serious about her?' Then he shook his head. 'I suppose you wouldn't be telling me if it was just a casual fling, would you?'

'We've seen each other a few times, Adam. It just seemed to make sense that you should know about it.'

'But... Ann?'

My irritation obviously showed because he held his hands palm up and shook his head. 'Sorry, sorry, you know what you're doing, I suppose.' Then he shook his head again. 'I don't want anecdotes about your sex life doing the rounds. You remember the story about Tony?'

'Yes.' I grinned at him. 'But I don't have a small cock.'

He covered his face with his hands. 'I don't want to know. You want to shag my sister, go ahead, but don't tell me the details. And don't blame me when it goes pear-shaped, okay?'

I felt a dart of irritation... or was it disappointment... at his attitude. I'd hoped he'd be pleased. After all, his sister was doing well for herself. And I, well, I was going to have the most stunning woman hanging on to my arm. More importantly, although he didn't know it yet, Adam and I were going to be more than friends... we were going to be brothers-in-law.

I'd be part of the family.

41

For the next few months, I didn't see Adam for lunch for a variety of reasons. Some even genuine. When we did speak, it was a brief *how are you, sorry, just manic these days, yes, we will meet soon, no, no news, love to Jane.*

And then, two months later, I asked Ann to marry me. Of course, she agreed. There was never a moment's doubt. By that time, she knew exactly how much money I earned, what my prospects were, the kind of lifestyle I could offer her.

As I said, she got what she wanted.

And I really thought, then, that so had I, that it didn't... wouldn't... matter that I didn't love her. Despite cooing words of love whispered in my ear, I knew she didn't love me either, knew if all my money vanished, so would she. But I didn't expect to lose all my money, did I? The world was ticking along quite nicely, thank you very much. I played my cards just right and didn't expect someone to come along and stick a joker in the pack.

After Ann had said yes, her next words were, 'The ring has to be from Tiffany's.'

I was still down on one knee, stupidly thinking the romantic gesture was a requirement, whereas she had already moved on. The speed at which she had jumped from acceptance to organising where to buy the ring caught me unawares. 'Tiffany's?' I said, genuinely puzzled.

'New York, darling. Everyone who is anyone goes there.'

Feeling stupid, I laughed, and stood up. The romantic aspect of the engagement was over. 'Okay, then. Tiffany's it is.'

We flew to New York, stayed in the Waldorf Astoria, and spent about three hours in Tiffany's looking at diamonds, until I was almost blind from so much sparkle. Of course, we didn't just buy a ring. As Ann rightly said, what was the point of travelling all that way *just* for a ring? And what was the point in buying earrings without a bracelet and necklace. What was the point indeed? Consoling myself by looking at the diamonds as an investment, I handed over my credit card. After all, my next bonus would easily cover the $75,000.

Ann wore all the diamonds for me that evening. Just the diamonds. And, my God, she looked stunning. 'You want me, Jake?' she whispered, sashaying across the room, her creamy skin lit here and there with fire that sparked as she walked, fire that caught me and made me hard. She didn't object when I pressed her to the wall and slid her upward, pushing her thighs apart. I held her there, fumbling with my zipper, and slid her quickly onto the erection that fell out, hot and heavy, hearing her gasp of pain or pleasure... I was past caring... and came almost at once, feeling my seed shoot into her.

'That was good,' I whispered into her ear as I slipped out of her and lowered her legs. I kissed her gently and stepped away.

Ann smiled perfunctorily. 'A bit messy, maybe.' She grimaced as my semen started to trickle down her thighs and a musty smell rose to envelop us.

My trousers had slipped down round my knees, and I

suddenly felt... what... dirty? Lecherous? Watching her move away, the glisten of moisture on her thighs catching the light as she went, just as the diamonds had a very few moments before, I knew, suddenly, she felt she had paid well for them.

Perhaps, this was the first time I questioned the wisdom of marrying a woman I didn't love to achieve the lifestyle I thought I did.

It might have been the first time; it wasn't the last.

42

Weddings, by their very nature, bring the question of family to the fore. Ann, of course, was under the impression that my parents were dead, thanks to the lie so casually told all those years before, a lie reinforced when I visited the Cotswolds to discover that Adam had told his parents all about me. Including the tragic death of my parents. They had been so sympathetic, and so kind, that if there had been a moment's guilt, a second when I felt like confessing, it passed as I basked in their care. And then it was too late. The lie was set in stone, and I was caught in that strange blurry world where lies and truth are inseparably tangled.

The first few years, I wrote an occasional brief letter to my parents imparting only the bare facts that I was alive and well, my reticence to tell them more of my life in Oxford a sulky boy's revenge – *you weren't interested in my going there; you won't be interested in hearing about it.*

There was also the rarely acknowledged hurt that, although they had to have known where I'd gone, they'd never tried to contact me. When I had money, I considered sending them some to help brighten their later years, but I knew they'd be more offended by what they'd regard as charity than by my neglect.

By the time I met Ann, even a letter had become too much trouble, and I did no more than scribble my initial on a Christmas card once a year.

So, I had no interest in inviting my parents to our wedding. Even if I could without exposing myself for the liar I was. But because weddings *are* a family thing, my parents, or rather my abandonment of them, began to weigh on my mind.

'I might have to go to Bristol on Saturday,' I said to Ann over dinner one evening. 'One of my clients wants to have a face-to-face.'

'On a Saturday?' she asked, surprised.

'It's the only day he can make, I'm afraid. It'll only be for a few hours.'

'Perhaps I'll come with you.' She smiled across the table at me. 'Shops in Bristol are supposed to be lovely. I'm still looking for that certain something to wear for the pre-wedding dinner.'

'He wants to meet at ten,' I said, thinking quickly. 'We'll have to leave about 7.45.'

She closed her eyes and shook her head. 'That's inhuman, Jake.'

'You stay in bed.' I reached for her hand. 'I'll be back in time for a late lunch in that new restaurant you wanted to try.'

And it was settled. I had the morning in Bristol to myself, or perhaps it would be more honest and truthful to say *we* had it to ourselves. Me, the boy who'd left all those years before, and me, the man who drove his Porsche slowly because he couldn't quite remember how to get to the road he had once lived on.

The lack of recognition caught me by surprise, sure as I was that it would all come flooding back to me as soon as I returned. It didn't. Stopping with a grunt of frustration, I keyed my old address into the satnav, followed its directions, waiting for the penny to drop, waiting for my brain to say, *ahh, yes, I remember now*. It didn't. Nothing looked the same to me.

Directed down a road as unfamiliar to me as any road in any town I've never been in, the final direction came to me, *you have reached your destination on the right*. I drove to the end of the road, and parked.

Getting out, I looked around, searching for something, anything familiar. There was nothing. The small town I remembered had been swallowed by the city of Bristol, and Bristol had put its mark on it. I noticed the cars. Ford Mondeos, BMWs, Volvos, solid middle-class cars. The gardens too, showed that certain air of expensive care; manicured lawns, box hedges, fancy paving, topiary shrubs on tiled doorsteps. Families, priced out of the upmarket suburbs of Redland and Clifton, had obviously drifted a few miles further and landed here.

Locking the car, I headed slowly down the road toward my parents' home. It wasn't yet ten, and it was quiet, curtains in most houses still firmly shut against a sun that was already warm. I took off my jacket and swung it over my shoulder, trying for nonchalance, feeling a shiver down my spine that I recognised as fear. Nothing was familiar to me. And if I hadn't known the number of my parents' house, I would have walked past without a flicker of recognition. As it was, I counted down the numbers and stopped outside twenty-four, double-checking the number, staring at the house with a feeling of puzzlement. The dull grey house of my memory was a smart terraced house with a glossy red painted door and a pretty garden bursting with colour. Hanging baskets cascading with colourful flowers hung each side of the doorway, drooping fronds almost touching blooms that grew up from pots on the step.

'Can I help you?' a voice asked, startling me. It came from the house, the owner of the voice peering from the upstairs sash window she had just opened. Even from a distance, I noticed her eyes were narrowed in suspicion.

'Yes, my name is Jake Mitchell.' I suppose I expected her to look surprised, pleased or even shocked, but her face didn't register any change of expression at all, as if she didn't know who I was, or care. 'My parents live here,' I elaborated.

She didn't move, her hands braced on the open sash window, her head slightly extended through the opening, looking down on me. 'You're mistaken. *I* live here.'

43

My heart, already pounding quicker than normal, started to beat double time. My gaze drifted back to the number. Twenty-four. Maybe it was the wrong street... of course, that was it. Satnavs... they really weren't to be trusted. I shook my head. 'I'm sorry. It's been a long time. I'm looking for twenty-four Primrose Terrace. I've obviously come to the wrong street.' Still shaking my head, I started to turn away.

'This *is* twenty-four Primrose Terrace.' The voice drifted down and stopped me mid-turn. 'Wait there, I'll come down.'

Moments later, the glossy red door slowly opened and a short slim woman beckoned me through the garden gate. 'We'll annoy the neighbours if we keep shouting,' she said, and standing back waved me into the house.

If the outside of the house bore no resemblance to the one I had known as a child, the inside bore less. It had been extended out into the garden, the small kitchen replaced by a huge open-plan living, kitchen and dining area. Spacious and elegantly furnished, it reminded me of a smaller version of Elgin Crescent.

No expense had been spared, and the furnishing was tasteful, sophisticated.

I followed the woman through, and she waved me to a seat. 'Would you like a cup of tea?'

'Coffee, if that would be okay.' I hoped a shot of caffeine would help me to understand what was going on. Where were my parents?

She filled the kettle, switched it on, took out some pretty china mugs and a small red tin that she opened and put in front of me. It was filled with biscuits. I reached and took one, nibbling chocolate off the edges while she watched me with mounting curiosity.

'Well, Jake Mitchell,' she said finally as I sipped on the coffee she'd poured. 'Why did you think your parents lived here?'

I swallowed the last of the biscuit. 'They did,' I explained. 'I did. I left seventeen years ago.' Shrugging, I added, 'I haven't been back since.'

Puzzlement creased her brow. 'You left home seventeen years ago, but your parents stayed here?'

I nodded. 'I went to Oxford.' When she continued to look puzzled, I added, 'University.'

'Yes, I understand, but you didn't visit?'

There was implied criticism in the words. What did she know about me, or them, or the life we led? 'We weren't close.'

'But you must have spoken to them over the years.'

'No, I wrote to let them know how I was doing. That was the sum of it.'

She rose and went to fetch the coffee pot, filled my mug, then her own, put the pot back and stood beside it as she looked across the room at me. 'My husband and I have lived here sixteen years. The house was on the market for a few months before we bought it.'

Coffee sloshed from my mug onto the table. 'I'm so sorry,' I said, watching as the coffee spread to the edge and dripped to the floor. I put the mug down, needing to use two hands to do so. I seemed to have totally lost coordination.

She moved to mop the mess up, watching me carefully as she did so. 'Are you okay?'

All I could do was nod, the power of speech traitorously abandoning me. My mind churned over the facts and couldn't make sense of them. If she was telling the truth, my parents moved from here shortly after I left. And all the letters and cards I had sent with no forwarding address. They had never had them?

'I wrote to them. At this address.'

She sat down across the table from me, her expression soft with sympathy. 'We got a lot of post the first few months after we moved in. I remember the surname on the letters clearly. Mitchell. That's why I let you in, I recognised the name. We had letters, every now and then, and for the last few years, at Christmas, we've had a card.' She shrugged helplessly. 'We just forwarded them all on.'

All the letters and cards I'd sent. They'd never had them, never knew I'd graduated from Oxford, or how well I was doing. I'd wanted them to be proud of me... despite everything... and they'd never even known.

Sorrow, regret and a sudden longing for the past I'd cast aside swamped me.

'Where did my parents move to?' Had they just forgotten about me? Moved on to better things? I couldn't reconcile any of this with the truth I had expected to find.

'They didn't move,' she said quietly. 'It was an executor sale. I'm so sorry, your parents are dead.'

44

Of all the scenarios I had expected and predicted, this was not one of them. My parents were dead? 'Are you sure?' I asked, hearing the emotion in my voice, unable to do anything about it, barely able to control the tremble that rippled through my body.

She, the nameless woman who sat opposite me with such pity in her eyes I wanted to get up and leave rather than face it, spoke gently. 'We forwarded all the post to the solicitor who handled the sale. He had grant of probate, as far as I remember.'

I couldn't help it; my voice came on the plaintive cry of an orphaned child. 'What about me? Why didn't someone tell me?'

'I'm so sorry. I don't know any more. The solicitor will be able to help you. I have his name somewhere.' She got up and left the room.

I heard her footsteps cross the floor above, then a long silence before she re-crossed, seconds later appearing before me, a thick file in her hand. 'It will be here somewhere.' She put the file on the table, opened it and flicked through a mess of information, assorted letters, documents, cards, flyers for this and that.

I stood up. 'It's all right, please don't bother. I can find out.'

'No,' she insisted, her fingers speeding up, as if finding the damn card was a form of restitution for having been the bearer of such bad tidings.

'No, really,' I counter-insisted, 'I've taken enough of your time.' I turned to leave; just wanting to get out and digest the information I'd been given, wanting to get out of this house just as much as I had done all those years before, and then more so, for suddenly, as if sent whirling back in time, I heard their voices, my mother's, my father's and felt an overwhelming loss.

'Eureka!'

The yell came from behind me, startling me, bringing me back from that night seventeen years ago, to the same house, different time.

I turned back to her. If she noticed the tears, she was considerate enough not to comment. 'Here it is, I knew I'd find it.' She held a business card out, held it in the silence between us, determined to pass on information I was equally determined not to receive. I didn't want to know, would drive back to London, forget all about this stupid, *stupid* idea. Seventeen years would become twenty, and thirty and everything, even today, would fade from memory.

And still she stood, and against my better judgement, against every fibre of me that screamed *no, you don't want to know*, my hand rose, and I took the blasted card that would damn me.

With a nod of thanks, I turned, card in hand, and left.

Back in my car, I turned on the engine and sat, unable to get past two thoughts. My parents were dead. And the lie I had told Adam all those years before, the lie I had lived with only the occasional smidgen of guilt, was a truth. And if those two thoughts didn't inflict enough pain, another came and turned the screw so tightly I couldn't, this time, stop the cry of anguish and despair.

My grief would have to be borne silently; I couldn't go home and tell Ann or Adam that my parents were dead. Because it didn't matter that I hadn't seen them for seventeen years, it didn't matter that I hadn't wanted to, they were dead, and my grief was genuine. And I would have to bear it alone.

45

The Porsche got me home somehow, negotiated all the twists and turns, parked me outside my beautiful house and allowed me sit there clutching that damn card in one hand. Finally, with a deep breath, I looked at it. Glossy but classy, a simple *Ian Carlton* with a phone number that, when rung, informed me office hours were Monday to Friday and offered another number to ring if my situation were urgent.

'Urgent,' I snapped out loud. Of course it was urgent. Listening to the message for a second time, I wrote down the number, and as I was about to phone it, hesitated. Was this the kind of conversation to have over the phone? Probably not. It would be better, easier, face to face. It would have to wait until Monday. Just a day and a half away.

My head flopped back wearily against the headrest. It would have been perfect to spend the day and a half in the comfort and peace of the Porsche, not having to speak to anybody. Pass the time, then drive to Bristol and speak to the solicitor.

Even as I decided it was impossible, I heard the front door open, saw Ann standing there mouthing words I couldn't read, but knew amounted to *what was I doing sitting there when a fancy lunch awaited?* I put on a correct, socially acceptable face and climbed out of the car.

'Sorry,' I said, coming up to her and placing a kiss on her cheek. 'Just needed to take that call. Give me two minutes to get out of this suit, and we'll be on our way.'

She kept her hand on the door frame barring my entrance. 'The Green Man is very upmarket, Jake. A suit would be most acceptable. And anyway' – she looked pointedly at her watch – 'we're already late.'

There was no point in arguing. 'Fine,' I said, and reversed my steps to the car, opened the door for her, climbed back into a still-warm seat, and started the engine.

The Green Man was new and full of its own importance. Acoustics were poor and the place incredibly noisy, so there was little room for more than the occasional conversational gambit that had to be repeated several times before being heard, losing any interest it might have had after the first or second telling. It didn't lead to a relaxing meal, but it suited me just fine. Food came and was eaten. It was probably good. It could have been terrible. I wouldn't have known the difference.

Ann complained several times, in her quiet but pointed way, that I was obviously distracted. Offering an elaborate excuse of complex financial doings made her shake her head and hold her hands up. 'All that stuff is completely beyond me, you know that. Just try and leave it in the office, will you?'

For a fleeting moment, a millisecond, a sub-atomic particle of time, I was tempted to tell her everything. Shouldn't she know the truth? Would it make any difference to her? Putting my knife and fork down, I looked across the table, opened my mouth to begin the telling, closed it again without uttering a word, seeing as clearly as if it had been written across her forehead.

She didn't care.

And beautiful as she was, I had to acknowledge I felt the same. Absolutely nothing, apart from a certain pride of ownership. My trophy wife-to-be. Her function was to look beautiful, to be the final piece of furniture for Elgin Crescent, never to be a soulmate, a confidante. Through the murky and warping mists of time, I remembered my parents, and thought with a deep sadness that they had had what Ann and I would never have. Banal, boring and dull as they were, they had loved each other.

And probably me.

And I had abandoned them.

Listening to Ann, her voice fading in and out as the surrounding noise invaded and receded, her monologue more interesting for the missing words, looking around seeing the wealthy and the glamorous, I realised this was it.

The pinnacle of success. Wealth. Sophistication. Glamour. They were all mine for the taking.

I had got *just* what I deserved.

So, of course, I said nothing to Ann. What would be the point? She didn't care where I'd come from, just what I had. She might have found it momentarily diverting and have added it to her repertoire of entertaining anecdotes. And she would tell Adam, of course, she wouldn't be able to stop herself.

'Is it true?' he would ask, and he would look stunned, puzzled and hurt. The look would turn to disgust as he understood the catalogue of lies I had told him for all those years of apparent honest friendship. It would be over then, of course, that friendship. No relationship could survive such deceit. We would be connected forevermore through Ann, but conversations, when they had to occur, would be stilted and uncomfortable, and our eyes would never meet.

There would be no point in trying to explain. No point in

saying it was a carelessly thoughtless choice, at a young and foolish age. There were years I could have told him the truth, years of chatting over pints when a confession might have been made and accepted. But not now.

Now, I had to bite my tongue and keep my dirty little secret.

46

Annoyingly, I had a meeting first thing Monday morning, so it was nearly eleven before I took out that glossy card and carefully rang the number under the name.

It was answered after two rings. 'Sheridan, Jones and Carlton, how may I help you?'

I took a deep breath. 'My name is Jake Mitchell. I'd like to speak to Ian Carlton regarding my parents' estate.'

'Hold for a moment, please,' the voice asked, and I was left listening to anodyne classical music for far longer than I wanted.

'Did you say Mitchell?' the same female voice asked.

'Yes, Jake Mitchell. Mr Carlton had probate for my parents' estate.'

'I'm afraid there must be some mistake,' the voice continued, firm if hesitant, 'we have no case under the name Mitchell currently being dealt with by Mr Carlton.'

'I'm talking about a case seventeen years ago. Emily and David Mitchell. I've been told Mr Carlton handled probate.'

'Just hold for a moment, please.' And once more I was left listening to the same irritating music. I was about to hang up and redial when she came back. 'I'm sorry for keeping you, Mr Mitchell. I've had a quick word with Mr Carlton. He would be delighted to see you this afternoon, at 3.30 if that's suitable.'

It was what I'd wanted. Now I wasn't so sure. 'Couldn't we handle this over the phone?' I bit out, letting my frustration show. 'I really don't have time to be swanning off to Bristol on a Monday afternoon.'

'Perhaps we could make it another day. Unfortunately, Mr Carlton insists it is handled in a face-to-face meeting, Mr Mitchell.'

'Fine,' I snapped, frustration winning over good manners. 'Fine. I'll be there at 3.30.'

I left the office without a word. Outside, unbelievable luck was running my way for a change, as an empty taxi was stuck in the traffic in front of me. A quick knock on his window got his attention. He nodded, and I climbed in. Brilliant, I thought, relaxing back into the seat. Five minutes later, I was swearing under my breath, sweating under my clothes. We hadn't moved.

'Is there a problem?' I leaned forward, trying not to sound irate.

His shrug denoted a non-English origin, dramatically elaborate, saying everything.

'Perhaps I would be faster taking the Tube.'

Mr Shrug waved a casual hand at the meter that was already clocking up pounds and then shrugged again, as if to say, *I don't give a toss what you do, mister, as long as you cough up the dosh.*

Unable to decide, I sat and eventually, as it always does, the traffic moved. Once outside Elgin Crescent, I quickly handed him a note, with an even quicker, *keep the change.* It wasn't until later that I realised I'd given him a fifty, not a twenty; the fare wouldn't have been much over fifteen. It's no wonder his face lit up. He didn't remonstrate, or say it was too much. Or maybe he had, but I hadn't waited to hear.

I hurried into the house, grabbed my car keys from the hall table drawer, rushed out again and climbed into the Porsche. Taking the solicitor's card from my pocket, I breathed a sigh of relief when I spotted the postcode on the reverse. Keying the code into the car's integral satnav, I started the engine. It purred, ready to go, but then I thought of Ann, and switched off again to ring her.

'That chap in Bristol wants a further meeting,' I said, when she eventually answered her mobile. 'I'll be home around eight. We can go to the Italian, if you like.'

'No. I'm bored with Italian, let's try the new Indonesian restaurant instead. I'll book a table for eight. Don't be late.'

Don't be late. I was driving to Bristol and back, and that's all she could think to say. A wave of exhaustion, or maybe it was terror, hit me and my head dropped back onto the headrest. A few minutes, that's all I needed. But it was no good, too many thoughts were rushing around willy-nilly to allow even a moment's rest.

Traffic was probably the usual mayhem; to be honest, I don't know that I really looked out the window of the car as I drove. I followed the directions, took the first, second, third exit off roundabouts as directed, but was never aware where I was. When the voice told me I had arrived at my destination, I was caught unawares and stopped the car in the middle of the road. The driver behind waited a courteous thirty seconds before putting hand to horn and waking me from where I lingered.

There were four parking spaces outside the offices of Sheridan, Jones and Carlton. My luck was in, because just as I pulled up, I saw the reverse lights of a car waiting to pull out. I waited, quickly drove into the space, and turned off the engine. The clock on the dashboard told me it was 2.45. I checked my watch, thinking it couldn't be correct; surely it had to be later than that. But my Rolex confirmed 2.45, I'd obviously made very good time on the road from London.

I left the car and wandered along the street in search of somewhere to wait. It didn't take me long; the first few shops I met included a coffee shop that looked hopeful. The barista looked bored as he did his thing, and even more bored when he handed me my double espresso.

I should have eaten something but felt too jittery. After the coffee, I felt even more so, but at least then I knew why. Emptying the tiny cup, I checked my watch and headed back down the street. I felt jittery but also numb, detached, still struggling to process what I'd learned on Saturday.

It was 3.30 on the dot when I rang the doorbell of the office of Sheridan, Jones and Carlton. A disembodied voice asked my business. 'It's Jake Mitchell. I have an appointment with Mr Carlton.'

The door buzzed, and I pushed it open and stepped into a spacious lobby. Moments later, I heard the sound of footsteps click-clacking across a wooden floor and one of the doors off the lobby opened. A slim brunette, the owner of the click-clacking heels, approached with extended hand. 'Mr Mitchell, I'm Sasha, Mr Carlton's secretary. He has asked me to apologise, he has been unavoidably delayed.' She shrugged and added, 'A complex court case.' With that, she stood back and indicated that I should precede her into the room behind. 'He should be here in about thirty minutes,' she said, leading me to a small sofa beside a real coal fire. 'Please, make yourself comfortable. I'll fetch you some coffee, or would you prefer tea... or something stronger, perhaps?'

Sitting, I shook my head, then changed my mind and nodded. 'Coffee. Coffee would be nice, thank you.'

She nodded and left, returning several minutes later with an elegant tray set with a small cafetière, a delicate china cup and saucer, and delicious-looking almond biscotti. I sat, dipped the biscuits into the coffee, and munched through the lot. The observant Sasha didn't ask, but she got up from her desk on the other side of the room and left, returning moments later with another plateful. She put them before me with a slight smile. 'They are good, aren't they?'

I poured more coffee, dunked more biscotti, and waited.

It was over an hour later before the solicitor arrived. I'd turned down more coffee, my heart was already pounding an erratic beat. I was beginning to think I should just leave, had even made a half-hearted effort to stand, before facing the truth that I couldn't go. Not without knowing the full story.

When Carlton did arrive, he bustled in, arms full of files, words of apology spilling from his mouth every which way. Either the years had been very kind, or he was a much younger man than I had expected, having imagined I would be dealing with a man around my parents' age. The father I remembered would surely have looked for a more experienced man to take care of his legal affairs, wouldn't he? Or had my memories become warped with time? What did I know about him really?

The solicitor dropped the files higgledy-piggledy onto the secretary's desk, where Sasha immediately reached a hand out to prevent the lot tumbling to the floor.

He approached me, hand extended. 'I'm Ian Carlton. My apologies for the delay. Please, come into my office.' He opened the door, waved me through, and then with a 'Hold all calls, please, Sasha,' he closed the door behind us.

His office was traditionally, comfortably furnished. A big desk dominated the room, making chairs positioned either side look tiny in comparison.

'Please,' he waved to one of them, 'have a seat.'

Before sitting on the far side, he opened a filing cabinet and extracted a large file that he put before him, laying his hand on top without opening. The smile he had greeted me with in his secretary's office had gone, and he looked sombre and serious, and suddenly older. I re-evaluated his age up a decade.

'Do you have identification with you, Mr Mitchell?'

Surprised, I reached into my inside pocket, took out my driving licence and handed it across the desk to him.

He took it, looked at it for a long time before handing it back. 'Mrs Youlden, the lady you spoke to on Saturday. She rang me first thing this morning, so I was anticipating your call.'

I nodded. 'She gave me your card.'

He put both hands on the file, tapped his fingers on it. 'The thing is, Mr Mitchell...' he stopped, cleared his throat. 'The thing is... you claim you are Jake Mitchell, son of David and Emily Mitchell who lived at twenty-four Primrose Terrace.'

This wasn't going as I expected. 'I'm not *claiming* to be, I *am* Jake Mitchell. My parents are... were David and Emily Mitchell. I didn't know they were dead.' The words caught in my throat even as I said them.

The solicitor nodded. 'Yes, Mrs Youlden told me.' He bit his lower lip. I could see him thinking what to say. Didn't expect what he *did* say. 'The thing is, Mr Mitchell...'

For an educated man, he wasn't very erudite. If he said *the thing is* once more, I was going to have to climb over the desk and squeeze whatever the hell *the thing* was out of him. I settled for an impatient, 'What?' the word spat out to float in a cartoon bubble between us. We sat, the two of us, the word sitting there unchallenged, unanswered, until *ping*, the bubble burst, and the solicitor, as if released, moved.

He opened the file before him, flicked through the contents. I knew a delaying tactic when I saw one, had used the very same one myself, too many times to mention. But never when the news was good. You never needed delaying tactics then. A bead of perspiration trickled down the side of my face. I reached into my jacket pocket, took out a linen handkerchief and wiped my face. I met the solicitor's eyes across the desk, swallowed frantically as my stomach cramped and hot burning acid shot into my mouth.

'What?' I shouted, wanting to be heard over the loud insistent thumping of my heart. 'What the hell is going on?'

'The thing is,' he said once more, but I was beyond caring, and too afraid to interrupt in case he never bloody told me what the damn thing was. But this time he continued, blurting it out as if he couldn't get the words out fast enough. 'Jake Mitchell was reported as having died in the crash that killed your parents.'

47

When the silence had worn itself out, Ian Carlton shuffled in his chair, cleared his throat, and started to explain. 'I hadn't been with the firm very long. It was just Sheridan and Jones then, I only became a partner a few years ago. Ben Jones had dealt with your parents and drawn up their will, but he was semi-retired when the accident happened. When the police contacted us, he asked me to take over.'

I was still gripping the edge of the desk in front of me, my body tense and leaning so far forward that I was within snapping distance of the fingers fiddling with the file and its contents. Suddenly, forcing a yelp from me, Ian Carlton stood and moved to the corner of the office where he opened the top drawer of a filing cabinet and withdrew a bottle and two glasses. He didn't ask but uncorked the bottle and poured amber-coloured liquid into each glass, filling both almost to the brim. The pungent smell of single malt filled the room. I wasn't a whisky drinker, but I took the proffered glass, downed it in one and held it out for a refill that quickly came, downed that, held it out once more. There was a slight hesitation before he filled my glass again.

This time, I took a sip and put the glass down. It had done the trick. Feeling the tenseness ebb, and welcoming the soft fuzziness that soothed my agitated thoughts, I sagged back in the chair.

'Is there someone I can call for you, Mr Mitchell?' Carlton asked, watching me over the brim of his still full glass. 'You've had a shock.'

I shook my head. It wasn't a good idea; the whisky had gone straight there and was doing a thumping good job. 'I'll be fine,' I told him, although all evidence was to the contrary. 'Please just tell me everything you know.'

He nodded, sipped a miniscule amount of whisky, and put the glass down at the same time as I picked mine up. He waited till I had emptied half, before continuing, 'It was a very bad crash. An oil tanker lost control – they think the driver had a heart attack – it skidded across the road and took three cars with it before exploding. The occupants of the cars... seven people... were killed in the subsequent fireball.' He stopped and took another sip. His gaze swept over me, as if to ascertain how well I was doing.

I must have looked okay, because he continued. 'The intensity of the fire made individual identification of the bodies virtually impossible—'

I gripped my glass. 'What about DNA?'

The solicitor shook his head. 'The bodies were burnt to such a degree... they used the term blue-grey-white... it seems when they're burnt to that degree that DNA obtained is unreliable.'

'Right.' I was struggling to sound objective. Blue-grey-white... they'd probably died immediately and hadn't known a thing. 'So what happened?'

'The police were able to trace the owners of the cars from chassis numbers and what was left of the licence plates, metal being more resilient than flesh and bones. Eventually they went to your home and neighbours were able to fill them in on who lived there.' He waited a moment, took another sip of his whisky, then went on. 'They told the police they had seen you and your parents the day before, but nobody remembered seeing any of you since.'

I held up my hand to stop him. 'The day before? Neighbours saw me the day before? My parents were killed the day after I left?'

The solicitor nodded.

I swayed in the chair as a terrible thought struck me. 'Where? Where did it happen?'

There was great sadness in Carlton's eyes.

'They were on the road to Oxford, weren't they?' My voice quavered on the words as I registered his nod of agreement. They'd been on their way to Oxford. To find me. All these years, I thought they hadn't cared. Only then, in that cold hard moment, did I understand how bitter I had been that they had never tried to find me.

Now I knew the truth; they had died trying. Died because of me. Disbelief fought with despair and left me with no words.

48

After a beat, Ian Carlton continued the story, 'Your father's employer told the police you were going to take up a position with them, so there was no reason to suppose you had gone elsewhere. Based on everything they had discovered, the police made the natural assumption that you were in the car along with your parents, and that along with them, you were killed in the accident. A memorial mass was held a few weeks later and' – he hesitated and looked at me across the desk before taking a steadying mouthful of his whisky – 'a gravestone was erected.'

My grip on the glass I held was so tight I wondered it didn't crack, cut me, and make me bleed regret. 'A gravestone?'

'In South Bristol Cemetery. It was where your parents had said they wanted to be buried.'

I nodded as if I had known that. I hadn't. Why would I? Death wasn't something we had ever discussed. Death wasn't something I expected, certainly not then. Not now.

A thought struck me. 'I've been writing to them. All these years. Did no one wonder?'

Carlton's hand moved to the folder, fiddled once more with

the contents, and withdrew a bundle of letters and cards. 'These?' he said, holding them up and looking directly at me, the first hint of censure in his eyes. 'You never included an address. You signed them "J". I had no idea who they were from. Thought it might have been a distant relative. I had no way of knowing it was you.'

I had been so careful to prevent my parents intruding on my Oxford idyll, so determined they wouldn't arrive unannounced and somehow spoil it. So bloody well determined to keep that part of my life separate from my wonderful new one. And I needn't have bothered. It had all been for nothing.

The solicitor looked at his watch, not bothering to be discreet. I suppose he usually charged by the hour, wondering vaguely if he would bill me for this.

My whisky-fuzzed brain was a few steps behind in processing all it had heard. There was something niggling, something important. Then it came to me. 'What about my National Insurance number? When I started working, wouldn't that have alerted someone?'

Carlton shuffled restlessly in his chair. 'I'm afraid an error was made at the time.'

'Go on.'

'Ben Jones was semi-retired. He worked part-time, helped with the routine paperwork.' Carlton hesitated, as if reluctant to lay the blame on a colleague. 'Your death was registered, obviously, but it appears he missed out informing the National Insurance contributions office.'

'So I was able to use it without alerting anyone to the mistake.'

'Yes. Of course, I will have to contact the authorities now.'

I had nothing to be afraid of, the mistake hadn't been mine, so my fear wasn't from the ominous word *authorities*, just what it represented. More people knowing and the horrifying idea that the lie I had told all those years before would escape. 'Is that necessary?'

He pulled his head in like a giant Galapagos tortoise. 'You have been declared dead, Mr Mitchell. This situation obviously cannot be let lie.'

'Fine, fine, as you wish. In that case, I would ask that you act for me. Let me know what must be done. I will pay a retainer, of course.' I reached into my inside pocket for my chequebook.

He mentioned a figure that made my eyebrows rise automatically, but I had neither the energy nor inclination to argue. 'I would prefer this matter to be settled as soon as possible,' I said, handing over the cheque. 'Send any mail concerning the matter to my office address.' My office address, keeping my secrets hidden away. I handed him my card with the relevant information.

'Of course,' he said, and then, 'There is the matter of your inheritance, of course.'

'My inheritance?'

'Your family home was sold, plus your parents had savings. All was left to you in the first instance, but as you too were deemed to have perished, the estate was left to the retirement fund of your father's factory.'

I shook my head. 'That's fine. I'm in no need of the money. Let it stay as it is. How much are we talking about, anyway? The house can't have been worth much.'

'No, it didn't fetch much, I'm afraid. But your parents had invested their savings well. Altogether their estate came to £300,000.'

49

Stunned, I stared at the solicitor. 'How much?'

'Three hundred thousand. As I said, the house wasn't worth much. It sold for just £55,000. But your father had shares in the factory. Didn't you know? They had increased in value over the years. He did very well with them.'

Shares in the factory? He had bought shares in the damn factory. Why had he never told me? 'I didn't know. I wasn't even aware the company had floated shares.'

The solicitor nodded. 'All employees were given the opportunity, although few took up the offer. Your father bought the maximum available, and he kept adding to them when he could. Three hundred thousand pounds is worth fighting for.'

I thought of the shabby grey house I'd grown up in, our dull boring life, and I hated my father then as never before. We could have lived a different life, and if we had... oh, God, maybe I wouldn't have sneaked off as I did, and they wouldn't have been on the road to Oxford that morning, wouldn't have gone up in flames.

My hand shook as I lifted the glass to my lips and tilted the rest of the whisky down my throat. It burned... and I thought of blue-grey-white and wanted to cry.

Carlton had taken a blank sheet of A4 paper and was making notes in tiny spidery writing that was impossible to read upside down. I guessed what he was writing, though, and held my hand up. 'No,' I said bluntly, 'I don't want it. Leave it as it stands. Just have my death declared an error. Can't that be done?'

He stopped writing immediately, the pen held mid-squiggle and looked at me, possibly weighing up my sanity. 'We're talking about £300,000, Mr Mitchell. More, if we make an argument for interest on that figure.'

My head shake made me dizzy. The room swirled and across the desk there was a kaleidoscope of solicitors all identical to Ian Carlton. I shut my eyes and took steadying deep breaths. When I opened my eyes again, it was to see just one solicitor regarding me with a worried frown. I smiled wryly. 'Perhaps I should have sipped that whisky.'

He picked up his phone. 'Sasha, can you bring us some coffee, please?'

It arrived within minutes, the lovely Sasha placing a heavy tray on the desk between us before taking herself off without a word spoken.

Picking up a delicate cup and saucer, he poured coffee, added milk and sugar without asking, and handed it to me. Just as I had with the whisky, I downed it and held it out for a refill. 'No sugar, please.'

I don't know if the caffeine worked as an instant antidote to the whisky, but I began to feel a little better almost immediately. Putting the empty cup on the desk, I smiled at the solicitor. 'Thank you, Mr Carlton. That seems to have done the business. But my mind is made up. I'm not interested in pursuing my inheritance. I simply want this matter closed officially, and my status confirmed.'

He crumpled the paper before him and threw it into a wastepaper basket in the corner, the wadded paper bouncing first off the wall before landing on target. He took a fresh sheet, did some more spider-writing and put his pen down. 'I'll get it sorted. If you're not contesting the inheritance, I don't envisage any problem.'

I nodded, satisfied, and felt a wave of exhaustion sweep over me. 'Thank you. Perhaps you could tell me, if you would, is there a hotel nearby? I don't think I will head back to London this evening.'

Carlton picked up his phone again. 'Sasha, ring Dobbin's, please, and book a room for Mr Mitchell for tonight.' Replacing the phone, he nodded at me. 'You can leave your car outside, if you like. Dobbin's is just a short walk, five minutes at the most. Outside, turn right, then the next turn left, and there it is. It would take a lot longer to drive.'

Standing, I held out my hand. 'I appreciate your assistance, Mr Carlton. Thank you.'

He stood, took my hand and held on to it. 'Go easy on yourself. Life throws curveballs all the time. You're just responsible for the ones you catch, not the ones you don't.'

I nodded. He let my hand go, and I took my leave.

Minutes later, I was walking towards the hotel, my mind buzzing with the events of the last few days. I checked in, made a quick phone call with an even quicker lie to Ann, spinning the tale of an investor who needed more time to decide. Lies and more lies, and worse, I couldn't see an end. I would have to lie forever.

50

I had something to eat in my room, ordering randomly from the room menu, shaking my head at what arrived. I picked at the mushroom risotto and seafood lasagne, enjoying neither. Opening the wine I'd also ordered, I did it more justice and finished half the bottle before I had eaten a mouthful of either dish. I left the food, took the rest of the bottle with me and lay on the bed, propped against the pillows.

With the TV blaring for company, I sipped the wine slowly, afraid to finish the remainder too quickly, knowing if I did, I would order more. Then I thought, what the hell, finished the bottle, ordered another, finished that.

If I had been thinking in any way straight, I would have stripped before starting the second. Instead, I woke next morning, far later than I'd expected, with a mouth like a camel's arse, my rumpled trousers and wrinkled shirt a testament to a debauched night. My jacket, thrown over the back of a chair, was my saviour. Putting it on, I checked my reflection in the mirror, noting the red-rimmed eyes, the unshaven face and uncombed hair, I thought the air of dissoluteness rather suited the lying murdering bastard that I was.

Breakfast didn't appeal to me, or my ill-treated stomach. I settled for instant coffee, making it from the supply in the room. After two cups, I felt alert enough to be on my way.

A call to my office sufficed to alert them to my absence using the same generic excuse I had used with Ann. The words *potential investor* acted like a magic key; I'd have been forgiven anything. When nothing came of it, there would be a *you win some, you lose some* shrug that was part of the financial vocabulary of the day.

My intention was to head back to London immediately. My satnav was set, engine started, the car nosing out into mid-morning Bristol traffic. Almost without thinking, my plan changed, my eyes instinctively following signposts to another part of Bristol, ignoring the satnav as it repeated, over and over, *recalculating, take the next... recalculating... recalculating.* I was still ignoring the irritating tinny voice when I pulled up outside South Bristol Cemetery and parked the car.

The cemetery staff were very helpful and informative. Armed with their directions, it didn't take long to find what I was looking for.

It was a plain granite stone, the sentiment simple.

Here Lie the Remains of Emily and David Mitchell and their Beloved Son, Jake.

It was all a lie, of course. The solicitor had made it quite clear. Each of the families had been given some remains, something to cremate or bury depending on the wishes of the family or the deceased. So, the remains within might, or might not, have been my parents. The bigger lie, of course, was that I was not there.

I stood there, looking down on my death marker, the death

marker of my parents and felt... what? Numb? Yes, I felt numb. Better to feel that way than to make room for the excoriating guilt that was lying in wait.

I felt in my jacket pocket for a handkerchief, pulled it out, spat on it and cleaned away some bird-shit that marked the edge of the stone. I brushed away pine needles that were caught in the deeply carved letters of the inscription. Giving my dead parents the care and respect I'd denied them in life.

It started to rain, big drops darkening the stone where they fell. I brushed them away with my now grubby handkerchief, smudging the dirt, making it worse than when I had started. I stood back, feeling an endless unshakeable harrowing loss. The drops... not rain, I realised now... fell silently to mark my suit jacket. My eyes filling, overfilling, leaking sorrow and shame, regret and guilt.

I wasn't sure what I was crying for... my parents, the stupid boy I had been... or the pathetic liar I had become.

51

Maybe if I hadn't been so determined to put a distance between my present and my past, I would have called a halt to the excess our wedding became. Not vulgar excess, Ann was far too classy for that.

She dismissed churches and cathedrals as being too banal, and a marquee on the Cotswold family estate, her parents' wish, too bourgeois for words. Wedding planners were interviewed and impatiently dismissed. 'They've no vision, no imagination, Jake,' she told me one evening over dinner. 'We don't want mediocrity, do we? I'll just have to do all the work myself.'

She entered into it with enthusiasm and determination, spending hours on the internet, visiting various venues, dragging me along as if she were the slightest bit interested in what I thought. It amused me, and certainly kept my mind from drifting back into the muddy waters of my past.

Finally, after exhaustive searching, she rang me at work one morning, her voice breathlessly excited. 'I've got it, Jake. We're going to hire a steam ship!'

'A steam ship? Fantastic. Listen, I can't talk now, I'm just heading to a meeting. Tell me all about it tonight.' I sat through the meeting, half my mind thinking of an old tugboat, imagining us chugging across the sea dressed in Aran sweaters and waders. Not what I would have thought she'd come up with. I liked the idea more and more. It had a certain outlandishness that appealed to me, and it would be small, intimate. Yes. A good idea, and my mind drifted from high finance to the high seas and back for the rest of the day.

Ann had moved into Elgin Crescent just after our engagement. I wasn't entirely keen on the idea, wanting the place to myself for a while longer, but she argued it was foolish for her to keep paying rent for her place when she could be making a home out of mine. I'd learnt very quickly that it was impossible to argue with Ann.

When I arrived home that night, my mind still adrift on a sea of saline metaphors and humming, if you believe it, an old sea shanty, she was sitting in the dining room, the huge table spread with leaflets and brochures.

'Hi,' she said absent-mindedly, lifting a brochure and firing it over her shoulder where it joined a mounting pile on the floor.

I kissed her neck and inhaled her scent. 'I'm looking forward to hearing all about this steamboat plan.'

'Ship,' she corrected me. 'It's a steam*ship*.' She fumbled with the pile of brochures that remained on the table and withdrew one. 'This is it.'

Of course I had it wrong. It was a huge vessel, more ocean liner than tugboat.

'I saw it originally in your *FT How To Spend It* magazine.' Ann turned the pages of the brochure, her beautiful fingers lingering over the glossy photographs of maritime excess, her red glossy nails tracing the outline of the ship. 'They sent me the brochures this morning and I knew... I just knew this was it.' She turned in the circle of my arms and reached her hands up, laying them on my neck, her nails tracing a similar outline on my skin, arousing me. 'It's a little more expensive than we had planned... well, a lot more, really, but...'

Her lips moved to where her nails had been, her tongue tracing the lines they had left. Her hands, relieved of their duty, moved lower, nails finding my zipper and running noisily up it before catching the clasp and pulling it slowly down, releasing my already swollen penis. She dropped to her knees before me, licked the length of me, swirled her tongue briefly around the engorged head, then stood, pulled up her dress and sat on the table behind, spreading her legs to allow me full and easy access. No underwear to get in my way; she never did wear it at home, preferring, she said, to let the air at her *foofie*, a euphemism I had never heard before I met Ann, one she had learnt from a nursing friend who in turn had learned it from a Somerset care assistant.

Whether this was a particular Somerset expression, we never did find out. We were even more amused to discover the same care assistant used the word *fandango* to cover the anal area, turning the whole female genital area into a *foofie-fandango*. It appealed to me, that expression, and I used it when I could, slotting it into the conversation at totally inappropriate times in front of people who had no idea what I was referring to. I'd still be using it, but Ann got bored with my *schoolboy* humour and banned the expression.

Unfortunately for her, by that time I had let Adam in on the joke and he, as amused as I, took to it like a babe to a tit. He used it in the posh restaurant where we went to celebrate Ann's birthday, asking the waiter in a very controlled prim voice if there was *foofie-fandango* on the menu. Of course, we then had to explain the joke to Jane, who insisted, to my amusement and Ann's chagrin, in trying to figure out the origin of the words.

'Perhaps *foofie* is a child's pronunciation of *fanny*?' Jane said, sipping her wine.

'Pretty big stretch,' Adam replied. 'And what about fandango? You're never going to get that from anus, are you?'

'Please, Adam!' Ann looked around to see if anyone could possibly have overheard, Adam's voice after several beers having a strong carrying quality.

He ignored her. 'Maybe it's Spanish? It sounds Spanish.'

Jane squealed suddenly, causing us all to look at her in concern, and heads to swivel from various other tables. The kind of attention Ann hates. 'Fandango!' Jane said, looking at us in excitement. 'You remember,' she continued. Her smile lit the room, making us all smile too, although as yet none of us knowing why. Then Jane started singing, 'I see a little silhouette of a man, Scaramouch, Scaramouch, will you do the fandango!'

And we all, even Ann, joined in without thinking, 'Thunderbolt and lightning, very, very frightening,' then we stopped and laughed until I thought we'd be ill, drawing smiles from other diners who didn't know what we were laughing at, but who were drawn in nonetheless by laughter that was innocently uproarious.

* * *

But there was nothing innocent that night about Ann's neatly shaved *foofie*, and I plunged in with enthusiasm, coming quickly with little thought for her satisfaction. It didn't matter, I could see from her expression she'd got exactly what she wanted... my agreement to pay for what was obviously going to be a very, very expensive wedding.

52

The minimum hire for the steamship was a week, and we made the most of it. The cost was astronomical but what was the point, Ann argued, in having money if we didn't spend it. We had a couple of soirées on it before the wedding. Ann's parents came, the first time I'd met them since our engagement. They were more than thrilled the way things turned out. 'Can't believe you two got together,' Giles said, so often, in fact, it became embarrassing, as if Ann and I were the most unlikely of couples.

I could have told him the truth, but I was struggling with reality following the revelation about my parents. Sometimes, when Ann was going on and on about the arrangements, I could swear I heard my father's voice, his scathing words, *ideas above his station*, and I would look around, sure I'd see him standing there.

So we may indeed have been the most unlikely of couples, but I clung to the idea that marrying such a beautiful woman would make my life all right again.

* * *

Two hundred people, the maximum the steamer could cater for, were invited to the wedding. Nine couples, including Giles and Clara and, of course, Adam and Jane, were invited to stay on board with us for the remainder of the week. An unusual honeymoon, maybe, but we thought it would be fun. We planned to go somewhere, just the two of us, later in the year.

The steamer was moored just off the coast at Hastings. Ann organised a fleet of limousines to drive everyone down from London and the steamer provided tenders to transport people for the ten-minute journey from the harbour.

The steamer sounded its horn in greeting as each docked alongside, and smartly dressed sailors assisted the guests aboard. I stood on deck in my white linen suit and greeted them, directing them toward the sundeck.

A harpist played while we waited for Ann to appear. Adam, my best man, of course, chatted about nothing. If he was surprised at my marrying his sister, he had never said. And it was certainly too late then. In fact, neither he nor Jane had ever mentioned being pleased or otherwise at our relationship. Wisely, Ann and I had waited a couple of weeks before letting them in on it. By then, it was too late anyway. The decision I had made in that appalling French restaurant had become fixed during those first weeks, and nothing then could have changed my mind.

The only person who might have influenced my decision was Jane. If she had left Adam. If she had looked at me with anything other than sisterly concern.

But she didn't. She never would. She loved Adam. I loved her. That was that.

And as I stood and watched Ann approach, slim, elegant, beautiful, I decided I hadn't done so badly. After all, as Tina Turner once sang, wasn't love *just a second-hand emotion*. With *what's love gotta do with it* playing in my head, the words ringing out as clearly as if I was hearing them, the harpist played some much more suitable tune and Ann joined me in front of the minister. Rows of friends and family, and people I had never met before, stood and listened as we vowed to love each other until death did us part.

Then we were married, and as the breeze ruffled my hair and Ann's dress, I saw how her hair remained fixed in place. I knew it would always be this way. She would be impeccable, in control, perfect, and the world and I would whirl around her. I shivered and the breeze wasn't to blame.

The reception was perfect. The sailors carried magnums of Louis Roederer Cristal Rosé with reverence, but poured as if it was sparkling water, and I lost count of the satisfying pops I heard as each magnum was opened. The food, inspired by the surroundings, concentrated on seafood, and there was crab and lobster and scallops along with fillet steak for the carnivores.

The steamer captain came to me around two and expressed his concern at the increasingly drunken antics of some of the guests, one of whom had decided to go for a swim in the sea, fully clothed, and who had to be rescued by two of the crew. 'Safety is becoming compromised, Mr Mitchell,' he said apologetically, but with a firmness I knew preceded a decision. 'I must insist that the guests who are not staying overnight begin to disembark.'

At that stage, I couldn't remember who was or wasn't staying in the steamer's ten cabins. We had invited Ann's parents and Adam and Jane, but that left seven free. The steamer gave a slight lurch, and I grabbed the captain's arm. 'I'll sort it,' I said, my voice an inebriated lisp.

I left him and headed shakily across the deck to where Adam stood chatting to a man I didn't know. I gave him a wave of apology, grabbed Adam's arm and steered him away to a quiet corner. 'The captain wants the day guests to start going ashore.'

I didn't have to say any more, luckily. I wasn't sure I could. Adam nodded and headed over to where the captain still stood, his face looking a little grim.

Within minutes, Adam's clear voice came over the Tannoy announcing the arrival of the tenders to take people ashore, and there were suddenly crew members everywhere handing guests their jackets, shawls, bags and other belongings, assisting them down the gangways and onto the waiting tenders before most were even aware what was happening.

Within a short while, the last tender had reached the harbour and all that was left were those privileged to remain with us for the remainder of the week. Apart from family, there was the couple who lived next door to us in Elgin Crescent, who Ann thought would be a good connection. There were a few people Ann had worked with in her public relations job, people who had the right connection, the correct status. There was, of course, a member of the aristocracy, an incredibly boring and amazingly dull man, and his roving-eyed wife. To my surprise, Francois Sebastian and his fourth wife, Cleo, came to the wedding, and to my greater surprise, they stayed. I thought it was a great compliment to me until I learnt he had a thing about boats.

I woke the morning after our wedding with a hangover that throbbed. Ann looked at me askance, wondering, I suppose, was this it, every morning staring at my ravaged face. 'You look awful,' she said bluntly, not being one who thought self-inflicted pain deserving of sympathy. 'Let's go and have a sauna, it will clear your head.'

I thought I might throw up, but didn't like to say so, thinking, at least she wasn't suggesting we go for breakfast. We found the sauna empty, and I sat on the highest wooden shelf. Ann, who liked her saunas far hotter than I did, picked up a scoop and threw some water on the hot embers, the sizzle causing me to wince. I closed my eyes, opening them, startled, when I felt the belt of my robe being loosened. Ann stood there naked, her skin glistening in the heat, her eyes heavy with sudden lust. She quickly fondled my obviously reluctant manhood, and when that didn't work, she lowered her mouth and gave a tentative lick. I had been right, fellatio wasn't her thing, and in all the years of our marriage, she never did fill her mouth with me, preferring when it was necessary for her satisfaction to give cat licks that, although not so pleasurable from my point of view, did the job from hers.

My erection wasn't the best but was sufficient for her to climb aboard with a cutting, 'I suppose I'll have to make do.' A remark that would have resulted in detumescence if she hadn't already been riding me with a dedication I found thrilling. She came quickly, and would have dismounted if I hadn't held her there a moment longer, my hangover forgotten, my erection hard inside her, my pelvis driving, my release coming in a grunt, sending semen shooting into her, semen that dripped when she did dismount to stain the pale wood with creamy globules.

We had just belted our robes and were sitting back in post-coital satisfaction when I was jolted from mine as the door opened. It was Ann's parents, Giles looking a little worse for wear, his belly hanging over the tight belt of old but rarely worn shorts. 'She said this would do me good,' he said, nodding his head toward Clara, who was coming close behind, pushing Giles through the door.

I hoped they'd blame the heat of the sauna for the rush of embarrassment to my cheeks and beckoned Giles on, pointing to the seat perpendicular to mine. I used my feet to hide the stained wood, reluctant to actually put my foot on the mess despite being sure of its ownership.

But, no, he moved over and sat right beside me, his ample

backside covering the evidence of our coupling. 'Don't like these things,' he said grumpily. 'And it smells awful.'

I coughed to cover the laugh, turning to catch Ann's eye to share the funny side of it, imagining it would be one of those edgy stories we would tell at dinner parties to demonstrate how shockingly modern we were. People would gasp in horror or disgust, and we would laugh dismissively as if we were always doing something daringly different, bending rules, sailing close to the wind, and they would laugh too and admire us. Post-coitally, don't all men have delusions of godliness? I rested my elbows back on the wooden step behind me, let my knees drop even further so I was all manly display, and I felt so damn good.

And then it happened. I had to turn further to catch Ann's eye, but when I did, it wasn't her face I saw but Jane's. Jane's animated features superimposed on Ann's rather colourless ones. Jane's eyes twinkling at me, joining me in a recognition of the ridiculousness of the situation. And when it faded, when I saw Ann's blank look, it came to me in a rush, my eyes widening in a dawning horror.

Ann was beautiful, a perfect ornament, but she'd never be a soulmate, we'd never share the daft crazy things that made life bearable.

I had made a terrible mistake in marrying her.

53

My Damascene moment. Perhaps I should have stood up, there and then, told her, told her parents. Instead, I did what I always did – I ran away – shut the thought behind the door marked *forget about this*, bolted it, and didn't look back.

My thoughts were given a different direction when Ann, suddenly complaining of feeling unwell, stood shakily and dry retched. 'I feel sick!' She held a hand over her mouth and stumbled through the door, making it to the rails before throwing up. The nausea and vomiting lasted all day, but the fear that we were going to have an outbreak of food-poisoning was, thankfully, unfounded. Nobody else was unwell and the next day Ann was back to herself.

The idea that I'd made a terrible mistake in marrying Ann never really left me, but I put it to the back of my mind where it danced and swirled with the revelations of my parents' death.

The rest of the days on board passed quietly. Finally, and none too soon for me and my quickly emptying bank balance, the week came to an end.

And then it was back to the normal grindstone of life.

* * *

Five weeks later, just when normality had settled back into a pattern and we were sitting over a mediocre dinner in a new Italian restaurant, Ann interrupted a story I was recounting about one of my investors.

'Forget about him,' she said peremptorily, dismissing the man and my amusing anecdote just before the punch line. 'I'm pregnant.'

'Pregnant?' I said, as if it was the most impossible thing. And for the moment it was, our sex life being most remarkable by its absence. In fact, the last time, and I had to give it some thought, had been in the sauna on the steamer. I remembered vividly the spurt of my semen as it shot into her and realised one of the buggers had hit home. 'Pregnant.' I was in awe that such an inauspicious joining could have had such an outcome.

'Keep your voice down,' she hissed, with a quick look around the packed restaurant.

I hadn't realised my voice had risen and looked around apologetically. But no one was paying attention to us.

'My God, Ann, that's fantastic.' I could feel tears welling. 'My God.' The doubt I had over our marriage was dissolved in an instant. This was what we needed. A child.

'For goodness' sake, Jake, He had little to do with it. Anyway, I'm not sure this is the right time.'

I looked at her, puzzled and trying not to show it. Was I supposed to know what she meant? I was swimming in uncharted waters here but wanted to say, do, the right thing.

Ann picked up her wine glass and took a mouthful. I wasn't sure she should be drinking. I was almost sure she shouldn't be; shouldn't I know these things? I thought, with a growing pleasure, I would learn, buy books; check out internet sites, find out everything. Then I looked across at the face of my beautiful wife, saw the set, mulish look, and bit my tongue. I wasn't married long, but I was married long enough.

'You're not sure this is the right time to...?' I ventured.

She looked at me with disdain. 'What are we talking about? I'm not sure this is the time to have a baby. I was on the damn pill. This wasn't supposed to happen.'

We had discussed children. Ann knew I wanted them. She had seemed to feel as I did. There was a conversation shortly after we got engaged, she'd talked about coming off the pill... I suppose I assumed she meant straight away. Obviously not. The smile of joy at the thought of a baby stayed hidden safely away, waiting for privacy to come out and shine. I looked across the table and tried to look understanding. I couldn't think of anything better to say, so I kept it simple. 'It's perfect timing, Ann.'

Her face was stony.

What was her problem? My head spun, trying to think of reasons. 'This is what we wanted, isn't it?' I could hear the note of desperation in my voice, hated to hear it, and hated more the pleading tone of my pathetic. 'We want children.'

'Yes, sometime,' she said through gritted teeth. 'But not yet.'

'Okay.' I was pleased I hadn't got it completely wrong. 'Maybe the timing isn't as you'd have chosen. But it's okay. We can have the children early, and then enjoy them growing up.'

The look she gave me was withering. 'Child, Jake. One child. That's it.'

One child... the noisy clatter of feet running through the house dwindled to the sad sound of a single pair. One child. An only child, as I had been.

Had it been my parents' choice? Sadly, I didn't know.

Regrets, they were becoming as much part of my life now as secrets had been before.

54

I reached across the table and held Ann's hand. She didn't pull it away. 'We'll get a nanny, anything else you need. You can redecorate one of the rooms as a nursery. You'd like that.'

I couldn't have said anything better. I saw her eyes brighten, the mulish look on her face soften and relax. 'Perhaps,' she conceded.

'And as much help as you need in the house.'

Her face softened completely. 'Well,' she said on a sigh, 'I am finding the cooking and housekeeping a bit tiring.'

'Absolutely.' I was horrified that my pregnant wife would be worrying about such things, and ignored the little voice that sniggered behind my back and asked what housework she had ever done, what meal she had ever cooked in our grand kitchen. 'We can get a cook or cleaner if that's what you want.'

'Meredith and Simon have a housekeeper. Meredith says she's a godsend, leaving her time to do more important things.'

I looked across the table at the mother of my future child. 'A housekeeper, absolutely. We'll get a housekeeper.' I squeezed her hand. 'You can concentrate on getting ready for our child.'

'And, of course, we'll get a Norland maternity nurse, Meredith swears by them.'

I had no idea what she was talking about.

As it turned out, it didn't matter. Ann organised everything, and over the next few weeks, I came home to find strangers walking around the house with clipboards, swatches of fabric, measuring tapes. I didn't mind, Ann was smiling, and I swear her bump was growing by the day.

Adam and Jane were delighted with our news, of course, even if their delight was tempered by the fact of Jane's second miscarriage, only a week after our wedding. They were sincerely delighted for us, and if Jane's gaze lingered enviously on Ann's barely rounded stomach, she said nothing, but I noticed she held Adam's hand a little tighter. I noticed too we saw less of them over the next few months, and if that spared Jane the pain of seeing Ann pregnant, it also spared me the pain of seeing her sadness and the bittersweet pain of just seeing her.

Within days, Ann was interviewing candidates for the role of housekeeper. She had made up a list of her requirements, and I frequently saw her lost in thought, pen in hand, stopping, nodding and then scribbling frantically as if she had to get whatever it was down before she forgot and it was lost forever.

The list of her requirements grew longer with each unsuccessful candidate interviewed. 'I'm not asking for much,' she said in frustration, after the third interview, 'but an adequate level of comprehension of the English language is a necessity.'

The fifth interviewee appeared satisfactory, at least from Ann's point of view. Unfortunately, when she was handed a list of the duties Ann wanted her to take on, this lady sniffed and stood, dropping the list onto the table. 'Madam, I am a housekeeper, not a slave.' She left without further ado, leaving Ann too stunned to say anything, a rare state for her.

She consulted Meredith, her new best friend and arbiter of all that was right and acceptable, and came home much more cheerful than when she left. Over dinner, she broke the news. 'Meredith says I am asking for too much from a housekeeper. We'll need to hire more help to do the cleaning and washing. It seems housekeepers don't generally do that kind of thing. Also,' she hesitated and then plunged right on, 'Meredith says we really should hire a chef for special occasions, entertaining, et cetera. The housekeeper will just be responsible for day-to-day cooking.'

A cleaner, housekeeper and chef. The light in the Asian fusion restaurant we were eating in that night was soft and flattering, and Ann glowed. She smiled at me and rested her hand lightly on a belly that hadn't, at that stage, begun to swell with my child. Just then, I would have promised her anything. 'Fine, whatever you need.' We could afford it, after all.

The due date was mid-September, so in August she interviewed for the Norland maternity nurse who, Meredith told her, was an absolute necessity.

End of August, weary beyond belief, I arrived home to find a uniformed woman holding forth in the front lounge.

'Jake,' Ann said, from the sofa she was trapped in by the bump of our child. 'This is Linda, our maternity nurse. She has agreed to start work straight away, isn't that wonderful?'

Pulling at the knot of my tie, wanting nothing more than to slouch in front of the television with a cool beer and an Indian takeaway – something I'd done generally every night pre-Ann but which she regarded as too working-class for words – I rustled up a smile. 'Nice to meet you, Linda.'

Ann, her swollen body clad today in soft-rose gossamer material that seemed to have floated down upon her, was lying against big soft cushions. She held her cheek up to me and accompanied it with a winning smile that belied the command behind it. It was so much easier to obey. I leaned down to kiss the smooth cheek and demonstrate to this stranger what a happily married couple we were.

Exhausted after a hard day, I felt less than thrilled at yet another addition to the household. 'I thought you weren't due for another two weeks.'

'I'm not, darling,' Ann continued, surprising me with a seldom if ever used endearment until I realised her unusual affectionate manner was to impress the nurse. 'But I've been feeling so low, so exhausted, that I thought it would be a good idea to have someone with me until then.'

I shrugged. 'If that's what you want, then of course it's a good idea.'

We could afford it.

We could, although my plan to pay off the mortgage in four to six years hadn't factored in a wedding for which I got little change from a million. Nor did it take into account having to pay salaries for a housekeeper, cleaner, occasional chef and now this, what was she again... some sort of maternity type nanny.

This year's bonus had paid for the wedding – well, almost, anyway. If the interest on the £8 million mortgage was accumulating at a scary rate, well, I would get a handle on that soon.

My confidence wasn't misplaced. It was the way it was. The future was warm and rosy, and the clouds that drifted across our blue skies were wisps that dissolved before they as much as dipped the temperature. None of us saw the storm clouds approach, but come they did, and they wreaked havoc on our cosy financial deals, investments, and portfolios. Changing the fiscal landscape forever.

People like me, who'd overspent for years, people who made the stupid assumption that the status quo would never change – we were sitting ducks for what followed.

55

Morning sickness in the early months of her pregnancy left Ann exhausted, and my tentative hand on her gorgeous swelling body was brushed away with no apologies or excuses. I was an annoying fly swatted away. The cessation of morning sickness was followed by a bizarre craving for lobster at all hours of the day and night, and the house acquired a fishy odour that lingered long after that particular craving had passed.

What didn't pass until after the birth was an absolute abhorrence to being touched, fondled or caressed in any way, her skin becoming, she said, as hyper-sensitive as her nature.

'I just can't bear it,' she said.

I moved into the spare bedroom for the remainder of the pregnancy. There was no discussion but, to be honest, I didn't mind. The lustre had already worn off our sex life, and it had become an occasional pairing that was more functional than passionate. Belatedly, I realised that my darling wife, contrary to the stories I had heard before we were wed, wasn't at all interested in sex – just in what she could get with it, a currency she had used quite well over the years. Now that she had everything she wanted, a beautiful home, a child on the way, a successful husband and as much money as she could spend, sex as a currency had become redundant.

* * *

If I hadn't agreed to all Ann's demands, the housekeeper, chef, cleaner, maternity nurse, nanny, and after Phoebe's birth, the masseuse and the personal trainer – both of which, Meredith told Ann, were essential if she wanted to get her figure back – she probably wouldn't have agreed to have had a second child. But I suppose she felt I had conceded so much, she had to do her bit, and thus it was that a year later Peregrine was born.

I hated the names, had wanted to call our daughter Joyce, and our son after me, as is the tradition in every damn family but ours. Ann thought my choices were so lower-middle-class. 'So suburban,' she said, as if that was the greatest insult that could be levelled at anyone.

The alternatives I offered to the names *she* chose were either too common or too middle/lower/working-class, take your pick. I wanted to yell at her that I *was* working-class, but I didn't because I knew it wouldn't matter. She didn't care about me, she cared about her image. Anyway, she had decided and, as usual, what Ann wanted, Ann got.

So, my daughter and son were lumbered with Phoebe and Peregrine. I got my revenge, though, and by the time Peregrine was born, it had come to that, jab and counter-jab. Ann had insisted I move back to the spare bedroom early in the second pregnancy, citing her hyper-sensitivity again, but we both knew the truth. The fat woman may not have sung, but it was over all the same. Neither of us had ever pretended we were in love and for a time, I'd regretted marrying, but then Ann had become pregnant and we'd made plans and had dreams. If they weren't made with love, they were built on common sense, and I thought, as a foundation, it would be strong enough.

I was wrong.

I don't know who stopped pretending first, or when, but suddenly we were strangers who looked at one another as you would someone you thought you knew, but couldn't quite place, someone you were certain beyond any doubt you didn't like.

Following Peregrine's birth, I suggested I move back in with Ann, but although she didn't refuse, it didn't happen. A few weeks later, feeling horny, I followed her in and made amorous advances that she accepted without much enthusiasm. We made passionless, loveless love; sex that left me feeling empty and unsatisfied. Each time, after I emptied my seed into her on a cry that was part release, part desperation, I swore never again. After maybe the third or fourth time, when I opened my eyes to see her lying there under me, unmoving, her cold eyes fixed on mine with an expression of disdain, I never did go back.

But we stayed together. Why wouldn't we? I was busy trying to keep my position with Sebastian et Sebastian; she was busy finding new ways to spend money she didn't realise was running out. I started to criticise her spending, to find fault with her constant demands, and she became more dismissive, more derisive. We jabbed and counter-jabbed instead of speaking, avoided each other as much as possible, made polite small talk when we had to spend time together.

But as I said, I got my revenge on her choice of names for our children. The awful Phoebe, and ludicrous Peregrine, became Fi and P, the nicknames catching despite Ann's best attempts to prevent it. 'It's Peregrine,' I heard her snapping at the housekeeper one morning and chuckled to myself. By the time he was almost two, he wouldn't answer to anything else except P, and even Ann had had to give in. She remained the only person to call Phoebe by her full name.

Adam and Jane adored them both. They were delighted godparents and willing babysitters when Ann was out with Meredith or some other friend, and I was, once again, working late.

By this time, Jane had discovered she was unable to carry a child. Adam broke the news to me over lunch, told me Jane was distraught. He didn't say but I could tell he was pretty devastated himself.

'What about... what do you call it... IVS or something?'

'IVF,' Adam corrected me, shaking his head. 'No, I'm afraid she's not a candidate for it. She has no problem getting pregnant, you see. It's the hanging on to it that's the issue, some unusual abnormality in her uterus.'

'Poor Jane,' I said, reaching out a hand and gripping Adam's arm, trying to convey, in the way men do, that I felt for him too.

Jane never mentioned it, of course, and in her company, neither did I. But I watched her playing with my children and I thought, not for the first time, and not with any degree of originality, *life wasn't fair*.

P and Fi loved them both and were only too happy to go with them anywhere, and it was Adam and Jane who took them to the pantomime, to the circus, to visit Santa. And if it wasn't them, it was the Norland nanny or one of a succession of Norland nannies we had had since P was born. Ann treated the children like pets; she picked them up, cuddled or played with them, then put them back, forgetting about them almost immediately. She was too busy organising the social soirées she had become renowned for.

I played my part, loving husband, doting father. But the truth was, I wasn't the first, and hadn't time to be the second.

56

As my marriage was falling apart, the world started to crack, and I was struggling to make repayments on the colossal mortgage that now stood at nearly £10 million.

And then the crack widened, and into it fell Northern Rock, Lehmann Brothers, Fanny Mae and Freddie Mac. They fell like dominoes taking so many with them, so many little people caught up, so many lives changed irreparably. And if that wasn't all bad enough, along came Madoff to finish it all off.

Was it bad luck or judgement that I was caught up in it all? I don't honestly know. Like so many others, I'd been a willing prisoner of this wonderful glitzy slingshot of a life, the band stretching further and further, the excitement building and building. We thought we'd be shot into the stratosphere, our world a constant twinkle, and instead with a snap it all gave way, and we were dumped unceremoniously into the sewer, fighting for survival with all the other rats.

Everything I'd worked all my life for was bouncing out of my reach, and when I tried to grab hold... there was nothing but dust.

I sold my apartment to the current tenant for half what I'd paid for it six years before. The money barely put a dent in my debts.

There were those, of course, who got out in time, who escaped to watch from the sidelines. The previous owner of Elgin Crescent, for instance, sitting prettily in alpine splendour in Switzerland and thanking his lucky stars he had sold his house for 10.255m – a house, incidentally, that was now worth eight. If I could find anyone stupid enough to buy it.

When Lehmann Brothers hit the fan, it sent a waft of debris across the ocean to take the lustre and sheen off our gold, turning it once more into filthy lucre, tarnishing all of us who had worked hard to milk the system of every penny with the same viscous mess. My consultant status, of course, offered me no protection. Sebastian et Sebastian were very up front, very polite, but the bottom line was they were retrenching and huge retainers, never mind six-figure bonuses, were out of the question. No contract, no argument. It was okay for a while. I still had my clients and I worked hard, looked after them well, made the best choices I could under the circumstances but, no matter what I did, no matter which way I turned, they dropped like flies, fell like dominoes, dried up like puddles on a hot London day.

It was over, way before I realised, or certainly before I accepted the finality of it.

Seb n Seb – the full title I had insisted on for years was the first to go, and I took to using the abbreviation Adam always used – kindly kept me on in my consultant capacity, offering a pitiful retainer that was supposed to indicate some version of loyalty. I suppose it did hold out an element of hope. But hope didn't pay bills. And for the moment, any mention of a bonus, just the mention of the word, had senior management rearing back as if from a scatological obscenity, tut-tutting and shaking their heads as they headed back behind their hand-carved solid mahogany desks.

It was all stiff upper lip, and we're all in this together, and joking about the Blitz spirit. Meanwhile deals were being done under those hand-carved tables, shares were sold, money moved, fortunes lost, jobs chopped, lives changed utterly.

I thought about Elgin Crescent and wondered how long I'd be able to keep it; and how soon Ann would leave once everything fell apart.

57

The view from my office window at Sebastian et Sebastian was breathtaking... London... no, the world was at my feet. Eight years before, I couldn't believe my luck when I'd landed a position here. I remember staring out of this window, looking down on the tiny figures scurrying below, feeling powerful. I was going to be rich, and money was a god.

Now, well, everything had changed, hadn't it? I was waiting for the phone to ring. All morning, staring out of the window, waiting, yet when it did ring, it startled me. I jumped and my heart – I swear it stopped and started out of sync – hammered a *thumpty, thumpty thump*, a canter that became a full-on gallop as I reached for the phone, my hand trembling, a sudden burning in my solar plexus, my other hand moving automatically, the heel of my hand pushing in to close the door on the flames.

Picking the phone up, I forced my voice to sound the way it should – busy, but not too busy to deal with the caller, concerned but not overly so at the earlier email dispensing with my services, dismissing me, dumping me. Bitterness shot through me, put a bite in my voice.

'Jake Mitchell.' Good, my voice was businesslike. Cool. No hint of the tension, the determinedly unacknowledged desperation that pinged beads of sweat on my brow, beads that gathered and ran their course down the sides of my nose.

'You free for lunch, Jake, old buddy?'

The cheery voice in my ear brought a reluctant smile to my face. Stress lines that had been tightening all morning took an anti-clockwise half-turn, and I breathed *Adam* on a quiet exhale, as if he were the answer to a prayer, I hadn't known I'd wanted to make.

I should have said no, really should, but then thought, *why not*. Taking an hour out to meet an old friend for lunch, taking an hour of time to play at normal, it wasn't going to change anything. And for that hour I could, maybe, relax or at least pretend to. 'Sure, Adam, usual place?'

'Yes, that'd do. See you at one?'

'One, perfect, see you then.' My smile died before I put the phone down, my hands moving tiredly over my face, tracing lines I was sure hadn't been there till recently. I sat heavily behind my desk and picked up the email that had come earlier. I'd printed it out, hoping that my computer screen was being traitorous and lying to me, but on paper, no matter how many times I read it, it read the same. My last, my *only*, client was dispensing with my services. No explanation. After... how many years was it...? Nine? Maybe more? I had brought him with me to Sebastian et Sebastian, had nurtured him, nursed him, given him my expertise and time, and now I was getting dumped like a one-night stand. Tempted to reply to his email with a succinct *rot in hell, you bastard*, instead I sent a polite businesslike email, asking him to ring me so we could set up a meeting to discuss matters. That was three hours before.

I finally faced the truth. There was nothing left but the pitiful retainer Sebastian et Sebastian paid me, and even that mightn't last, not when I broke the bad news about my last client. Nothing left... I'd had *ideas above my station*, and I'd lost. I could almost see my father nodding, almost heard his voice. It made my head hurt... or maybe it was exhaustion. I hadn't slept more than a couple of hours a night for several days.

There didn't seem any point in doing anything, so I didn't. I sat and stared at my desk, unblinking eyes becoming dry until I forced myself to close them, only to open them quickly because in the darkness I could see the emptiness before me. I sat until it was time to leave to meet Adam, threw on my coat and left my office door to click shut behind me.

The receptionist ignored my forced cheery wave. There seemed to be no point in telling her when I'd be back. Nobody was going to ask.

Minutes later, I was on the Tube to Charing Cross, standing, one hand holding on, one hand in my raincoat pocket, making myself small, trying to avoid the hoi-polloi as they brushed past me, clambering on and off. I tried not to breathe too deeply, conscious of the expelled breaths of the masses that made up my air, catching the faint whiff of garlic, the merest hint of alcohol. From an elderly lady, dressed in a suit and yellow-tinged white gloves, her outfit a remnant of a bygone era, a faint but not unpleasant hint of camphor drifted up and tickled my nose.

The next stop was mine, and at Charing Cross I joined the mass of bodies that swept toward the exit, taking my card out as we moved, reaching the barrier and doing the usual tap-and-keep-walking routine we all know so well.

Instead of exiting the station immediately, I stopped to check my mobile in a last burst of hopeless optimism. I'm not sure how long I stood staring at it, but when I did eventually leave, I ran up the steps of Exit Five alone. The tap of my leather-soled shoes on the steps was a sound I was sure I'd never heard before, lost as it usually was in the chorus line of other tapping feet. The concrete tunnel felt suddenly sinister, otherworldly, and I gave a quick glance behind, seeing nobody, feeling strangely unnerved, my feet speeding their ascent until I was running, as if the hounds of hell were at my heels. I exited into the sunshine, still alone.

If I hadn't been alone, if things were the way they were supposed to be, I might never have noticed the woman sitting at one of those wooden tables outside Paul's café. She sat unmoving, brake lights of passing cars making the red coat she wore glow and shimmer. I rubbed my tired eyes, wondering if she was a mirage, if she'd vanish. But she was still there. And now I could see she was eating a pastry from the café and drinking a coffee... and in the noise and hullabaloo of the street, in the chaos that was my life, she suddenly looked so normal. A normality I so desperately craved.

If I had just moved on, if I had shaken my head at my own foolishness and walked on... well, then things might have been different, and I might not have done the things I did.

58

But I didn't walk on. I moved to the chair opposite the woman, put my hand on the back of it and, raising my voice a little to compete with the road noise growling behind me, I leaned towards her a little and asked, 'Would you mind if I sat here?'

Her eyes opened, warm hazel eyes that met mine while her small, slightly prominent Hollywood-white teeth closed down on the pastry again. Tiny flakes broke away to float and flutter down around her like falling blossom from a cherry tree. They speckled the front and sleeves of her coat, but she made no attempt to brush them away.

There was something almost bovine in her concentrated chew, her lower jaw moving in a slow anti-clockwise cycle... around... stop... around. I was mesmerised, standing with my hand on the back of the chair, my eyes locked on hers. Waiting for her reply. Wanting her to say *please sit down*. Traffic sound faded into the far distance and there was suddenly no sound, just a vacuum waiting to be filled.

A strange sensation crept over me, making me shiver. This woman, whoever she was, might be exactly what I was looking for.

She might have the solution to the mess my life had become. I didn't believe in God, but in that moment of desperate need, I had the oddest thought that she'd been sent to help me.

She broke her gaze then and slowly raised one shoulder in an elegant shrug, her face twisting in casual acceptance, polite indifference. It was less than an invitation but enough for me, and I rushed to pull out the chair and sit.

'Hi,' she said. Just the one word but said on an outward breath that wafted across the table, smelling sweet and luscious, and the flicker of desire I'd felt when I saw her caught and became a flame.

Mental desire quickly became physical, and I felt my body stirring with a sense of disbelief. Small beads of perspiration broke out on my forehead as I concentrated on controlling the response this woman provoked in me. For goodness' sake, I was almost forty, not fifteen. I was supposed to be past all this adolescent nonsense, wasn't I? Whether I was or not, the truth wasn't out there, it was tenting the front of my expensively pleated trousers. Grateful for the cover of my Burberry, I leaned forward, elbows on the table and, all articulacy and eloquence failing me, said simply, 'My name is Jake.'

'Joyce,' she replied with a slight nod.

'Aah,' I breathed, 'that's my favourite name.'

Joyce smiled, and it wasn't just in the gentle curve of her lips but in the twinkle in her eyes, the softening of her face, and in her soft, melodious voice when she asked, 'Really?'

I nodded foolishly, searching in vain for a pithy quip or clever witticism, the kind of thing you can come up with while lying awake at three in the morning but never, *never* can think of when needed.

Just then, the phone in my pocket vibrated, and I gave the casual shrug that conveys apology and took it out. Adam's name flashed on the screen, I pictured him immediately, a slight frown on his face as he checked his watch, worried suddenly because I was never late.

'Sorry, have to get this,' I explained, as if our exchange of names made such courtesies necessary. Opening my phone, I spoke rapidly, 'Adam, listen, I'm sorry, I'm running late. I'll be there in five, okay?' Then didn't wait for an answer but shut the phone and pocketed it.

'I have to go,' I said. She sat unmoving, watching me, the smile gone and in its place a curve of her lips that I couldn't interpret. Women are so much better than men at reading faces. Ann, I thought, without the slightest pang of guilt, would have been able to tell me exactly what that enigmatic smile implied. But thankfully, Ann wasn't there, so I chucked objectivity out with the bathwater and read the curve of Joyce's lovely mouth as a sign of sympathetic interest. 'I have to go,' I said again. 'Will you be here tomorrow?' The odd idea that his woman could somehow help me persisted. 'I'd love to have time to talk.'

Her warm hazel eyes transfixed me.

'Please,' I said again, and reached across the table to where her hands now rested, one atop the other, touching her gently with the tip of one finger, feeling the electricity fizzle. Then, because I could think of nothing else to say, I took my finger away and put it into my mouth, sucked it, tasting her sweetness.

Her eyes narrowed and the curve stretched back into a smile that dazzled. 'Tomorrow,' she said, nodding.

With great reluctance, I stood, then reached across and patted her hand, the second pat drifting into a caress. Her smile didn't falter, and I took it with me, went off to meet Adam with a bounce in my step that hadn't been there since I don't know when.

59

Adam accepted my excuse for being late without question. Why wouldn't he? Mind you, Adam was good at avoiding confrontational topics. He had never, for instance, asked me if I was in love with his sister. Perhaps if he had, things would have turned out differently.

I watched as he fought to hold his club-sandwich together, a slice of tomato edging its way out as he bit in. He caught the sigh I made, and hesitated, his mouth full, eyes questioning. The tomato slipped further, poised to take that leap onto his trousers. I pointed it out to him, and he slurped it up and chewed noisily, but didn't lose his train of thought. He could be persistent when he wanted; a family trait, his sister was the very same.

'Things okay with Seb n Seb?' he asked. 'Don't tell me there's trouble in the highest of the high.'

I wasn't sure if I had been sighing about work or the woman I'd just left, in any case, it was easier to smile and say nothing.

It was always a relief having lunch with Adam. I tried to explain what I did for a living, once in the earlier years when he might have been supposed to be interested, just a little. His eyes had glazed over. Even now, with news of the economic meltdown everywhere, on everyone's lips, in every newspaper, he had little interest. We talked football, movies, beer. He asked about Fi and P, and I told him the latest funny thing one or other of them had said. He never pointed out that he and Jane spent more time with the children than I did, that he knew more stories, more anecdotes.

We parted with the usual arm slapping and back thumping that was as much part of the ritual as the lunch itself. He headed back to his teaching, and I headed back to the office where I tried to look busy. I read over memos I knew by heart, looked at share prices until the numbers blurred, looked at my computer screen as if somehow the very act of looking would somehow change the way things were. I closed my eyes against the futility of it all. In the back of my mind, the one constant thought. I would see *her* again tomorrow.

Ann didn't notice that I was more than usually distracted that evening, in fact she seemed a little distracted herself, but I didn't ask her why. I knew she would tell me if she wanted me to know. I spent the time before dinner playing with the children, listening to their happy babbling, making them laugh by pulling silly faces, picking them up and smelling their addictive baby smell. Rosario, the current Norland nanny, arrived to take them away just before dinner was served, it being one of Ann's many rules that we had dinner undisturbed by the children's cries.

'We need *adult* time, Jake,' she would say, when I asked that they be allowed stay. She would add, with a complete lack of irony, 'After all, I've had the children all day.'

We rarely, if ever, ate out any more. Or at least not together. Truth was we rarely ate together, full stop. Until recently, anyway. My long working days meant I hadn't arrived home some nights till after eight, nowadays I was home by six. In the early days, if I managed to get home early, we'd sit out on the veranda in the summer or watch some television. But now, the house was big, and we rarely spent time in the same part of it. I excused myself immediately after dinner and spent the evening in my office, supposedly working, but actually just waiting for the time to pass, every dreary tick and even drearier tock.

I arrived earlier than usual in the office the next morning, desperate to get out of the house, only to find myself equally desperate to get out of the office. As a consultant, I could come and go as I pleased but, like my fellow consultants, I hung around watching for crumbs to fall from the desks of our illustrious bosses. Like ducks, we would pounce, fighting over who got the scrap, the crumb, grabbing it and taking it back to our desk to work it, sometimes for hours, in the pitiful hope it would give us sustenance.

It was important to look busy, to play the game. Rather than sending emails, I wrote some completely unnecessary letters to people who were unlikely to read them before putting them straight into the shredder, letters that, in fact, were so innocuous, so banal that shredding was too good for them. I made small talk with other consultants, watching their eyes, like mine, slide to the doors behind which the powers sat, knowing that our conversation would be terminated, even mid-word, if we got the slightest sign. Some consultants had left, of course, at the first sign of trouble. Others, and I count myself in this group, were under the stupid, arrogant, foolish belief that what had happened to the iconic Lehmann Brothers couldn't happen here – that was over there, after all – for God's sake, we were talking about England.

But, of course, it did. And then it was too late.

No crumbs fell during the morning, and I left for Charing Cross early, unable to wait a moment longer. I bounded up the Exit Five steps knowing it was far too early, but she was already there, and I sat facing her, feeling as if I hadn't taken a breath since leaving her the day before. I did then. Took a deep breath and let it out on a sigh.

She was in the same seat, wearing the same red coat. She had obviously ordered the same pastry, one corner missing, crumbs on her lips. 'I'll just get...' I had no idea what I wanted apart from her, so I just waved toward the inside of the café, went in and joined the queue. It was long, as usual, but I didn't mind because it gave me the chance to stare through the window at Joyce.

Coffee in hand, I headed out into the sunny London day and sat opposite her.

We probably took turns to stare. Certainly, when her eyes dropped to her cup, I stared at her intently. I only supposed, hoped even, that when my eyes dropped to my cup, she did the same.

She wore the same coat as the previous day, and around her neck a string of beautiful pearls.

Once I had spotted them, I couldn't take my eyes away, my stare becoming intent and probably embarrassing. She didn't look embarrassed, though, she caught where my gaze went and her hand went to the pearls, and she brought them more into view, pushing back the collar of her coat where they were partially obscured.

'They're beautiful.'

She let the strand drop back against her skin, warm cream on blush. 'I wear them all the time. They're not particularly fashionable but...' She shrugged elegantly.

I knew they weren't. I'd wanted to buy a similar strand for Ann to celebrate Phoebe's birth, but she refused. 'Fuddy-duddy,' she had said dismissively, choosing instead an exorbitantly expensive modern diamond and emerald piece that *was* stunningly beautiful, but a long way from the understated elegance of pearls.

'Classics don't go out of fashion,' I said to Joyce. 'Anyway, they suit you.' She smiled at the compliment. I sat back, surreptitiously checking out the rest of her. A black skirt peeped out from the open edges of her coat, black-clad legs ended in neat black shoes that had seen better days, the heels worn down, toes slightly scuffed. Not a shoe person, obviously, thinking of Ann's vast collection, the Imelda Marcos of Elgin Crescent.

As my eyes ran up her legs, she uncrossed them, stretched them out and languorously crossed them again, her movements feline and incredibly sexy. I wanted to reach my hand out and just touch her, anywhere, to feel a connection, to make sure she was real, that I wasn't dreaming.

'I'm glad you came back today,' I said instead, sitting forward in my chair, leaning across the table. Closer but not touching.

'I wanted to see you again,' she said, simple and uncomplicated, taking my breath away, so all I could do was nod and nod again until it came back, and I squeezed out a *me too*.

'You're married.'

It wasn't a question. I had made no attempt to hide the wide gold band that ringed my third finger. Hers were unadorned. 'Yes.'

'Children?'

'Two. Phoebe is three and Peregrine is two.'

Her eyebrows rose but she said nothing.

I shrugged. 'My wife, Ann. The names were her idea.'

'They're different.'

'They're terrible. I wanted Joyce and Jake, but Ann tends to get her own way.' I grinned conspiratorially. 'I call them Fi and P, it really pisses her off.'

She smiled in response, then lifted her cup and drained it, tilting her head back, her throat stretching, pale and vulnerable. I wanted to put my mouth over the pulse I could see fluttering, taste her, feel her vitality. She put the cup down. 'Tell me more.'

'Yes.' It was what I needed. Someone with no agenda to listen to my tale of woe. Maybe if I got everything out, I'd be able to see a way out of the mess. She was a good listener, didn't interrupt, nodding occasionally and now and then giving a murmur of sympathy. 'And that's about it.'

She didn't comment, instead she reached a hand across the rough wooden table and clasped mine before sitting back with a sigh. 'No wonder you look so sad.'

'Talking to you helps.' I couldn't believe how much it did. I felt lighter than I had in days, maybe even weeks. It wasn't a miracle, I still couldn't see a way out of the quagmire I was wallowing in, but maybe I had found somewhere to rest... just for a bit.

She smiled. 'Good, but now I'm afraid I need to get back.'

'Back?' I had told this woman my life story and I didn't know anything about her.

'To Bristol. I came today to see you.'

Bristol? I wanted to ask her to be specific, to see if perhaps we'd met when we were both younger. Something to account for the strange draw she had for me. But suddenly, inexplicably, I was afraid to. It didn't matter, I only needed to know one thing. 'Can you come back again tomorrow?'

She nodded, got to her feet and vanished down the steps to the station.

60

We met every day after that. Monday to Friday, at the same time, in the same place. 'Magic,' she told me, when I asked her how she was always there when I arrived, and I believed her because it was just that, magic.

We talked over our coffee as if tomorrow didn't exist; filling each other in on the small minutiae of the lives we lived without the other. She was an artist, I learned, and she described the detailed canvases she sold in a tiny gallery in trendy Clifton, her voice becoming more animated as she spoke. 'I like to pick something ordinary, something mundane, and try to subvert proportions and people's expectations.' She used her hands as she spoke, sketching in the air, using her fingers to outline what she drew. 'I once did a six-foot canvas. A Yale key, painted in gold, copper and burnt umber. It was bloody amazing.'

'A Yale key.' If I sounded puzzled, well, it's because I was. A painting of a huge Yale key sounded just a little bizarre. It also rang a distant bell in the back of my head. Hadn't I seen an exhibition of something like that a few years before? Something Ann had dragged me to? I had a vague memory of a big keyhole, one I fancied trying to climb through, just to see what was on the other side.

I wanted to ask her if it sold, this six-foot painting of a key. Then her scuffed shoes caught my eye, and I decided against it.

The next day we met, I handed her an envelope. She looked at it, puzzled. 'It's a gift,' I said, hoping she wouldn't be offended. 'You come here just to meet me; I wanted to show how grateful I am.'

She opened it and took out the ticket that lay within, her eyes squinting slightly to read the small print.

'I know it's a bit cheeky to buy you a yearly commuter ticket, but for however long we meet like this, I wanted to make it easier for you to keep coming.'

I'm sure I saw a tear in her eye or maybe I just wanted to. She tucked the ticket into the small black shoulder bag she always carried.

We'd been meeting a week before I suggested we go somewhere. I'd already checked out nearby hotels. The Northumberland was only ten minutes away, I'd rung the evening before and booked a room, hoping she would say yes.

I felt sixteen again. Practised what to say a million times; what to say if she said yes, what to say if she said no. I paid a visit to a pharmacy on the way and bought a packet of condoms, feeling sleazy and guilty as I handed them to the young sales assistant, who took them without as much as a second glance. She scanned them, bagged them, took the money and turned away to deal with the next customer who likewise paid not the slightest attention to my transaction.

I felt I had the word adulterer tattooed onto my forehead as I put the packet into my inside pocket, thinking what a nightmare it would be if I forgot they were there, if Ann found them. Then, of course, I started worrying about performance. It had been a while. What if... you know... I couldn't get it up, or something? But then I arrived, and she was there, and I knew *that* at least wasn't going to be a problem.

'Hi,' I said, as I sat down and smiled across the table at her. She had her usual coffee, her usual pastry, and she mumbled a 'hi' back, flakes escaping to fall around her.

'I'll just get a coffee,' I said. 'Would you like another?' I always asked, she always said no.

Sometimes I got a pastry for myself, tempted by the display as I queued for my coffee. More often than not, though, I just got a coffee, not wanting to be distracted by the need to eat.

I wasn't sure how to approach the hotel idea, but as it happened, I didn't have to. We were on the same wavelength, you see, our minds, thoughts, in perfect harmony.

'It would be nice if we could go somewhere,' she said, and I put my coffee cup down and stared at her in amazement.

'I was thinking the same thing.' I reached for her hand. 'In fact, to be honest, I did more than think about it. I booked a room in the Northumberland. I was going to ask you.' I laughed. 'I was trying to find the right words.'

She laughed too, and we sat there, hand in hand. And on the back of the laughter, lust rode in at a gallop, wiping the smiles from our faces, filling our eyes with desire, heating our bodies, making me hard. We stood, our hands still clasped, and walked without taking our eyes from one another.

The Northumberland was, as I expected, a luxuriously elegant hotel, its colours muted, its furniture a seamless mix of antique and reproduction. The lobby was a very grand spacious area with a very long reception desk behind which several receptionists waited to assist. Before long, I had a key card, and we were in the elevator heading to room seven on the second floor.

I wasn't nervous any longer and, looking at Joyce, I guessed neither was she.

As soon as we were inside the room, we started undressing. She wore a simple shift dress under her red coat. It didn't seem to have buttons or a zip, she just pulled it over her head and let it drop to the ground. I was still fumbling with buttons, but I reached out for her, my fingers closing on skin so soft my mind was catapulted back to P, and on the back of that thought, a lick of guilt that disappeared instantly as her hand slipped down to unzip my trousers.

And it was just as I expected. And she was just as I hoped. And it was sublime.

'Magic,' I said to her as she lay in my arms, and I felt her laugh, her body quivering.

'There's a lot of it about,' she replied, her voice low and husky.

'Can we do this again?'

She laughed again, reached for me, and caressed me until once again I was hard, and she straddled me. 'This, do you mean?' And she moved on me and this time it was even better, and I called out to whatever gods there may be.

61

When I ate at home, I would have preferred to eat in the kitchen, at the small table beside the window that overlooked the garden. Ann insisted, however, that we maintain what she liked to call a 'certain decorum'. So we bracketed the huge table in the dining room, and the staff enjoyed the comforts of the intimate space in the kitchen.

I would have preferred, too, to fetch my dinner myself, even to have dished it up myself, to feel some element of control in my own damn house. But it wasn't to be. I think Julie, our house-keeper, preferred it that way, a strict delineation of what was her job and what was our place. A latter-day, and totally incongruous, upstairs/downstairs.

Ann, of course, was perfectly happy with the arrangement and never, to my knowledge, as much as stepped into the kitchen, happy to ring through on an internal line and ask Julie to bring her a cup of tea or glass of water. Ann, slim and porcelain-skinned as she was, gave an impression of ethereal frailty and Julie, like many people, fell for it, hook, line and whatever. I'm not saying that Ann pretended, she didn't have to, she just looked the part and allowed people to believe what they wanted, especially when it suited her. When she really wanted to milk it, when manipulation was essential, she wore one of her collection of fine, pastel-coloured silk dresses, the material sighing when she moved to be in such close contact with an angel.

She was wearing one now, a pale pink, almost transparent silk that shimmered in the soft light from the antique chandelier hanging overhead. I wondered without any real interest what she was after, my sensibilities not the least affected by her angelic appearance. After all, when you got to know her, when you got to see beneath the very, very thin veneer, you saw a woman as tough as old boots and hard as nails.

Julie played maid and carried our dinners through. She placed Ann's plate before her with a slight curtsy, receiving a nod from Ann that had me grin. Mine, Julie put in front of me with the air of someone who didn't care if I ate or not. My grin faded to a sigh, and I picked up my fork and started to eat.

'Knife, please, Jake.' Ann's voice was sharp in the quiet of the room. I sighed louder, moved my fork to my left hand and picked up my knife.

'Happy now?'

'There is no need to become slovenly.'

'Americans eat with their fork all the time.'

She smiled the smile of the victorious. 'I rest my case.'

It was the longest conversation we'd had over dinner for a long time. A huge floral arrangement, delivered fortnightly from a very avant-garde florist, was set in the centre of the table, filling the emptiness between us, and blurring the distance that had slowly grown to be too much trouble to travel. Sometimes the arrangement was such that we could barely see one another. Conversation, generally desultory, became impossible, and we sat and ate and left as if we'd eaten alone, sometimes with only a bare acknowledgement of the other's presence.

This fortnight's floral arrangement was a low round yellow mound which was so large as to cover the four-foot-wide table side to side. I hadn't really paid much attention to it. I never did. But it caught my eye as we spoke and I took a closer look, leaning forward over the table, holding my tie to prevent it flopping into my dinner. Then I sat back in disbelief. I wasn't very up in the world of floristry, but I recognised a dandelion when I saw it.

'Where did that come from?'

Ann, about to embark on whatever it was she was going to tell me, raised an eyebrow. 'The same place as usual, Jake. Chez Fleur. We have used them for months. They do Kate's, you know, we were lucky they were able to fit us in.'

'Kate Middleton?'

Ann frowned. 'No, not her,' she said dismissively, as if I were stupid not to realise she meant someone more important than the girlfriend of the heir to the heir to the throne. 'Kate Moss.'

I tried and failed to remember who Kate Moss was. 'But they're dandelions.' I used my knife to point at the arrangement. 'Just weeds.'

A tut-tut was followed by an impatient sigh and a shrug that sent pale pink silk rippling. 'It's a floral statement. It challenges our notions of what is, or what is not, acceptable and pushes the boundaries of horticultural restraint, subverting the traditional and forcing us to see beauty in flowers hitherto considered unworthy.'

I closed my eyes. What twaddle. 'Unworthy? They're bloody weeds.'

'You just don't get it, Jake,' she said shaking her head, her voice sanctimonious.

I might not, but I was bloody well paying for it. 'How much are they charging us for these *statements* then?' If she was going to do sanctimonious, I was going to do sarcastic.

Ann held her knife and fork, and considered me across the table, her look contemptuous, as if I had committed a major social blunder by bringing up something as sordid as money.

I wasn't backing down. 'How much?' I put my knife and fork down and sat back in my chair, arms crossed.

'We were lucky to get them. They don't agree to work for everyone—'

I interrupted her with a harsh laugh. 'Just fools who'll pay for that nonsense.'

Ann hated to be interrupted, and she frowned across the table. 'If you would let me finish,' she said cuttingly. 'We were lucky to get them. There is a waiting list for their services. Of course, to engage them we had to commit to a regular delivery before they would consider entertaining our request.'

She was stalling. I let her waffle on, hearing the odd word... desirability... cost-effectiveness... ambience... waiting for the only words I wanted to hear. The cost. The dandelion arrangement caught the light and glowed, and for a moment I thought, *actually, it's not bad.* Then I thought, they're bloody dandelions and shouted, 'How much?'

'Four hundred pounds a month.'

She said it as if it were a perfectly reasonable amount of money to pay.

'For that?' I pointed at the dandelions, appalled.

'Hardly. We get a new arrangement every two weeks.'

I was still pointing at the dandelions. Now I stood and walked around the table, moving closer to see what on earth we were paying 200 quid for. I poked it. It didn't move, or bite, or sing. I leaned closer and sniffed. It smelt okay; smelt like any dandelion you pick on the roadside. I pulled one out of the arrangement, ignoring Ann's squeak of dismay. The flower had a one-inch stem. It wasn't dipped in gold. It was just a dandelion.

I pulled another flower out, then another. 'We paid £200 for a bunch of weeds?'

'Jake, for goodness' sake, leave it alone. You are ruining it.'

I threw one of the dandelions at her, it landed in her dinner. Without batting an eyelid, she picked it out of her sauce and put it on her side plate, saying, in a voice devoid of any emotion, 'Chez Fleur provides a repair service. I'll give them a call tomorrow, tell them Phoebe is to blame for the damage.'

I had to smile at her self-control. I picked up the dandelions I had pulled out and brought them to her. She took them without looking at me and put them with the other on her side plate. 'Maybe you could just stick them back in,' I suggested, remembering she had done flower arranging in the distant past. Her look was withering, so I shrugged and returned to my seat and my dinner.

I had to keep things in perspective. After all, we were only talking about £400 a month. Compared to the money I owed, it was a piss in the ocean.

Anyway, Chez whatever-the-hell would soon stop delivering the arrangements when the funding died.

62

Ann took a mouthful of water, then cleared her throat. 'I've arranged for us to visit St Andrew's.'

I waited for enlightenment, but it didn't come. Perhaps this was the follow-up to a conversation we'd had before. One I had nodded along to, made those listening noises we all make, the hmnnns and the uhhuh-uhhuhs that are supposed to show agreeable interest while our minds fly elsewhere.

'St Andrew's?' I said, giving up on attempts at recollection.

Ann shrugged her shoulders, picked up her cutlery, and proceeded to load her fork with a tiny piece of everything that was on her plate, cutting a shaving from a carrot, a sprig from a broccoli floret, a smidgen from the pork, and finally adding a grain of rice. She held it before her like an offering to the gods before explaining. 'The preparatory boarding school where we are going to send Phoebe and Peregrine.'

A preparatory *boarding* school? Suddenly I lost my appetite. I put down my knife and fork, picked up my wine, drained the glass, reached for the bottle and refilled it. 'We've never discussed boarding school.' I was certain I was right. I would have remembered something so catastrophic. 'Ever,' I added with finality.

She reached for her glass, took a mouthful of water and sat back. 'There is nothing to discuss, is there? Unless you prefer a different school to St Andrew's, although it has been highly recommended.'

'By your friend, Meredith, I suppose,' I said, my voice heavy with sarcasm.

She ignored me. 'St Andrew's is a feeder school for both Eton and Marlborough College. They'll take Phoebe next year and Peregrine the following year.'

Was I hearing things? 'Next year? Phoebe will only be four.'

She nodded.

'You want to send our children to boarding school at four? Are you mad?' I hadn't realised I was shouting until I saw her hands go to her ears, and she held them there with an exaggerated look of pain on her face.

'Please, I can't talk to you about this if you are going to shout.'

I took a deep breath. 'I'm sorry, but honestly, Ann, four is far too young. Isn't it?'

'You wanted children. I gave you children. Now, I want to concentrate on a life for myself. It's all right for you, you go out to work, but I'm stuck here. There are things I want to do.'

I took a deep breath, trying to keep my temper. 'For God's sake, you have a housekeeper and nannies. It's not as though you are tied to the house or the children. And P would be devastated if Fi went off to boarding school. They're inseparable.'

'Yes,' she agreed reluctantly. 'They are, aren't they.' She took another mouthful of her dinner.

I realised I was holding my breath and let it out on a heavy sigh.

Then Ann nodded. 'Perhaps we should wait until the

following year, and send them both together. Would that be a better idea, do you think?'

Relief flooded through me, and I babbled agreement. 'Yes, I think that would be a much better idea.'

'Good. I'll make the arrangements for us to go and visit, and we can enrol them both for the following year.'

I saw a look of triumph on her face, and I knew I'd been had. I'd agreed to send my five-year-old daughter and four-year-old son off to boarding school to be brought up by strangers.

Ann ignored my silence. 'They'll get into Eton and Marlborough College easily from St Andrew's.'

I'd been had... but then so had she. There would be no money for fancy preparatory day schools, never mind boarding. It would be state schools for our children. The idea didn't bother me, I'd done okay by them. Ann, though, would be horrified.

She was still talking, her voice fading into the background. Where would we be in two years? Looking at my wife over the mound of that ridiculous floral arrangement, I thought how very wrong it all was.

I thought of P and Fi, and smiled sadly.

I thought of Jane, and nearly cried.

I thought of Joyce.

Then, I looked at Ann, her mouth moving as she spoke to the wind, and I knew something had to be done.

63

Again and again, day after day, hour after hour. Whether I was standing sardine-like on the Tube or standing staring across the London skyline from my office window, my every thought was of that *something* I needed so desperately to do. Every conversation I had with anybody, the usual meaningless drivel that makes up social intercourse, the *how are you*, the *nice day, isn't it*, the *how's the family/wife/mother*, every damn word came from a small part of my brain that was switched to autopilot while the rest of it was searching for a solution. But every solution it came up with became a problem I couldn't solve.

I wondered if I should take Adam into my confidence; see if maybe he could think of an exit strategy, but even as I thought it, I discounted the idea. There was no exit. No way out. And if there was a strategy, if there was some plan that would work... well, I couldn't find it.

If I just left? If I packed my bags and walked out the door, walked away from Elgin Crescent without a backward look? I closed my eyes and thought about it, imagined myself closing the heavy door behind me, the catch clicking, a full stop ending a chapter. Getting lost in the moment, I could almost hear the tap of my leather soles on the pavement, almost feel the wave of relief with every tap, the wave becoming a tsunami, overwhelming me with longing to do just that, to go, put it all behind me. To forget. Start again. Do it better.

But it wasn't that easy, was it? The relief only lasted till I opened my eyes. Then it was shredded, torn to tiny little irreparable slivers by the piercing, trusting, neon bright eyes of my children, until even the thought of abandonment was erased.

Take Fi and P with me? I pictured myself walking down the road, one little hand clasped in each of mine, the three of us setting out on a new life together. What a pretty picture I painted in my head, the fond, doting father, his adorable well-behaved children. But money had bought more than a pampered, indulged lifestyle. It had brought incalculable degrees of separation, so that I had never bathed either of my children, had never dressed them, never fed them. I had never even seen them unwell, never had to manage their tears, had no idea what they ate, what they liked to play with, what their favourite toy was. Isn't that something fathers should know? Yes, I adored my children, but couldn't take them with me without the succession of nannies I could no longer afford.

A formal separation? I shook my head and rested my forehead against the cold glass of my office window. Out of the question. Not because Ann wouldn't agree. She'd agree and be in her solicitor's rooms before the final sibilant consonant of her delighted *yes* had faded. Her demands would be extortionate; the house, money for its upkeep, for her, for the children, for their education, for the lifestyle to which they had become accustomed, the nannies, the dietician, the masseur... on and on. All of it. None of it. There was money for none of it. I couldn't afford the mortgage any more. The bank would foreclose. Soon... tomorrow... sometime. It didn't matter when, it mattered that there was no way out.

What if I told Ann the truth? What if I sat her down, told her everything? The thought brought a rare smile of humour to my face. I could see it clearly. She would sit, ankles crossed, beautifully manicured hands resting palm-upward, one on top of the other. And she would listen attentively, her face, courtesy of regular Botox, calm and absolutely rigid. Blue eyes would turn glacial as I laid it all out, every sad little detail, my pathetic cry for support and understanding. She would laugh that derisive laugh she had, the one that would tell me in no uncertain terms that they were *my* debts, not hers, *my* problems, not hers, and she would walk away and leave me to it. I would wait and watch, see her footsteps slow, see her turn again to face me, realisation in her eyes that in this there *was* no hers and mine. If *I* had debt, there was no money. If there was *no* money, her cosy indulgent life was going to come crashing down.

And finally, at last, she would hate me.

64

The phone rang. Lost as I was, it startled me. I tripped over the leg of the chair in my haste to answer, caught my elbow a painful blow that brought a grimace to my face as I put on my best investment banker voice and said my name. 'Jake Mitchell.'

'*Oui.*' And in that one word I heard derision, disappointment, disgust. '*C'est Francois Sebastian,*' the voice continued before, with a sigh of irritation, a sigh that said *and he doesn't even speak French,* he switched to English. 'We need to have a meeting. Friday, midday, my office.'

My knees suddenly gave way, and my free hand smacked loudly down on the desk, elbow locking to support my weight. I groped for something to say, for a response. I needn't have bothered. Francois had hung up. My locked elbow wavered as I continued to hold the phone, holding it to my ear as if taking it away would be the last disconnect, and I would be unplugged and float away weightless. I pivoted around on my wavering arm and sat on the corner of the desk.

So, I thought with a self-deprecating smile, no heavily embossed invitation this time. No fancy lunch with expensive wine. I pulled over the chair and swung heavily onto it, my knees still refusing to do what they were supposed to do. I gave a snort. Nothing was the way it was supposed to be. I cupped my hands and let my face fall into them, hiding in their darkness, somewhat comforted by their touch.

I needed the comfort.

Friday.

I could hear the fat lady singing now, and the words were clear. I was being cut loose from Seb n Seb, would lose this rather grand office and the pitiful retainer that kept the rock and the hard place from grinding painfully. No longer. Friday, the rock and the hard place would grind and grind, and all that would remain was the dust of my dreams.

Yet even there in my desperation, I grabbed the glimmer of light that lit the darkness.

Today was Monday. I had three days to come up with something.

I tested my legs. They seemed to be in working order again, strong enough to get to Charing Cross. On the Tube, they weren't really required, and I stood sardine-like for the packed journey, swaying with my neighbours, propped against their warm bodies, breathing their body smells, taking comfort in being part of the hoi-polloi, grateful for their unknowing support.

I closed my eyes as I swayed, my mind chugging back to where it had left off its earlier thinking. Leaving alone wasn't an option. Neither was taking the kids and leaving. Asking Ann for a divorce was a definite no-no. The Tube stopped, bodies moved, shuffled, readjusted. Everything changed. Nothing did.

The carriage jerked suddenly, and my eyes opened. I was briefly disorientated, startled. Between the heads of those around me, I caught sight of a reflection in the window. My smile had long since faded, but surely that haunted face wasn't mine. Had there been room, I would have raised my hand, touched my face to prove it wasn't me, there wasn't room, my arms strait-jacketed by the masses, so I winked instead, saw the face wink back, smiled again, saw my reflection grimace.

The crowd surged around me, and I broke my stare with a panicked glance around. Had I missed my stop? Was this it? In my panic, I joined the surge for the door and exited, saw the station sign, realised my mistake, and tried to swim against the tide to reboard. The door slid shut, and I was left behind, shouting at the departing Tube as if it were the last stage from Dodge City.

Ignoring the sideways glances from other commuters, glances that brushed over me trying to gauge whether I was in serious trouble or just another irate commuter who had let things get the better of him. None of the glances offered support, none offered comfort. If I tried to meet their gaze, they swiftly turned their heads, moved away. If I had reached out a hand, if I had beseeched them to help me, their looks would have turned to horror, and they would have run. I was on my own here, as in everywhere else.

It wasn't supposed to be this way. My life was supposed to be perfect.

Another Tube stopped, and I felt and heard the crowds move off and on, their bodies brushing mine, meaningless, comfortless body contact. I couldn't find the energy to open my eyes and join them. No energy, no desire. No wonder I couldn't think of a plan. Who was it that said apathy was the scourge of the twenty-first century? I was too apathetic to remember.

I'll get the next Tube, I told myself, or the one after that. There is a certain strange peacefulness about Underground stations when a train has just left. For a few seconds, I was the only person there. I looked down the track, a black hole gaped. I looked up the track, there it was again, an empty maw calling, inviting. For a moment, I was tempted. It would be an answer. It would definitely be a plan. Walk into that hole, never come back – at least not in one piece. And it would be quick and there was a lot of consolation in that – better a quick death than this long drawn-out leprosy that was taking me piece by piece.

Once again, the eyes of my children came to mind. Innocent and trusting. Depending on me to rescue them from a life of nannies and boarding schools. I had failed them so far. My only legacy was their names. That was all I had done for them. Reduced the ridiculous Phoebe and Peregrine to the slightly less ridiculous Fi and P.

I owed them much more than that.

65

Joyce was where she always was, sitting in the same seat outside Paul's, waiting for me. Wearing the same red coat. Odd that she was the only stability in my life.

The traffic was playing its usual gentle rumble as I sat opposite her. I had suggested several times that we meet somewhere else, somewhere quieter, more salubrious. But she always refused. 'We met here,' she explained, 'it's as if this is where we are most real.' And I loved her for that, for seeing it as I did.

So, we continued meeting there despite the noise, adjusting our conversations to the lulls, remaining happily silent and content to gaze at one another when the traffic roared just that little too loud, ignoring the dust that swirled and coated us. 'Fairy dust,' Joyce would laugh, rubbing her eyes after a particularly dramatic swirl rose and enveloped us.

It wasn't fairy dust that was making my eyes water that day.

Joyce knew me so well; I didn't have to tell her I was in trouble. 'Talk to me,' she said, reaching to hold my hands in hers.

The warmth of her hands gave me strength and the words stumbled out, slowly at first, then with a gush, falling over themselves in their haste to be heard. I told her about Ann, and her plan to put Fi and P into boarding school. 'There's no money, but I've no doubt she'll find it.'

'From her parents, probably.'

I had told Joyce about my parents-in-law and their comfortable lifestyle. She was right. Clara and Giles would happily pay for their grandchildren's education. 'Yes, you're probably right.' My sigh was lost in the traffic rumbling past. It didn't matter, she gripped my hand tighter as if she'd heard. I raised my voice to continue my tale of woe. 'Francois has called me to a meeting on Friday. I don't need a crystal ball to know what he's going to tell me.' A trundling bus forced another pause. I shook my head, grimaced my frustration and before I was once again interrupted by a mechanical roar, rushed out, almost shouting the words. 'It's all over. Late next week, the banks will foreclose on my loans. It'll all come out.'

Her grip on my hands tightened, calmed me, her strength wicking up my arm, infusing me. 'I've gone over every option,' I said. 'I thought about just leaving, but I can't abandon Fi and P. I even considered throwing myself on Ann's mercy, but that wouldn't work either. I need to think of a plan to safeguard the children, give them a future they deserve.' I shrugged sadly. 'I can't think what to do for the best.'

'Fi and P,' she said. 'They're the key, really. I know how much you love them.' Her grasp on my hands tightened further, almost painfully. 'It sounds like there's only one thing you can do.'

I'd spent a sleepless night trying to think of something. I shook my head and smiled. Joyce always surprised me. 'What's that?'

'You need to get rid of Ann.'

66

I looked at Joyce in disbelief. Get rid of Ann! Had she really said that? A three-bus convoy passed, and my pulse raced. Three buses together. Was it an omen? What was the mark of the devil? Wasn't it 333? Maybe I should take it as a sign. Beads of perspiration popped on my forehead, and a band tightened across my chest as the roar of the buses' engines echoed in my head. I rose, frantically looking around for an escape, chained to the spot by Joyce's hands holding mine, grounding me. *Or preventing my escape?*

'You know I'm right. It's the only way.'

My eyes, still searching, met hers, and as the roar faded, so did the panic, and I knew she was right. It *was* the only way.

'Yes,' I said, sitting so heavily the chair almost overturned. One hand was still held in hers. I reached across with my other, held on tightly, anchoring myself and waited for her to speak.

When she did, her voice was calm and startlingly reasonable. 'If Ann isn't in the picture, Fi and P will get the future they deserve. Not with us, though.' She shook her head sadly. 'That won't be possible. I think you know that.'

Did I? I was no longer sure what I knew. Bizarrely, what was clarified in my head was the mark of the devil. 'It's 666,' I said, but although I'm almost sure I said the words aloud, they had no impact on the woman whose hand I clasped so desperately.

'Adam and Jane will love them as if they were their own,' she said, her eyes fixed on mine, her words filled with irrefutable logic. 'You're always saying how happy they are with them.'

I frowned. Was I? I didn't remember. I rubbed my free hand over my forehead. It didn't matter, Joyce was right, Adam and Jane would be far better parents than Ann and I ever were.

'We can leave, go abroad and spend the rest of our lives together.' Joyce slipped her hand from my grasp and sat back. 'I could paint. We could get a nice little house, get married, have children of our own. A new start. A new life.'

A new life. The chance to start again. Get it right this time. Reinvent myself... again. 'It would have to be somewhere without an extradition arrangement.' I didn't have to think for long, I'd had some dodgy investors over the years. 'Venezuela.'

'Sounds perfect.'

'We'd need some money.' I was almost horrified at the way I was thinking about the practicalities... could I really do this? Did I have a choice? The answers to both questions came staccato. *Yes... No.*

Joyce was speaking. 'Have a look for flights.'

I blinked. 'Flights?'

She was always patient. 'To Venezuela.'

'Yes, of course.' I took out my phone and did a quick check. 'Friday afternoon.'

'Can we be ready by then?'

Leave before the shit hit the fan. Yes, why not? 'It doesn't give us much time to get ready.'

She smiled and shrugged. 'I don't have much to pack, Jake.' She tilted her head and stared at me. 'You sure you can do this?'

Dust swirled as a van drove past. Magic dust casting a spell on me. 'I have no choice.'

'Friday, then?'

'Friday.' The one word a confirmation of all I was about to do.

She got to her feet, leaned over and kissed me on the cheek. 'I won't be able to see you till then. I'll meet you here, we can start our new life where we first met.'

With a smile, she walked away, looking back moments later to wave to me. I stood, looking after her, oblivious to the belching traffic and the motley passers-by, watching her with hungry eyes until she moved out of sight.

Then she was gone, as if she had never existed. I wouldn't see her till Friday... the longest we'd been apart since our first meeting. I listened to the noise: traffic, footsteps, wisps of conversation, meaningless words caught in passing, a lingering note of laughter at a joke never heard, and I thought about the new life I was going to make.

Incapable of moving, I stood with the grey dust of the London street eddying and swirling around my feet, turning the glossy black leather of my shoes dull and lifeless. *Lifeless...* I thought of Ann, of what I'd committed myself to doing. I stood unmoving until Exit Five belched out the contents of the latest Tube, the hurrying, destination-intent travellers diverting around me, as if I weren't there.

'*Ux*oricide.' I said it aloud, feeling the shape of the word on my tongue, hearing it before it was lost in the rumble of traffic, the jostle of passing people. *Ux*oricide, it sounded like some type of insecticide. Perhaps it was pronounced differently. I changed the stress and tried again, '*Uxoricide*.' Better.

I had a plan, and my plan had a name. Uxoricide. The act of killing one's wife.

67

Had there been another way, I would have taken it. But there wasn't. Joyce was right, it was the only way. It wasn't as if killing Ann was an end in itself. I wasn't planning to kill her for kicks. It was simply a means to the only possible end.

I would leave, go abroad with Joyce. Fi and P would stay with Adam and Jane and be happy with them. Happier. Jane would have the children she so desperately wanted. Clara and Giles would survive Ann's death, and would grow closer to Adam, Jane and the children. Win-win all around.

Except for Ann, of course.

Once the decision was made, it was necessary to choose the method. It's surprising how much knowledge is acquired, despite yourself, from television crime shows. Off the top of my head, I could think of several ways of doing away with Ann. The classic blunt object sprang first to mind, but I shuddered at the thought of smashing her head in. Worse was leaving her body, brains strewn across the floor, for some poor soul to find. Mind you, it would probably be Julie, the housekeeper, and I had never taken to her. But what if I didn't hit her hard enough, and she survived? I ditched the blunt object idea.

Should I make it look like there had been a burglary? Mess up the place a bit, take some of the jewellery she constantly left lying around instead of locking it away in the safe. Problem would be trying to anticipate when she would be in. And then I was back to how to kill her. Unlike the people in every US crime drama I'd ever watched, we didn't own a gun. Even if we did, my hand-to-eye coordination was such that I would probably miss her skinny frame.

No. It needed to be simple. Fi and P had to be out of the way. So would Julie and the nanny. Plus, I'd have to come up with a ruse to keep Ann at home. If I went to all that trouble, they'd never believe it had been a burglary. Especially since I'd have disappeared. It didn't matter, in fact it made things easier.

It was after midnight. The house was quiet. I was lying, fully dressed, on my bed, planning. Ann wasn't home. I only knew because I had asked Julie earlier. She had looked at me, and I swear her lips moved in a sneer before she answered, or maybe it was just a knowing smile. 'Mrs Mitchell is out for dinner. She said she wouldn't be back until very late.'

'Oh, yes,' I said, shaking my head at my stupidity. 'I remember now, she said she'd be out.'

We both knew I was lying. I don't know why I bothered, it had been a long time since Ann bothered to tell me where she was going – or with whom. It was possible she was having an affair, of course, but if she was, I really didn't care.

I got up from my bed, walked quietly in my bare feet down the hallway to her bedroom. In the bathroom, one ear cocked for her arrival, I rummaged through the array of packets in the cabinet. There were far more than I expected, and I let out a groan of frustration. I had no idea what they were for, none of the names looking familiar and none of the names of the many packets contained the word sleep, or any euphemism for it.

I was holding several packets, peering at the small print, when a distant creak made me jump and drop the lot on the floor. Hurriedly, squatting down, I gathered them up and stuffed them back into the cabinet, closing the door with difficulty. Switching off the bathroom light, I crept across the dim room to the hallway, stood and listened, until the silence was loud and persuasive. Nothing was moving.

Jittery but determined, I crept back, opened the cabinet door again, remembering too late the way I had stuffed the packets in only moments before, and they came tumbling out. I juggled, foolishly trying to catch one, then the other, catching and dropping until all were strewn in a mess at my feet. 'Shit!' I was tempted to kick them aside and just leave them there, after all, she would hardly guess what I was up to. She wouldn't see the packets on the floor and immediately deduce I was planning to use her sleeping tablets as part of my plan to kill her.

But I still hadn't found the damn things. She definitely had them, vague memories of her moaning about being unable to sleep, trips to a sympathetic doctor, packets of pills left by her bedside, then nights when she would sleep like the dead. Her bedside table... damn, of course, that's where the bloody things were. Quickly picking up the packets from the floor, I arranged them in a vague semblance of the way they had been. Tidy enough, she'd never notice.

I waited for my eyes to adjust to the dimmer light of the bedroom, then padded across the deep-pile carpet to her bedside table. Two books of the chick-lit variety she preferred, the rare times she did read, sat neatly, one on top of the other. My fingers felt for the drawer handle and eased it gently open. It was cluttered with sundry items including an unopened packet of condoms. I wondered, without much interest, who she had bought them for.

I finally found what I was looking for and took out a packet of pills. The name meant nothing to me, but I was almost sure I was right. Pulling out the two cards of pills, I fished out the information leaflet and scanned the small print till I saw the word *insomnia* that confirmed my guess. Of the twenty-eight pills the packet originally contained, there were twenty-four left. I checked the date on the label. Six months before. Obviously, she rarely took them. Probably wouldn't miss several. How many would I need? No idea. Erring on the side of caution, I took a full card of fourteen. Surely that would be enough for my needs.

Pocketing the tablets, I closed the drawer and turned to leave. I'd left the bedroom door open, light flooding in from the hall, shining onto the huge king-size bed Ann now slept in alone. We'd never been a couple who curled up together, spooning, convex and concave slotting together. From the beginning, we would couple, then drift to the further reaches of the bed, never touching, the distance a chasm we never thought to cross, then it was more than a physical chasm. Or maybe it always was.

I went back to my room, hid the card of tablets in a drawer, undressed and got into bed.

Exhausted, I fell into a disturbed sleep, tossing and turning as I crossed an eerie landscape. When a woman appeared, and I saw it was Joyce, I calmed, maybe even smiled in my sleep as she came closer, my smile dying as a strange tattoo on her forehead came into focus.

I woke on a scream, the 666 I'd seen cut into her skin staying on the back of my eyelids till I opened them and reached for the bedside lamp. In the bright light, I brushed the nightmare away. It was unfair of my subconscious to cast Joyce as the bad guy, she was simply being a realist. What I was about to do was horrifying, but she was right, I had no choice.

68

Bankers and priests have a lot in common. Historically they were the people you trusted without question. The priest with your children. The banker with your money. Turns out, of course, neither was to be trusted with either. But there was a hangover effect, and people still tended to trust priests and bankers they knew, assuming they were the exception, and it was the other ones who did all the bad stuff. But trustworthiness is easy to feign.

It helps if you have a solid reputation. The good thing about going down the tubes was that people knew I was honest, because if I hadn't been, I would have been in Switzerland like the guy whose house I bought, or sunning myself on a beach in Barbados, not going down for the third time, fighting for air that was quickly running out.

Although there were only a few days left before Seb n Seb pulled the plug, I still had access to many of the company files. In fact, unbeknownst to either the great Guillaume or Francois, I had access to a lot more than I should. They operated under the old-fashioned and very noble idea that none of their employees would think of cheating or doing anything deemed dishonourable. As a result, their passwords were ludicrously easy to crack. I cracked them first because I could, but didn't look at the accounts from the kind of noble good manners that would have pleased them. Then, as my days became more of a nightmare, I looked at the accounts as a form of self-flagellation, because, surely, if I'd been any good, I would have accounts like these. Hell, I would *be* one of these accounts.

I would sit and drool over them, see the bottom line drift marginally up and down, criticise how the accounts were being managed, sneer at investments made, thinking I could have done so much better.

As I criticised and sneered, somewhere deep in my subconscious, the glimmer of a plan was being formed, so that when something had to be done, it was there almost ready. All I had to do was take it out, smooth out the creases, sand down the rough edges, and get on with it.

My meeting with Joyce had given me the needed impetus. Suddenly my plan was a viable proposition, not something airy-fairy with no prospect of fulfilment. It was going to happen. But it needed careful organisation.

My first step was booking those flights to Caracas. That brought up the problem of payment. No point in trying my cards, they were maxed out long ago. Moving money this soon was risky. Tomorrow, I'd calculated, was the earliest to do that to ensure we got away on Friday without being hauled off the plane by law-enforcement personnel. In the end, I shrugged and used my company credit card to pay, smiling at my reluctance to do so. I was going to rip Seb n Seb off for millions, and I was balking at diddling my expenses by a measly grand! It was so plainly stupid that I made up for it by booking first-class seats, using the old sheep as for a lamb maxim to justify my decision. No doubt the company accountant would open her eyes in horror at the cost, but by then, it would be way too late. Anyway, I had often spent as much on a lunch with clients as on the flights – hard to believe now, didn't seem in any way odd then.

Sighing loudly for times past, I spent the next few hours making my future financially stable. There were a number of accounts to choose from, and I chose carefully. Some clients liked to spread their risks with multiple investments, liked to try new markets. These accounts were more likely to be looked at over the next few days. I avoided them. I went for the conservative accounts where the client liked to know exactly where his money was, exactly which investments he had, a client who rarely, if ever, speculated. These accounts could go for weeks without changing. These were the ideal. Finally, I found just the right account. And I was ready.

On Wednesday morning, with less than two days to go, my fingers were poised over the keyboard. Almost despite me, they started clickity-clacking and before I knew it, it was done. Simplicity. That was the secret. People were programmed to see what they expected to see. What they wanted to see. If you look at a figure, and you expect to see £3,597,000, you look and see the numbers 3, 5, 9, 7. Do you count the zeros? Do you check that there is a comma and decimal point in the right place?

Of course not. You see the numbers, and you think all is well with your world, and you don't realise, until it is way too late, that some pilfering bastard has relieved you of millions and you now only have £359,700. What a difference a zero can make.

I simply moved a decimal point and moved the excess money, so that at first glance, the account had the same balance – the numbers were unchanged. Just their value. Opening an account in Liechtenstein, I transferred money there first, and from there had it transferred to an account in Venezuela. Years of international finance had taught me well. I was unable to stop smirking when I considered the denouement, imagining Francois's face, his inability to understand what had happened, the penny finally dropping. Would he panic? Or remain very French and shrug. He would have to ring Guillaume. They'd call in accountants; have all the accounts analysed, and eventually all the evidence would point to me. Would they be surprised? Shocked? Resigned?

The police would probably be called. Probably, but not definitely. It depended on whether Sebastian et Sebastian could absorb the loss, whether they would lose more by exposing the embezzlement than they would by absorbing it. After all, we were only talking about £3 million or so. Chickenfeed. The loss to their reputation would be a lot more.

Sitting back, I smiled in satisfaction. Three million, two hundred and thirty-seven thousand and three hundred pounds was sitting in my account in Liechtenstein. It would be transferred within twenty-four hours to another account in Venezuela.

The easy part was done, my future financial stability assured. The difficult part lay ahead. I stood at my office window, gazing down at the little people below, wondering if any of them were planning equally horrendous deeds.

'Uxoricide,' I whispered. My warm breath misted the glass and hid the view.

69

I picked up the phone, and when Adam answered, I jumped straight in. 'Hi, it's me. Listen, I want to do a special dinner for Ann, Thursday night. I know mid-week's not the easiest for you, but would you be able to take the kids, maybe keep them till the weekend?'

'Jake, hi, it's been ages. What've you been up to? Thursday...' I heard him move around, imagined him going in search of Jane to sound her out, never willing to risk making a decision without consultation.

For the first time, with a clarity that was almost painful, I realised I could never have married Jane. I would never have been so accommodating, so selfless. How well she and Adam were suited. I could have saved myself a lot of angst if I'd recognised this years before.

'Jane,' I heard him calling, his voice muffled, then suddenly louder as he held the phone back to his mouth, 'Yeah, Jane says great, she has some leave to take, she'll take Friday off and spoil them. She's already excited; you know what she's like. Will you drop them over or would you like me to pick them up?'

I thought quickly. 'I'll drop them over. About six? That okay?'

'Perfect. We'll really enjoy having them, you know that.'

And I did. I knew having the children was just what they needed. And my children would be happy... no, happier... living with them.

A call to Elgin Crescent got me the current nanny, a Filipina called Rosario whom the children loved, but I never took to. 'Rosario, the children are going to Adam and Jane's on Thursday night for the weekend. You can have the weekend off.'

'Mrs Mitchell never told me,' she said.

'That's because she doesn't know. To be honest, Rosario' – my voice slipped into conspiratorial mode – 'we've been drifting apart a little recently, and I thought a weekend when we had the place to ourselves with no staff around to distract us might do us good.'

I waited for the penny to drop, hoping it would, that I didn't have to spell it out.

'Okay.' Her voice slightly hesitant. 'I could go and visit my aunt, if I could borrow the car.'

Borrow? She could keep the small run-around we had bought for her and Julie's use. 'Fine, yes, no problem. Take a few days, don't rush back.'

'Perhaps I will stay with her until Sunday?'

'Yes, yes, fine.' Then, afraid she might get suspicious, I added, 'Not too late, though.'

'No, Mr Mitchell. I'll return early afternoon.'

'Great, have a good visit. Can you put me through to Julie, please?'

I wiped perspiration from my forehead as I waited, heard the click as she transferred my call to the extension in the kitchen.

'You wanted to speak to me, Mr Mitchell?' I could hear the surprise in the housekeeper's voice.

Thinking of tangled webs and all that, I'd decided to stick to the same story in case she compared notes with Rosario. 'Yes, I'm planning a surprise romantic weekend at home – just Ann and me, no visitors, no guests. Adam is taking Fi and P. Rosario is taking the weekend off. We won't need you to come in at all over the weekend.'

Silence.

'Julie?'

'Mrs Mitchell never mentioned anything about this to me.'

Her voice was deeply affronted. You'd think the stupid woman would be delighted with a weekend off. And I'd said 'surprise'. Didn't she understand the concept? 'It's a surprise, Julie. She doesn't know.'

There was silence as she digested this. Finally, she said, 'And what, may I ask, are you going to do for food?'

As if, before her arrival, we'd never eaten. 'I've organised caterers, Julie. The same ones we used for our wedding. Romance, you know?' Knowing full well the nearest the old battle-axe got to romance was folding Ann's ridiculously expensive and incredibly sexy underwear.

'Caterers.' Julie sniffed disparagingly. 'They'll make a mess that I'll have to clean up, I suppose. I don't know why you don't let me cook up something on Friday before I go. Makes more sense.'

Friday? 'N-n-n-no,' I stuttered helplessly, trying to remember what I had told her. Of course, I had said *weekend*! 'That's very kind of you, but I have it all organised. And it's going to be a long weekend. If you could make your excuses and go after lunch on Thursday, that would be great.'

'Thursday?'

'Thursday,' I said firmly. 'And don't forget... it's a surprise.'

The audible long-suffering sigh that came loud and clear down the phone told me what Julie thought of surprises. If there was a moment's guilt for what I was going to put the woman through when she found Ann's body, it vanished then.

The third call was going to be the most difficult. The success of the plan depended on Ann being home on Thursday evening, but staying home was a rare occurrence for her those days. Nights we had dinner together, she would normally go out somewhere afterwards, sometimes she told me, sometimes she didn't. It didn't matter either way. We drifted by each other with a bare acknowledgement of existence, neither knowing nor caring what the other was up to. It wasn't that we hated each other, it was never stronger than plain old disinterest.

On Thursdays, she played badminton, leaving the house around seven, getting home sometime around ten. Her partner was a woman called Laura, an athletic, strikingly beautiful woman, endless legs, expensively streaked blonde hair, mesmerising turquoise eyes that I was convinced were contacts. When I asked Ann what she thought, she just raised her eyes to heaven, let out a long-suffering sigh, and walked away shaking her head. Whether that meant *of course they're contacts, you idiot,* or *how could you think such a thing,* I had no idea.

Ann never missed badminton. All I had to do was to convince Laura to go along with my *surprise.*

I picked up the phone again and slammed it back with a groan. I didn't have her blasted number, did I? Okay. Calm. I dialled home again. 'Julie, sorry, it's me again. I meant to ask you to give me Laura's number.'

'Laura? Laura who?' Julie's voice was chilly.

Laura who? I'd no idea. 'The woman Ann plays badminton with every Thursday. I need to get her help in this surprise I'm trying to organise, you know.'

'Ah,' the non-word injected with all the superiority of a woman who thought she knew Ann far better than I did. 'You mean Laura

Bradley, I think. Just hold for a moment and I'll see if I can find her number for you.' She put the phone down with a clatter, heavy footsteps fading slowly as she moved away. Ten minutes later, my patience see-through, a distant rustle grew into her heavy tread before there was a noisy scrabble for the phone that made me wince. 'Here we are,' she said, making no apology for the length of time she had kept me waiting. 'Laura Bradley, 483356.'

I repeated the number back. 'Thanks, Julie. Is there a mobile number as well?'

'Yes. Do you want it?'

No, I want you to write it across your face in indelible ink, you stupid woman. 'If that wouldn't be too much trouble.'

The irony was lost on her. 'No trouble at all, Mr Mitchell.'

Hanging up, I breathed a sigh of relief. Almost there.

70

People believe what they want to believe. It makes deception easy.

Laura answered her own phone. She was rich, of course. Being rich was the sine qua non of being Ann's friend, but she wasn't quite rich enough to have a full-time housekeeper.

'It's Jake Mitchell,' I said, quickly following up with, 'Ann's husband.'

'Hi, Jake,' she replied cautiously. 'Is Ann okay?'

'Yes, yes, she's fine. I'm ringing to ask a favour. I'm trying to organise a surprise weekend for us. I was going to take Ann away, but then I thought of a better idea. I've organised for the children to be away, the staff too, and I've organised caterers to supply Ann's favourite food... you know, lobster, caviar, and champagne, of course. The whole works.'

'Gosh!' She sounded so surprised, I was immediately suspicious that Ann had told her enough about the state of our marriage to make my romantic weekend proposal sound unbelievable.

Taking a deep breath, I let it out in an audible sigh. 'We've been drifting.' I hoped Laura would pick up on the pathos I was desperately injecting into each word. 'I've let work get in the way.' *See, I'm man enough to accept all the blame.* 'I want to make it up to her, treat her the way she deserves to be treated.' *Well, I had that all sorted.*

I explained the trouble I had taken to get the house to ourselves, and described the sumptuous meal I had arranged to be delivered. 'You know how much she loves lobster.' I waxed lyrical about the meal I had quickly ordered the day before, not at all surprised at how she swallowed it, it sounded amazing. As I said, people believe what they want to.

'She'll love it, Jake,' she said finally when I had exhausted the details, adding and elaborating when I thought I wasn't getting through to her. 'She'll absolutely love it.'

'Thanks, Laura. I have tried.'

'What can I do to help? It sounds like you have every "i" dotted already.'

My laugh was mechanical. 'I'm so desperate for this to work, you know?'

'Of course, you are,' she soothed. 'Don't worry. It will all be fine. What can I do to help?'

Swallowing the sigh of relief, I told her. 'Something simple. Just before Ann leaves for your game tomorrow, ring and cancel. Make up whatever reason you like. It will be too late for her to make alternative arrangements, and she'll have to stay in. The food is being delivered during the afternoon, and I'll set the scene in our dining room. When you cancel, I'll show her what I've done.'

'She'll be thrilled. I just know she will. Yes, of course, I'll think of something believable to tell her. I hope you have a fantastic weekend.'

It was all arranged.

The planning and organising, phone calls, elaborate lies. All exhausting. All filling my time, so I never had time for doubts, for all the what-ifs that make decisions so annoyingly difficult. Now, everything arranged, they slipped in, cunningly appearing late at night in a brief waking moment, growing there so that when I woke, they were there full-on, blinding me, combining their parts to form a full colour photomontage of what I was about to do.

There was no question of any of my arrangements going awry; since Rosario and Julie had already agreed, it was easy to persuade them to pretend to Ann it was their choice to take time off, all in the spirit of keeping it a surprise. I coached them in their various parts, asked them to tell Ann their plans on Wednesday.

If the coincidence of both wishing suddenly to take time off, at the same time, struck Ann as unusual, she made no comment to them or, over dinner on Wednesday night, to me. It was a rare event for us to dine at the same time. We made desultory conversation, me trying very hard to appear relaxed and normal, Ann responding monosyllabically, when she responded at all. Sometimes her response was a shrug, or a raised eyebrow that I would catch or not depending on whether I was loading my fork or chewing. I stopped both, when she mentioned, in a casual by-the-way voice, that Fi and P would be staying with Adam and Jane for the weekend.

My fingers white-knuckled on the cutlery.

She continued eating.

'Really,' I said, calmly. 'Why?'

She looked at me. I'm sure she would have frowned, had she been able. 'Because Rosario is going away. You must know about it' – she looked suddenly suspicious – 'she said you told her she could take the car.'

I hadn't thought Rosario would mention that I'd given her permission to take the damn car. I put my cutlery down noisily. 'Oh,' I said, adding a tut-tut, 'I'd forgotten all about that. She mentioned something to me a couple of days ago; I told her there'd be no problem. I assumed she would have discussed it with you.'

'She only told me earlier today,' Ann said, her voice tinged with annoyance. 'It might have been most inconvenient.'

'But Adam and Jane are taking them, aren't they?'

'Yes, but not until tomorrow evening. Who's going to look after them until then? Rosario is insisting she has to leave after lunch. It really is most inconvenient.'

Good girl, Rosario, I thought. At least she got that bit right. 'I'll take some time off and take them over to Adam's in the evening.'

'You?' Ann laughed as if the idea was unbelievable, ridiculous.

I shrugged. 'Why not?'

'You've never done so before.'

'So? A first time for everything and all that...'

Pushing her plate away, she stood and looked across the room at me. 'You're behaving very oddly these days, you know.' Her gaze was analytical, sharp, then dismissive, as if she suddenly remembered she didn't care anyway. 'Fine, I'll leave you to it. I'll make sure Rosario has everything they need packed up. They only need clothes, no toys, there's plenty there already.'

'Adam complained once they'd have to move out if any more toys got left behind.' I smiled as I remembered Jane picking up one of Fi's forgotten dolls, unconsciously trying to restore order to its child-battered clothes, maternal fingers smoothing down unmanageable curls, fixing frills, unbending the desperately bent, before posing it carefully in the corner of the sofa to await its less-than-careful owner.

The thought of how much she would love my children strengthened my purpose.

Ann stopped at the dining room door and turned, an elegant hand resting along the edge of the glossy white door, scarlet nails tap-tapping. 'I almost forgot, to add to the inconvenience, Julie needs the weekend off too. You'll need to eat out.'

No invitation to join her for dinner, no mention of where she was going to dine. It wasn't going to make what I'd planned any easier... but it wasn't making it harder either.

71

I didn't leave work early on Thursday. I simply didn't bother going in. Instead, I wandered around London, hopping on and off the Tube, drinking endless coffees in a series of expensive forgettable cafés, watching the normality of it all, and wondering once again why it was so hard to feign when it looked so easy.

Finishing my last coffee, I reached into my inside pocket and pulled out my mobile, watching my reflection in its blank face for a long moment before pushing the button that reconnected me to the world. Surprisingly... or maybe not... there was no missed call from Seb n Seb deploring my absence. They probably hadn't even noticed.

Ann had left a message, short and succinct. 'Don't forget you are watching Phoebe and Peregrine this afternoon. Rosario is leaving at two.'

I didn't think it necessary to reply.

There was a message from Jane, asking me to bring the children over as early as I wanted. It did deserve a reply, and I pressed the speed dial that quickly connected me. 'Jane, hi, it's Jake. Thanks for that. It would be great if I could bring them over a little earlier, as long as you're sure.' As I held the phone tight to my ear, trying to close off the chattering masses around me, her tinkling laugh pealed in my head, and I had a tantalising glimpse of what would be when all my plan was complete.

The realisation that we'd never have suited as man and wife hadn't stopped me loving her. I wondered how she'd judge me when everything came to pass. Would she realise *why* I had done what I had done? Would she look at my children and judge their genetic make-up as wanting?

But then her words followed on the back of the laugh. 'You know how much I love to have them. As usual, I won't want to give them back when Sunday comes around.'

I'd seen it so often, her last tight hugs, the last lingering glance, and the shade of longing in her eyes that she could never hide, especially from me. This Sunday would be different. And I knew it would be all right. She would never judge; it wasn't in her nature to place the sins of the father onto the tiny shoulders of babes. Maybe, someday, I would have the chance to explain.

'How about five?' I asked, thinking it would leave me plenty of time to set the stage for the final act.

'Perfect.'

'Great, I'll drop them over then.'

'Just beep, I'll keep an eye out, don't bother trying to find parking. It's murder at that time of the day.'

Thanking her again, I shut my phone and stood. For a moment, I had no idea where I was, looking around in confusion, trying to see some point of reference. Once out on the street, a glance around orientated me, and I headed off to the nearest station to catch a Tube. I arrived home with minutes to spare, catching a sharp look from Ann, who was heading out at the same time I was going in. 'You made it,' she said, and left without waiting for my reply.

The children's playroom was down beside the gym. A small windowless room, I think it was originally designed as a storeroom, but as it was near Rosario's room, Ann thought it would be ideal for the children and keep all their paraphernalia from cluttering the house. It certainly kept them out of her sight. Sometimes, wandering around the vast reception rooms, you could forget there were children living there.

As I descended the stairs, their laughter drifted towards me. Despite our dubious parenting, they were happy kids.

'Hi, Fi, hi, P,' I called. Opening the door, I was gratified by the instant pleasure on their faces at my arrival, a pleasure that faded as quickly when they realised my arrival meant Rosario's departure. They clung to her hands, a look of desperation on their faces, casting looks of horror in my direction as if to say they were pleased to see me, but to be taken care of by me… that was a different story. One so beyond their understanding that their looks of horror quickly descended into tears of terror. Rosario shot me a look of utter triumph. I was only prevented from physically pushing her out the door, telling her to be on her miserable way, by the thought that she would soon be out of a job anyway. If my triumphant expression confused and puzzled her, it didn't faze her for long and she bent to console my children. *My* children.

I did push her then. Gently, of course, I didn't want to rouse suspicion and have her ring Ann with a complaint that would not only have roused *her* suspicion but might have scuppered all my carefully laid plans. No, I gently pushed her, and told her to go on her way, that I was taking Fi and P to Auntie Jane and Uncle Adam and we didn't have time to delay. Of course, as I knew they would, Auntie Jane and Uncle Adam's names consoled my children, as the names Mummy and Daddy never did.

Reassured as they were by the promise of being in my company for only a short while, they smiled and waved happily as

Rosario collected her bags and left with scarcely a glance in my direction.

'What shall we do?' I asked them, hunkering down, meeting them eye-to-eye, their clear blue eyes so like their mother's, their guileless innocent gazes so unlike hers.

Fi darted a look at P, then back to me. Suddenly I saw a hint of the woman she would become, her smile dazzling, her gaze flirtatious. I smiled, an automatic programmed response to innate female cajolery. 'Ice cream?' she whispered.

'Ice cream it is.'

First, of course, I had to find it. Integrated kitchens look fabulous but there is no hint as to what is behind each door until you open it. As it turned out, I couldn't have planned it better. Fi thought it hilarious that I didn't know where the ice cream was kept, and it turned into a game, both children laughing hysterically as I tried each door in succession, a clownish, confused look on my face when I pulled out pots and other kitchen paraphernalia. 'Is this ice cream?' I asked each time, and as with children everywhere, they didn't tire of shouting 'no' and they rolled around the floor in laughter.

Eventually, I hit on the right door and found a wonderland of ice cream. I took all the tubs out, the Luscious Lemon, Sizzling Strawberry and Riveting Raspberry. There were half-full tubs of Caramel and Candy, and an almost empty tub of one with the glorious name of Chocolate-to-Die-For. Fi found bowls; judging from their size, they were ones designed for pasta rather than ice cream, but the kids weren't complaining and their eyes grew wider by the second. I'm sure we possessed a scoop, but I couldn't find it and improvised with a soup ladle, opening the tubs and waving the ladle over them like a wand.

'Right,' I said, 'which flavour would you like?'

'That one and that one and that one!' P shouted, carried away by the excitement, waving chubby hands about, pointing at everything.

'No!' Fi joined in. 'That one and that one and that one!'

'Why don't we have a taste of each?' I proceeded to fill their bowls until, big as the bowls were, they overflowed and melting ice cream dripped lava-like from the edges.

They didn't eat it all, and ended up wearing almost as much as they ate. But I don't think I have ever had so much fun. I hoped the memory of that day would last, so that in the years to come, they would say to each other, *do you remember the day of the ice cream*, and they would smile and think of me.

When they could eat no more, and ice cream had crept into every anatomical crevice, I swept their giggling sticky bodies into my arms and carried them wriggling all the way to their bedroom. In their bathroom, I showered them together, lathering them with soapsuds and getting myself soaked in the process. I wrapped them in fluffy towels, rubbed them gently dry and listened to their childish babble, soaking it in, wanting to remember it all. All through it, I fought back tears, a fixed smile on my face. I caught sight of it in one of the bedroom mirrors and saw an edge of mania that scared but didn't surprise me. What sane man, after all, would plan what I was planning?

Soon the children were dressed again. Neat and tidy, and ready to leave.

And it was time.

They were still laughing and giggling as I strapped them into their seats in the car. After all they'd consumed, I hoped they wouldn't be sick. Half expecting them to be, I grabbed a china bowl from the hallway as we left. Just in case.

Forty-five minutes later, I was pulling up outside Adam's house. I didn't need to honk my horn. Jane must have been sitting in the window waiting, probably had been waiting all afternoon.

The door opened almost before the car had stopped, and she came rushing out, a smile on her face, in her eyes, arms extended, welcoming, always welcoming. I reached back to undo the children's seat belts and unlocked the door. They grabbed their little bags, piled out, and ran into the curve of her arms. They didn't look back.

Jane didn't come to the car. I was always in such in a hurry when I dropped them off, it had become a habit for us just to nod or wave, then I'd drive away.

All I had missed.

All I *would* miss.

I was compelled to follow my usual course and, with a wave, as casual as I could force it to be, I drove away. My eyes glued to the rear-view mirror, I drove as slowly as possible. My last glimpse, just before the curve of the road took them away, was of Fi and P still babbling, Jane leaning down, an arm around each.

They were meant to be. Life wasn't fair. But sometimes, we can make it so.

72

It took me nearly thirty minutes to clean up the mess in the kitchen. Ice cream had dripped from the table to the floor, and from the children as I'd carried them from the room. In fact, when I looked, there was a faint trail of ice cream leading up the stairs and along the corridor. Small spots of Sizzling Strawberry or Riveting Raspberry marked the cream carpet of the landing. It was definitely Chocolate-to-Die-For that streaked the walls, P's fingerprints standing out in high relief. For a moment, I was tempted to leave them there, but I remembered my plan. Grabbing a damp cloth, I reluctantly wiped away all traces of the day's exuberance.

I had just finished when the doorbell rang to announce the arrival of the caterers. They didn't need me, so I left them to it and headed up to change my ice cream-stained clothes, choosing smart-casual dark trousers and a crisp white shirt. Very Tom Ford, I thought, admiring my reflection. Just the look that had always appealed to Ann. A splash of the eponymous cologne, and I was set for my leading man role.

Downstairs, the caterers had finished and were taking their leave. A final check that all was as it should be, and I was ready. It just needed my leading lady to arrive. Checking my watch, I realised she was late. 'Damn,' I said, just as I heard the front door open and the click-click of her shoes on the hallway tiles.

Fifteen minutes later, on cue, I heard her mobile ring.

I imagined the conversation; Laura would have thought up some plausible reason for pulling out of the weekly badminton. Ann would be silently fuming and trying not to sound so; she would pretend it didn't matter that she had so many other things she could do instead. I waited ten minutes before I headed up the stairs, concentrating on breathing slowly, trying to stay calm.

Outside her room, I took a deep breath before knocking, trying for commanding, coming out the far side of tentative. There was no answer, no sound, the doors heavy and designed to minimise the passage of sound. I clasped the doorknob and pushed gently just as it was pulled firmly from the other side, so that I stumbled and fell into the room. Not the suave entrance I had hoped for.

Ann stood glaring at me. She was still wearing the outfit she usually wore for badminton, so I guessed she had been trying to find an alternative partner. I hoped she hadn't had any luck.

'What do you want, Jake?' she said curtly, turning and undoing the buttons of her shirt as she moved. I guessed with a smile of relief that badminton was off the agenda. Dropping clothes as she moved across the room, uncaring that I was watching, she opened her wardrobe and took out a silk kimono. She stretched her arms up and slipped on the wildly coloured garment. For a moment, she looked like an exotic butterfly. As so often before, she took my breath away.

She couldn't resist a glance of triumph as she saw my reaction, preened a little, thrust her breasts out so her nipples stood proud under the fine soft silk. Then she obviously remembered the abandoned badminton game and scowled. 'That bitch Laura rang to cancel our game. Some lame excuse about one of the children being sick. As if the nanny couldn't have sorted that out. Honestly, some people really take the biscuit. Letting me down at such short notice too. Impossible to get a substitute at this late stage. And you know how much I look forward to my badminton.'

Putting on my best sympathetic look, I crossed the room and held out my arms. 'Oh, you poor thing, how annoying for you.'

She looked surprised, and her glance was sharp. Had I over-done it? I kept the sympathetic glance pinned firmly in place, felt it examined for sincerity and intent, and then saw her face relax. I had passed. With a sigh of self-pity, she melted into my arms and gave a little sob.

'Oh, don't be upset,' I whispered into the ear that nestled close to my mouth. 'Laura doesn't deserve a partner like you.'

I felt a sigh flutter through her. She moved closer. I'd forgotten just how slight she was, how fine her bones were. Then she moved again, and I knew what she was doing... feeling to see if I had an erection. For a woman who always had a hidden agenda, I suppose it was normal to suspect everyone else of the same thing.

But beautiful, desirable as she was, it had been a long time since she'd had that effect on me, and all her deftly moving knee could find was as soft as her silk.

No badminton, no sex. She wasn't having a good evening. I could hear the thought running through her head as she moved from my embrace, pushing my arms away impatiently, moving back to her dressing table. 'What did you want?'

What did I want? Shit, I hadn't thought to arm myself with a reason for coming to her room. I wasn't supposed to know about Laura's cancellation. 'Ah... ah,' I stuttered, playing for time, my brain stalling. 'I noticed you hadn't gone out and wondered if you were okay.' Beads of perspiration were gathering on my brow; I took a surreptitious swipe at them while she wasn't looking. 'You always go out on Thursday.' I left it at that, hoping it didn't sound half as lame as I thought.

'Yes, well, thanks to that stupid bitch, and her stupid child, I won't be going out tonight, will I?'

I put the sympathetic look back on. 'You know what you need?'

Her glance was cutting, lingering on my groin in a dismissive way. 'Luckily not a fuck.'

I hoped my smile didn't look as forced as it felt... hoped it didn't look manic. 'Better,' I said, 'food.' I nodded towards the door. 'Why don't you join me for dinner? I've had some food delivered.'

She crossed to her dressing table and sat. 'What kind? I'm not in the mood for Chinese or Indian.'

My smile broadened. 'Well, how about lobster thermidor and Beluga caviar, all washed down with a chilled bottle of Cristal? And there are a few side dishes of salads and things.'

The chair creaked as she turned to stare at me in disbelief. 'You're kidding?'

'Nope.' I shook my head.

'You ordered all my favourite food.' Her voice was heavy with suspicion. She wasn't a woman who liked to be made a fool of. 'I don't believe you!'

'It's food I like too. I thought since Julie was away, I'd treat myself. I ordered enough for the weekend, so there's more than enough for two.'

She stood, weighing me up. I could see her taking in how I was dressed, her eyes widening slightly in what I decided to take as admiration. If there was a catch, she couldn't figure out what it was. Why would she?

Finally, after what seemed to be a very long consideration, she nodded slowly. 'Well, I think that sounds like a very good idea,

Jake. It's been a long time since we've had a romantic meal for two.' She'd made up her own mind about my agenda, obviously thinking I was looking for some kind of reconciliation.

Just as I had hoped she would. My plan was going so well, it took my breath away, and I gasped, startling her. 'What...' she said, looking over her shoulder for whatever it was that had alarmed me.

I forced a laugh, brushed it away. 'Sorry, a shadow...'

'Honestly, you're such an idiot,' she said cuttingly, and brushed past in a flash of coloured silk. More hornet than butterfly.

As she continued to sweep ahead, I wondered how to keep her out of the kitchen. My plan needed some sleight of hand. I wasn't sure how good I was at that. It would be so much easier if she weren't in the vicinity.

But I needn't have worried. With a casual, and definitely rhetorical – 'You don't need my help, do you?' – she went directly into the dining room and sat in her usual seat at the table. Long ago, when we mattered, we used to joke as to who sat at the head and who at the foot of the table and compromised by referring to ourselves as the bookends. Now, as she relaxed back into her chair, she was most definitely at the *head* of the table. And I knew my place.

I closed the dining room door behind her and crossed to the kitchen. The players were assembled. The stage was set.

Let the last act begin.

73

The caterers had left everything ready. I simply had to serve. Obviously used to catering to the culinarily challenged, they'd even numbered each container. Idiot proof. There was also a three-page written guide, in case I didn't know what to do.

Turns out they were right. I didn't know not to use metal spoons with caviar, for instance – it seems metal can impart a nasty taste. Instead, they had included small wooden spoons for us to use. Reading on, it appeared that small triangles of toast would have been the correct accompaniment, but for my convenience – read, designed for lazy people like me – they had included thin wafers of home-made brown bread.

I put a slice of bread on one plate for Ann, and two on another for me. Opening the container of Beluga caviar, I looked at the little wooden spoons. Use one of them? It would take forever. Opening a drawer, I found a big wooden spatula. Perfect. Within seconds, half the fish eggs were on my plate.

Soft music drifted through from the dining room, something with guitars that wasn't familiar. It was romantic, sexy, even. Music for romance, not tragedy. Ann had come to her own conclusions about the evening. Why wouldn't she, I'd done my job well. I waited a moment in case she might come to offer assistance, not really thinking she would, but you never did know with Ann. Or at least I never did.

The card of tablets was in my pocket, I took it out. I needed to crush them. Damn, I should have done that earlier, should have been prepared. I needed a whajemacallit... I looked around the kitchen. We had every piece of equipment known to man, there had to be one. I saw it, the name popping into my head with the sight, a pestle and mortar.

There was a corner of the kitchen out of sight of the dining room door. I popped four tablets from the card into the bowl, then, with a to-hell-with-it shrug, I popped the lot. Fourteen tablets. That would surely send her to sleep within a short space of time. Speed wasn't essential but already tension was knotting my gut. The sooner it was all done, the better.

It took seconds to grind the fourteen tablets to a fine powder, seconds more to mix the powder into the remaining Beluga caviar. I remembered to use the wooden spoon to do the mixing and scooping, smiling at the irony as I did so. God forbid she wouldn't eat the blasted stuff because it was tainted.

Spooning it onto Ann's plate and comparing the two portions of caviar, I couldn't see any difference. Both piles glistened blackly. My tension-knotted gut squeezed and gurgled. It may have been a favourite of Ann's, but fish eggs weren't a favourite of mine at the best of times. And this definitely wasn't one of them.

No point in worrying about that now. There was more to do. I checked the instruction sheet. *Spoon the sieved egg white and yolk onto the plate beside the caviar.* I searched the box, found the containers, opened and scooped. Then, as directed, stuck a little wooden spoon into each mound of glistening caviar.

The final addition to this course, as recommended by the

instruction sheet, was a small glass of frozen vodka. But they hadn't included that, and we didn't have any. What I did have in the fridge was a bottle of Cristal, I guessed that would do as well.

Balancing the two plates in one hand, and with the champagne in the other, I kicked open the door into the dining room, put the champagne down and then, with a voilà, placed a plate in front of Ann. Of course, I put the wrong plate down. Luckily, noticing immediately, I picked it up and replaced it with the other. 'Less bread.' I excused the exchange blithely. 'But there's more if you'd like.'

'No,' she said, with a shake of her head. 'This is perfect.'

I opened the champagne and poured us both a glass. Ann lifted hers towards me, leaving me no choice but to acknowledge the gesture with one of my own, and our glasses clinked.

'Happy days,' Ann said smiling, and took a sip. 'Delicious.'

Forcing the corners of my mouth upward into some semblance of a smile, I echoed her toast, 'Happy days.'

Retreating to the other end of the table, I sat and looked at the caviar. Perhaps she wouldn't notice if I didn't eat any. But when I looked down the table, she was watching me warily. Perhaps my smile had looked as false as it felt.

'This is delicious.' I picked up the little spoon, dolloped some over-priced gelatinous fish eggs on a piece of brown bread and popped it into my mouth, relieved to see her do the same. I ate the lot, afraid to leave any in case she followed my lead. If she left any, how could I be sure she'd had enough of the sleeping pills? But it must have been good stuff because she emptied her plate.

74

Ann put the last of the caviar into her mouth. 'That was delicious.'

'Yes,' I agreed, trying not to gag on my last mouthful, swallowing it without chewing so as not to burst the little buggers. At that stage, the knots in my gut had knots.

Reaching for my water glass, I took a small sip and a few slow breaths. I managed a smile across the table. 'Ready for the next course?'

'There's no hurry, is there?' She smiled flirtatiously and waved her glass. 'More champagne, perhaps?'

'Of course.'

Filling her glass, I returned to my seat, sat and watched her closely. Were her eyelids starting to droop? The sleeping tablets should start to kick in around twenty minutes after consumption. I'd done some research. But the studies were based on taking the recommended amount. Exceeding that would surely speed up the process. Wouldn't it?

'I had coffee with Jane on Monday.'

This was so unexpected, I thought I hadn't heard right. 'Sorry?'

'I said I had coffee with Jane, on Monday. At their place.'

'Really?' I couldn't keep the surprise from my voice. I didn't think Ann and Jane were on meet-for-coffee terms.

Ann drained her glass and smiled sleepily. 'Don't sound so surprised. We do, you know. Meet, that is.' She shrugged elegantly, sending the silk of her gown rippling and shimmering in the candlelight. 'Not very often, granted, and usually down-town. But this time, I went over to hers.' She stopped and held her glass up to the light, staring at it, watching the bubbles rise and pop. 'Their house is so cosy, isn't it? We sat and chatted, and I thought how lovely it was.'

'Small, though,' I ventured, not really sure what to say, not having the slightest idea where, if anywhere, this conversation was going.

'Oh, yes. I wouldn't want to live anywhere *that* small, but...'

I waited. Her eyelids were drooping. 'But?'

Her eyes flew open, and she laughed. 'I think I've had too much of this delicious champagne. Maybe we should have the lobster, it might sober me up a bit.'

I hesitated. 'What were you going to say?'

She waved toward the kitchen. 'Lobster.'

There was no point in insisting she finish whatever it was she was going to say. I don't know why it suddenly seemed so important. What did I expect?

I couldn't figure out how to turn the oven off, so I left it on, took out the dish holding the lobster thermidor and put it on the counter. Tinfoil had been crimped tightly around the edges of the dish, thick, good-quality tinfoil that cut me twice before I was able to remove it. There I was, trying to serve up a very posh, designed-to-impress meal, with two of my fingers staining everything they touched with blood. I grabbed a teacloth and wiped the traces away, wrapped my fingers in the towel and held the gashes for a few seconds, willing the blood to stop. Removing the fabric slowly, I swore loudly when blood bubbled up once more. I looked around frantically. A first aid kit, we must have a damn first aid kit. And we did. There it was, a bright red box clamped to the wall. Could I get the damn thing off? Of course not. Who designs a first aid box that is impossible to remove when you need to access the contents? I took a meat-tenderiser from a drawer, and with a swing knocked the whole thing off the wall, shattering the clamp, breaking open the box and drawing a shout from the dining room.

'Jake? Are you okay?'

'Yes,' I shouted back. 'Everything is fine. Be there in a tick.' I picked up some of the disgorged sticking plasters and struggled to get them from their wrappers. Seriously, who designs these things? Finally, I had the lacerations bandaged and got back to the lobster. Thankfully, there wasn't much to do with it. Using the bloodied towel, I lifted half onto each plate, and following the instructions, sprinkled some chopped parsley over each half. And that was it. Using my thumb, I wiped traces of blood off both plates and carried them in.

Ann looked distinctly heavy-eyed, but she greeted me with a smile which widened considerably when she saw my bandaged hands, the blue dressings standing out clearly. 'Lobster attack?'

I nodded. Sounded so much better than the truth.

The lobster was very good, but after the first mouthful, I just played with it, moving pieces around my plate. Watching Ann, it seemed to me she did the same.

'What had you wanted to say?' I asked her, curious despite myself.

She looked up from her plate, puzzled, until I reminded her.

'You wouldn't want to live anywhere that small, but...?'

She nodded, and looked across the table at me with an expression I hadn't seen for a long time, or had I ever seen it? It was a mixture of appeal tinged with longing, regret touched with melancholy. She put down her fork and waved her long slim fingers around the room. 'This is a beautiful house, Jake, but I'd like a home.'

Flabbergasted. It was the only word I could think of that went anywhere towards explaining how I felt. 'I thought you loved this house, loved living here.'

'You had just bought it when we started dating, remember. You were so excited about it. So happy to be living here. I could hardly have said I didn't, could I? I suppose I got sort of used to it. But it would never have been my choice. It's all a bit big and cold for my liking. Adam and Jane's house is too small, but so much more homely.'

Flabbergasted. The word kept popping into my head. 'You'd like to move from Elgin Crescent. I'm flabbergasted.'

She pushed her plate away and smiled humourlessly. 'You've always made assumptions about me. You never took the time to ask what it was I wanted. It's time that changed. The children would benefit from a more homely environment, I think. Perhaps moving out of London...'

'Out of London.' I almost screeched the words. Was I hearing things? 'I thought you wanted to send them off to boarding school?'

'I did... for a time.' She shrugged. 'You were working all hours, you never saw them, barely saw me. But then, recently you've been coming home earlier, and I wondered' – she shrugged again – 'if maybe we could do better.' Her elbow slipped, sending champagne flying in a golden arc over her silk robe, the glass hitting the table and shattering into a million crystal shards that spun dizzily across the table.

'Oh, blast,' she said, pushing her chair back and standing. She swayed alarmingly, reached quickly for the table and shook her head, closing her eyes tightly. She opened them, looked at me across the table and gave a wry smile. 'How clumsy of me. I'll have to go and change.'

Still staggered by what she'd said, I tried desperately to get myself back on track to follow my carefully laid out plan. I rose and crossed the chasm between us, holding out my hand. 'You do look a bit shook. Why don't I run you a nice bath, you can soak while I clean up this mess.'

She looked at me from under heavy eyelids and smiled. 'That sounds like a good idea. Why don't you give me five minutes to calm down in it, then join me? Maybe bring another bottle of Cristal?'

I leaned closer, then closer still. Like kissing dolls, our lips touched and parted. We both nodded agreement of what would follow. I turned and, with a final glance at Ann, ran up to her bathroom, where I turned the hot tap on full and added her favourite bubble-bath. The bath was half-full before the door opened and Ann walked in.

She had shed her robe but still wore her three-inch heels and she sauntered towards me, hips swaying, naked and stunning. My breath caught, and I felt myself suddenly, unexpectedly, and completely inappropriately, hard as a rock.

Ann was back to being the woman I knew so well. She stepped close into my embrace and before I could stop her, she had cupped my balls in her hand, and ever-so-slowly moved her hands upward, trailing her clever fingers along my length, squeezing just enough to take my breath away. Her hand continued up my stomach and when it reached my chest, she gave a firm push. 'Give me five minutes to relax,' she said, her voice husky. 'Don't forget the champagne.'

Back in the kitchen, I took the bottle from the fridge, found two glasses, and sat, my head spinning. Everything had gone to plan, but at the same time, nothing had gone the way it was supposed to have done.

75

I opened the champagne carelessly, the cork flying across the room. It hit a small vase of flowers on the kitchen table; it wobbled once before falling to send a stream of water dripping to the floor.

I poured a glass of champagne and drank it in one. Poured another. Drank that. Poured a third, and wondered what the hell I thought I was doing. Seriously, what was I doing? I was planning to murder my wife, so that my best friend and his wife could have my children, then I was going to run off to South America with a woman I barely knew. That was my great plan? Was I nuts?

Why had I never realised Ann didn't want to live in Elgin Crescent? And if I didn't know that, what else didn't I know? Or to quote Ann, what other assumptions had I made about her? I would never have thought she'd be interested in us *doing better*. Never realised my long hours bothered her. Maybe I'd been so lost in my fantasy about Jane that I'd never given Ann a chance.

Bitter regret shot through me.

Maybe we could do better, and maybe if I told her we were broke, she'd be okay. We could sell this damn mansion, buy or at least rent a smaller house in the country. I'd have debts, but I could work with the bank, reschedule my loans and repayments.

Finishing the champagne, I stood shakily. I didn't know what to do any more, but I knew what I couldn't do. I couldn't murder my wife. We had been happy, maybe we could be again. And Joyce... she was just a dream. I'd meet her tomorrow as planned, one last time. I would explain everything, and she would understand.

A huge sense of relief flooded me, almost knocking me off my feet.

I was exhausted. Pretty drunk, but mostly just exhausted. Ann would be waiting. Hopefully the sleeping tablets would have taken the edge off the desire I had seen in her eyes. Maybe we had a future together, but I didn't think I was up for a night of unbridled passion.

I trudged up the stairs, glasses and the half-empty champagne bottle in hand. 'Sorry,' I said, pushing open her bathroom door. 'It took a while. I'm not used to domestic duties.' I was about to make some quip about champagne bubbles slowing me down when I realised I was wasting my breath. She wasn't there.

She'd lit candles after I'd left. They flickered now in the draught from the door I'd left open. The scene had been set but the male lead had dawdled off stage. The leading lady must be pretty pissed.

Or maybe not. Maybe she'd gone to the bedroom to prepare a different scene. Imagining her lying languorously across the bed waiting for me brought memories of our early days together. And despite my exhaustion, I felt something stirring. Maybe I wasn't that tired, after all. I was smiling; a genuine smile of pleasurable anticipation. I laughed out loud. This day wasn't turning out at all as planned.

The candles flickered again as I pushed the connecting

bedroom door open, a vague idea that I should blow them out remaining just that. Carrying the bottle and glasses, my eyes slowly adjusting to the darkness of the bedroom, I made my way over to the bed, prepared to see her displayed in all her glory, her long lean legs stretched, arms casually akimbo the better to show off her breasts.

But the bed was still neatly made, sheets tucked in, pillows plumped. Putting the bottle and glasses down on the bedside table, I looked around, foolishly aggrieved that the setting I'd imagined wasn't provided. I laughed again and shook my head. Exhaustion or champagne, something was certainly affecting my thought processes.

A rim of light showed around the door of the walk-in wardrobe, the one she had admired so much all those years before. She was probably searching for something killer to wear. Sitting on the bed, I pulled off my shoes.

'Sorry, Ann,' I called, walking across the room in my stockinged feet. There was no reply. I gently pushed open the door, preparing to retreat if necessary. But, although the light was on, she wasn't there.

For goodness' sake! She must have gone downstairs to look for me, leaving by the bedroom door as I had entered the bathroom. How very slapstick comedy. I went out onto the landing, calling her name as I went, trying to inject a note of amusement into my voice, although I felt far from amused. I was tired. I wanted to find her and go to bed, curl up with her, and sleep. Sexual gymnastics could wait for another day.

'Ann,' I called, going back down the stairs. 'Ann, where are you?' Back in the kitchen, the hum of the oven reminded me I still hadn't been able to switch it off. I looked at it briefly but, being none the wiser, left it and went into the dining room. There was no sign of her. Surely she would have heard me call.

Running back upstairs, I checked the bedroom again, then with a smile of relief realised she probably had gone to mine. She wouldn't have heard me call from that side of the house. Checking my watch, I frowned. She was probably sound asleep. Those sleeping tablets would have kicked in by now.

But my smaller bedroom was also in darkness, and undisturbed. The sight of my bed was tempting but I needed to find Ann, she must have fallen asleep somewhere. When I found her, should I wake her up, try to keep her awake? Damn, how many of those bloody tablets had I given her? Not enough to kill her. That had never been the plan, after all. The plan... and I shuddered to think I'd even considered killing my wife... the plan had been to push her down into the bath water; she'd have been too sleepy to struggle.

The bath. A hideous thought crossed my mind, and I reeled, my hand reaching out for the wall to steady me. The bath!

I ran, bursting through her bathroom door, candles flickering madly. The thick layer of bubbles in the bath looked undisturbed, pristine, virginal.

It couldn't be, could it? Carefully, hesitantly, I reached down, used my hand and cleared a circle of foam, then cried out in horror, falling back, foam dropping from my hand, soft snowflakes falling. I stood, overwhelmed, my hand held out, staring at the remnant of the foam as if it were to blame for the calamity I had caused.

It seemed I stood for a very long time. I don't know, but when I did move, my hand was empty. Had I imagined it all? Moving back to the bath, the layer of bubbles was, once again, complete, pristine. But as I had always known, things were never what they seemed. Carefully, once more, I pushed the foaming bubbles away. And there she lay.

I hadn't had to push her under; she'd fallen asleep waiting for me, sank down in the too-deep water of the too-big bath, sank down and drowned. I had murdered her after all. Bubbles tried to close over her face once more, I scooped them away. How beautiful she was. I thought of her, such a very short time ago, standing there in those ridiculous heels, looking stunning and so full of life and I screamed until my throat was hoarse.

76

When I woke, I was in my bed.

My first thought was relief that I'd come to my senses to prevent myself making the biggest mistake of my life. When I tried to move my head, it thumped painfully, so I didn't try. I just lay there, trying not to move or think. Memories of the night before came back in flashes. None made sense and they were messed up with the hideously graphic nightmare I'd had. It was easier to blame the mix of caviar, lobster and champagne than to blame an overindulgence in the latter.

Ann would laugh when I told her. I remembered what she'd said the previous night. Perhaps there was hope for us. It would be hard. There wasn't going to be any money for a long time.

Joyce would understand me abandoning that crazy plan. Joyce... oddly, her face was already beginning to blur. She'd been a dream. It was time to wake up.

Despite my aching head, I dragged myself from the bed, surprised to see I was naked. I saw my clothes; they peppered the floor between the bed and the door, a sock here, a sock there, my shirt in the doorway. Vaguely wondering where my trousers were,

I tried to piece the flashing memories of the previous night together in some semblance of order.

Dreams usually faded and bounced away when you tried to grasp hold, but this was a nightmare, and it wasn't letting go. Graphic images continued to flutter behind my eyelids with every blink.

I went to Ann's bedroom, knocked politely on the door and went in. The bed was as I remembered, still dressed, undisturbed. Ann hadn't slept in it; she never made her bed. Even when the housekeeper was away, she'd leave it unmade, climb back into it that night and every night, until Julie came back to tut-tut, take all the sheets off and redress it with fresh linen.

So, Ann, my wife, hadn't slept in her bed.

I stood a moment, staring, before turning slowly. The bathroom door was ajar. Suddenly, although I don't remember moving, I had my hand on the edge of the door and was moving with it into the room. Holding on tightly when my knees collapsed under my suddenly too heavy body, sliding down the door until I was sitting on the floor, the marble cold under my bare skin.

The graphic images hadn't been a nightmare. Hadn't I known? Deep down. Perhaps, but I was so fucking good at fooling myself.

I pulled myself up and swayed, or maybe the door moved. Nothing was certain.

In the images that had taunted me... that would probably haunt me for the rest of my days... the bath was deep with bubbles, white foam that covered what lay beneath. But the bubbles had dispersed overnight. Ann's body was on full display, looking strangely beautiful and almost serene. Sitting on the edge of the bath, I looked down at her for a long time, feeling numb.

What was I going to do? My eyes swept her from head to toe. Could I lift her out? I didn't think so and anyway, where would I put her? It was better to leave her there. But not like this, I decided, seeing the tell-tale discolouration of the water as her body rid itself of waste. How she would hate to be seen like that.

So, naked, I cleaned Ann's body, pressing the button that emptied the bath, using the hose attachment to spray her skin with water until it was clean. I dried her, as much as I could, her face, hands, feet. Her breasts and stomach. Her hair. I found a comb and combed it back, tried to make her look as presentable as possible. Finally, I went downstairs, took the flowers from the hallway and brought them up. Standing a moment, flowers in my hands, my heart thumping, I had one clear thought. *My God, what have I done?* And then, one after the other, I placed the flowers around and over her body.

There was nothing left for me to do then. And there were no options open for me. This was the end that was expected, after all. This had been my plan. *Joyce's plan.* What had I been thinking to have listened to her... a woman I barely knew, whose face I was finding hard to visualise... what had she been thinking to have suggested such a thing... and what did it say about me that she thought it was something I would do... did do? I stood, still naked and gazed down upon the wife I had murdered.

The plan had worked, despite my change of heart, and now it appeared I had no choice but to follow it through.

Joyce. It had been a crazy plan, but she'd had my welfare at heart, hadn't she? And I did love her, didn't I? I ran a hand over my face. Unsure of everything.

What was certain was I couldn't stay here. I'd make a life with Joyce, start again. My children's future was with Adam and Jane. I just had to make sure I didn't cock up anything else.

Returning to my room, almost robotically I showered and shaved. It was hard to care, but necessary, so I chose clothes carefully: navy trousers, casual button-down white shirt, navy jacket. Should I pack a case? I shook my head. If I did, I'd be bound to bump into someone... possibly the postwoman who'd been delivering our post for so long she knew everyone... she'd ask where I was off to, would ask if Ann and the children were going with me... and I knew I'd blurt out the truth... that Ann wasn't coming, that she couldn't because she was lying dead in the bath. I could almost picture the colour draining from the postwoman's face and gave a harsh laugh that morphed into a cry of despair.

No, I'd leave everything behind, start anew. New clothes for my new life.

Checking the time, I decided to give Adam a ring, see how the children were, maybe get to have a final word. The phone rang several times before it was picked up by a breathless Jane. 'Hello.'

'Sorry, Jane, have I interrupted something?'

'Hi, Jake... no, I was playing out in the garden with the kids, didn't hear the phone. I thought it might be you, checking up on us.'

'Don't let them exhaust you, you have to pace yourself, you know, or you'll never manage.'

Her laugh was drowned by the screams of Fi and P in the background. 'That's them now,' she said, laughing harder. 'They have Adam down on the grass and they're pouring water on him with the watering can. It's taking both of them to lift it. You should see them. It's so funny.'

'Well, give them my love. Tell them I miss them. Tell them...' I stopped. Tell them what... that I really hadn't meant to kill their mother. It would all come out, how I'd got rid of the nanny and housekeeper, how I'd organised for Ann to be home. Nobody was ever going to believe it was an accident, and I wouldn't be around to plead my case.

'Are you okay?' Jane sounded slightly worried. 'They're fine, you know, and we love having them.'

'Yes, I know. And that you'll always love them. Just remind them that I love them too, okay?'

'Jake, you're worrying me. You'll see them day after tomorrow, won't you? You're not planning to go anywhere. I know you and Ann have had your problems, but everything is okay, isn't it?'

'Yes, of course. Perhaps the weekend didn't go exactly to plan. I had to think on my feet, but I think the end result is best for all concerned.'

'Are you sure, because you sound very odd?'

'I'm sure. Trust me.' I wanted to tell her how much she meant to me... how much both of them did. I didn't because Jane wasn't stupid, and I didn't want her or Adam rushing over. Didn't want them to be the ones to find Ann.

'Right, then,' she said, sounding far from convinced. 'We'll see you on Sunday. Around five?'

I agreed and hung up, standing there with my hand on the receiver, wanting to ring again, talk to her for longer, and insist on speaking to Fi and P, just to hear their voices. But then I moved away, the memory of her genuine concern and their happy shrieks would have to do.

The oven was still humming away. This time, I didn't bother even trying to figure out how to switch it off. I made a coffee and sipped it, looking out of the window. There was an underlying fishy smell in the room that would get worse over the next day or two. The place would stink by the time Julie got back on Sunday. The place would disgust her and she'd be too busy cleaning up to venture upstairs at first.

When she did go to check the bedrooms, she'd be suspicious when she saw the neatly made bed, guessing immediately it hadn't been slept in. Would she check the bathroom then or go around to my room?

Expecting maybe to find Ann asleep.

Never expecting to find her lying in the bath.

Would she scream then, as I had done... as I was doing, the force of the sound sending me slamming into the wall, my fists pounding, pounding, pounding until I slid to the floor in exhaustion.

77

I had no choice but to pull myself together and leave Elgin Crescent for the last time. I shut the front door behind me and walked down the steps. At the gate, I turned. It was my second time to be leaving a house to start a new life. How strange that this life had begun unbeknownst to me with the death of my parents, and the death of my wife was the beginning of my next.

Three deaths. The thought made me shudder and reach for the wall to anchor myself.

I had to get to Charing Cross. Once there, everything would be all right. Joyce would make it so.

She was sitting where she always sat, her red coat taking on an almost unholy glow from the brake lights of passing cars. Tears welling in my eyes made her figure blur and even when I sat opposite, they made her face seem out of focus.

'I've done it,' I said. The words came out in a whisper. Mental self-flagellation... beating myself up for what I'd done, or what I'd failed to do... I was no longer sure. Joyce didn't need to know the details. I took out the airline tickets and put them on the rough worn table between us, the wood warm from the sun that cut a path between the surrounding buildings to shine on us. On us. Our time in the spotlight. Our last time. Soon we would be different people, we would take to the shadows, would have to live there for evermore, but we would be together.

I thought of all the lies, deceit, blood and death it had taken to get me to this point... to the gateway of my second chance at happiness. Joyce didn't comment on my announcement. She sat silently, her eyes fixed on the tickets. Unusually, she hadn't bought a coffee or her usual pastry. Perhaps she'd been too nervous, waiting for me, waiting to see if I could really do what she'd suggested. *Kill my wife.*

'I'll go get us coffees,' I said, jumping to my feet. She needed time to absorb the news, that was all. It was all going to be fine.

There was a queue inside the café. As I stood, waiting patiently, I watched Joyce, admiring the curve of her chin, the sheen of her hair in the light from the shop, the stillness of her body as she sat and waited. The sheer normality, the ordinariness of the scene. No hint in it of what I had done to achieve it.

'Can I help?' Irritation in the crisp voice hinted that it wasn't the first time she had asked. I dragged my gaze from Joyce reluctantly and smiled. Nothing could possibly annoy me now.

'Two lattes and one of those apple pastries,' I said, pointing to the ones I knew Joyce liked.

Moments later, I exited the shop, my lips already parted to speak, the words already rolling, 'Busy as u...' I stopped, transfixed by the empty chair, the empty table, the colossal vacancy where there had been a scene, a story, my life. I think I drooled, the unfinished words spilling as spit from my open mouth.

I put the coffees and pastry down on the table. The airline

tickets still sat where I had left them. Confusion blinded me. Then I shook my head on a half-laugh, a self-deprecatory whinny at my stupidity. She'd gone to the ladies'. Of course. Where else?

I took a sip of coffee that was too hot, burnt my tongue and swore under my breath. I put my hand on the tickets. It was silly to have left them there like that. 'Careless,' I muttered, my voice a little louder.

Tapping my middle finger on the tickets, I took a careful sip of my coffee. Tapped again, the tempo increasing, the middle finger joined by the first, tapped faster, more fingers joining until all the fingers of my left hand were dancing a tango on the airline tickets as my right hand beat a different tune, rising and falling with the coffee cup until it was empty, and it lay there redundant.

The chair screeched as I pushed it back and got to my feet, my empty cup falling to the ground where I left it to blow away and litter the streets of London. I didn't care because a sudden horrible fear had crossed my mind. Maybe she'd been mugged. All the stories I had ever heard about people being mugged on the Underground, in public toilets, anywhere, came rushing across my mind, littering it with what might have happened. I pocketed the tickets and stepped uncertainly towards the entrance to the station. Surely the closest ladies' was down there.

I ran down the steps, eyes flitting back and forward, looking for the sign, seeing it, running to follow its directions, hoping with every breath to pass Joyce on her way back, a tale of some sort on her lips, a tale of any sort... I didn't care, I just wanted to find her safe.

Outside the ladies', I came to a halt, my gaze reaching inside, unable to see very far, searching among the faces coming out standing in their way, forcing them to veer around me, causing them to stare at me with cautious looks.

An elderly woman approached, pushing a trolley laden with

the accoutrements of cleaning. I breathed a sigh of relief. I could ask her to find Joyce for me.

Her trolley was being pushed with the slow pace of the down-trodden, her feet broad and flat in shoes that had seen long service, her progress marked with the *shush shush* of dragged feet and the *clink-clink* of her tools of trade as they rattled against the metal trolley. I stood in front of her, and without as much as a glance, she swerved to push the trolley around me as if I was just another bothersome bit of dust. I moved again, put my hand on the trolley, pushing back as she pushed forward until finally, she woke from her self-induced apathy and met my piercing gaze.

I pointed to the entrance of the ladies' toilets behind me. 'My friend went in and hasn't come out. Can you look for me, see if she's okay?'

The woman's shoulders rose in a shrug and she muttered something I couldn't hear.

'Sorry, I didn't hear what you said, it's noisy in here.' I waited for her to repeat herself, bending down to bring my ear closer whilst trying to keep the entrance under surveillance, afraid I would miss Joyce, that she would somehow get by me and find the table outside Paul's empty, and panic at my absence.

I waited impatiently for the woman to speak, barely heard her when she did, her voice low and guttural and completely incom-prehensible. Then she moved on, pushing her trolley, her feet *shush-shushing*, her backside swaying inelegantly as she got smaller and smaller, disappearing into the bowels of Charing Cross.

What now? I did a 360-degree turn on one foot, the leather sole spinning with ease on the tiled floor.

'To hell with this,' I muttered. With a final glance around, I lowered my chin and walked into the ladies', avoiding startled looks, and kindly meant comments that I was in the wrong place. I called Joyce's name in a loud whisper that became a hysterical yell by the third repetition. 'Joyce. Joyce, Joyce!'

There was no reply but there was a reaction. Just not the one I expected. Instead of rushing up to me to offer comfort and assistance, to put a kind hand on my arm in a gesture of united humanity, instead of any humane gesture at all, the other occupants gave me a swift sideways glance and rushed to the exit, some walking briskly, some running fearfully, all looking at me as if it was *me* who was at fault. *Me.* I wanted to shout after them, to tell them there was nothing wrong with me, but that something terrible had obviously happened to Joyce. But there was nobody standing to tell.

Some women had remained in the cubicles, and I banged on these closed doors. 'Joyce, Joyce, Joyce. Are you in there?' From some came the echo of silence, from others the muttered cries of fright. I shouted louder at these, 'Is that you, Joyce? Are you sick? Come out, please.'

I'd worked my way through the four rows of cubicles before I heard heavy footsteps approaching. I turned to see a large well-muscled security man. His face was grim, his hands moving in a gesture meant to pacify, as if he were patting small children on the head. 'You shouldn't be in here, sir,' he said quietly, his voice light and high-pitched. I wondered how it would be heard out in the station, where the noise of the trains must surely have drowned it. 'You are not allowed in here,' he continued, as if I had stupidly mistaken my way, as if the sight of screaming women wouldn't have given me a large and unmistakeable hint.

I nodded at him. 'It's my girlfriend, I can't find her.' I ran my fingers through my hair, pulling at it to show, in case he was in any doubt, that I was worried. 'I've been pulling my hair out with worry,' I said, just in case he didn't get it. 'We were having coffee, and she just vanished. I thought she had come in here.'

He shrugged broad shoulders. 'She can come in here, mate – you, on the other hand, can't.'

The silence was filled with the distant sound of trains, the noise a sorrowful moan that seemed to surround me, reverberating through me, as if Charing Cross was the only sympathiser. Why would nobody help me?

I tried again. 'She could be collapsed behind one of those doors, there's no answer from some of them,' I said, pointing to a few doors that were shut tight. 'There's more the other side too. She could be dying!' My voice had risen, an edge of hysteria I didn't try to hide. I couldn't have anyway.

The security man was one of those bulkily built men with no neck, but I think he nodded in recognition of my argument. 'Stay here,' he ordered, and went to the first of the shut-fast cubicles and knocked. 'This is station security. Is there anyone in there?'

It didn't take him long to check. 'She's not here,' he said, relocking the last door and stating the blindingly obvious, his tone almost accusatory. Perhaps I looked as distraught as I felt because he sounded more sympathetic when he spoke again. 'If I was you, I'd go back to where you were having coffee. I'll bet she's gone there looking for you.'

Maybe he was right. Thanking him, I left, passing through a gauntlet of irate women on the way out.

I rushed off, back the way I'd come, almost slipping on the steps as I ran, my eyes squinting as I caught sight of the chair I had vacated, minutes, hours, seconds before. I wanted to see her red coat, her lithe body draped in the chair, her head turned, straining as she looked for me.

But the chair was empty.

78

I stared at the empty chair as panic gripped my gut with an intensity that had me double over. A squeal of unbearable anguish forced itself through my gritted teeth, a high-pitched keening that stopped people in their tracks. It had them look around for the wounded animal that had escaped from somewhere, had them shiver and walk on a little more briskly, a little more nervously.

It was unfortunate for me that a young police officer, imbued with all the newest training and well-versed in customer relations and community integration, identified me as being the source of the noise. I had recovered a little by the time he reached me, but felt weak and didn't resist when he led me to the very chair outside Paul's that Joyce had been sitting on earlier.

Perhaps if the young officer hadn't been quite so sympathetic, I wouldn't have told him about Joyce. But he was. Concerned, and so very eager to be of assistance. I told him what had occurred, waving towards the station, the café, banging my hand on the table, patting the chair I sat on, my two hands getting tangled as they became involved in the tale. By the time I had finished, the concerned expression on the officer's face had taken on a harder, more knowing edge, and I had realised the stupidity of involving the police in my affairs. Any of them.

But it was too late. The policeman had got the bit between his teeth, and no matter how many times I insisted I was probably making a big to-do about nothing, that Joyce would probably turn up unharmed, he was having none of it. It quickly became more than difficult. He wanted Joyce's address, so I had to explain that she didn't, in fact, live with me, that I was married, but not to her. Then, of course, he wanted Joyce's address even more and regarded me with suspicion when I told him I didn't have it.

'We used to go to a hotel. That nice one on Northumberland Avenue,' I said, as if my taking her to a five-star hotel somehow made up for my not knowing her address. 'We went there many times.' I wanted him to know it was a proper romantic affair, and not just a cheap sordid quickie.

He didn't seem too impressed. 'But surely you must have some idea where she lives. Haven't you ever taken her home, sent her a gift, a card?' He watched as I shook my head, and I could see he thought poorly of me for what he saw as a slight to Joyce. He just didn't understand our relationship. I suppose he *was* young. 'Not to worry,' he said decisively. 'Give me her surname and I can soon find out.'

'Mitchell.'

He looked at me suspiciously. 'That's your surname, isn't it, sir?'

'It's not an uncommon name,' I replied, trying not to sound defensive.

'And you say you met her here, then she went to the ladies' and never came back. Is that it?'

'More or less. I went to get us both coffee and when I came

back, she was gone. I made an assumption she'd gone to the ladies'. I don't really know.'

He gave a little knowledgeable smirk. 'Maybe she just left you, sir.'

It was the smirk that did it. I should have agreed and walked away. But, dammit, he smirked at me. Me, who worked for Sebastian et Sebastian, who had a house on Elgin Crescent, two wonderful children, a beautiful wife, a life he couldn't begin to understand. The image of Ann as I'd last seen her made me shudder.

'Sir?'

I blinked and dragged myself back from an image that was crisp and clear as if I was still standing over the bath looking down at my dead wife, to the present and much more immediate worry. The officer was looking at me intently. I managed what I hoped was an acceptable smile. 'No, Joyce wouldn't have left. We're going to Caracas for a holiday. Caracas, Venezuela,' I clarified. 'Our flight is tonight. She wouldn't have left me, officer.'

He nodded. 'Wait here.' He walked a few feet away and pulled his radio closer to his mouth. I saw his lips move, his eyes glance my direction and immediately away. Then his lips stopped moving and his head started nodding. And all I could do was sit and wonder what had become of Joyce. What on earth could have happened? Our flight to Caracas was at eleven. We had to get away tonight.

I had to get away tonight.

79

My panicked thoughts were interrupted by the return of the police officer. 'There have been no reports of accidents in the general vicinity,' he said, taking the seat opposite me. 'They cross-checked with station security and there have been no incidents reported in the station either, other than that of a wild-eyed man causing some trouble in one of the ladies' toilets.'

I raised my eyes in disbelief. 'That was me, looking for Joyce. I wasn't wild-eyed, I was just bloody worried. Wouldn't anyone be?' I looked at him. Couldn't he see I was close to the edge... tottering on the rim so that one push would be all it took to send me over into the chaos and mayhem.

He stood again and indicated the café behind with a jerk of his thumb. 'I'll just go and have a word with the staff, see if maybe she came back while you were running around down in the station.'

He questioned them at length, and I was beginning to wonder what was going on. After all, what on earth could they have to tell him? The type of coffee we liked; the type of pastry Joyce liked? Perhaps they were telling him what a devoted couple we were, how we met every day at the same time, sat at the same table, how she always wore red, always smiled when she saw me coming, how she put a bounce in my step.

The officer spent some more time on his radio before returning and sitting once more in the chair opposite. *My* chair, the one I usually took to sit opposite Joyce. It should have my name carved onto it. And the chair I sat on should have hers. All those days of meeting and talking, the memories sweet but edged with despair.

I expected to see a slight smile on his face, to see a degree of envy for the romantic picture Paul's staff would have drawn of us. Instead, with a cold firm voice, he looked me square in the eye. 'They say they have never seen you with a woman. You come here every day and order coffee; you sit here for almost an hour drinking it. They said you sometimes order a pastry, but you never eat it, and leave it behind when you leave. They throw it out. Every day. They say,' he continued in the face of my obvious confusion, 'that you have never been here with a woman. In fact, you always sit alone and refuse to allow anyone to sit in the chair opposite.'

My knuckles grew white as I gripped the table in front of me as if, somehow, I could stay grounded when my world was twirling, falling, disintegrating. I looked up the Strand. It was as it usually was. I stared through the window of Paul's, saw the rows of pastries, the people in their orderly queue. Everything was as it was supposed to be, so what the hell was going on? I was tottering on that damn edge. I wanted to take a step back, maybe even a few, to a different time when everything seemed simpler... before Joyce, Ann and even Jane, back to the boy I once was, the one who believe the future was his for the taking.

'Listen to me, officer,' I ground out, my voice low and ferocious. 'I've been meeting Joyce here every weekday at lunchtime for a couple of weeks. Maybe the staff are new, maybe they have changed shifts or something. Maybe they are lying!'

His eager face had closed in and wore a pinched, mean expression. 'They are the same staff, sir. They all recognise you.'

'Then they're lying.' I leaned forward conspiratorially.

He shook his head, frowning. 'Why would they be lying?'

Why would they be lying? Why? I wiped a hand over my brow. 'They're hiding something,' I suggested, 'they're involved somehow.' I clutched at straws but couldn't grasp even one. 'I don't know... but they must be... they're lying,' I finished, and I know I sounded pathetic.

'But you were in the shop when she' – he lifted his hands and made that incredibly irritating quotation mark movement with his index fingers – '*disappeared.*'

I wanted to reach out and grab him. Hit him. Keep hitting him until something made sense. I wasn't a violent man, but anger was oozing up from somewhere inside, consuming me. It was hard to control, and I could feel it sliding into my words. 'Listen to me, Ann is missing, you have to find her.'

'Ann?' He frowned. 'Who's Ann?'

Had I said Ann? I slumped back in the chair. She wasn't missing. I knew exactly where she was. I could see her... I hoped she wasn't cold and regretted not covering her in towels instead of flowers. 'Or maybe I should have used both.'

'What?' The officer stared at me, his eyes wary.

What? I dragged both hands down my face. I needed to get a grip. 'I meant Joyce.' There was no anger in my words now. I sounded pathetic, broken.

The bright shining new life I'd planned... we'd planned, Ann and I... I shook my head... no, I meant Joyce and I... didn't I... that new life... it seemed to be fading.

The police officer had been staring at me. I saw his eyes flick over my shoulder, and a look of relief flood his face. *Joyce!* I turned in expectation. It was going to be all right. We could start again.

80

But it wasn't Joyce I saw when I turned, and as the bubble of excitement burst, it dropped me back to reality.

The police officer stood and walked to greet a raincoat-clad man. They were joined, moments later, by another man wearing a loud check jacket.

The young officer told his tale. I could see his mouth moving, but any sound he made was lost to me in the continuously heavy traffic of the Strand. He pointed to me and to the café several times. I wanted to run over, push him out of the way and give them *my* version of the story without his bitter, twisted take on it. Instead, I sat with my eyes on the threesome and waited.

Raincoat-man nodded several times and glanced my way, his face an unreadable mask. Jacket-man looked as if he couldn't be bothered even to listen, he stared around as if this was his first time in Charing Cross, as if it were a foreign city he wasn't sure he liked.

When the uniformed police officer left, without so much as a glance in my direction, the two men stood a moment, not speaking. Just staring at me. I sat and bore the onslaught of their eyes while, inside, the pain of my loss was eating away.

Where was Joyce? Had she changed her mind? Was that it?

They approached like hunting animals, and I felt the hairs on the back of my neck stand in face of the threat. It took all my willpower to stop myself rearing back in the chair, to remain calm, in control. Raincoat-man took the chair opposite... *my seat.* I was sorry I hadn't taken the opportunity to switch, but that would have had him sitting in Joyce's chair, so perhaps it was better I hadn't. Jacket-man stood slightly to one side but a little behind me; if I wanted to see him, I had to twist around.

Raincoat-man smiled. 'You've had an eventful afternoon, Mr Mitchell,' he began, his voice trying for sympathetic but failing dismally. Perhaps it was the incongruous smile or maybe the flinty grey eyes. I don't know, but something didn't gel.

He introduced himself as Detective Inspector Phillips, and Jacket-man as Detective Sergeant Dobson. 'We need to get some details.' He took out a cheap notebook and opened it. 'If I could just take your full name and address, to start with.'

My sigh was exaggerated for effect and his smile faded, a frown appearing between his eyes. He opened his mouth to say something, but I stopped him with a wave of a tired hand, 'Okay, okay,' I muttered, and trotted out my name and address mechanically.

His eyebrows rose slightly when he heard Elgin Crescent, as well they might. But if I thought he might treat me with more respect, now that he knew I lived in such salubrious surroundings, I was wrong. His voice got sharper, his eyes narrowing in tandem.

'And you live there with your wife and...?'

'Two children,' I said impatiently. 'They don't know anything about Joyce. And I would like it to stay that way.' I tried to inject some authority into the last few words, the attempt failing as my voice caught and squeaked to a finish. 'There is no reason for them to know, really. Is there?' I was sounding more and more pathetic. I had to get a grip. Find Joyce. Catch our flight to Caracas. Start again. Do it right this time.

The smile reappeared, a hint of cruelty in its curve. 'We've no interest in upsetting your family, Mr Mitchell. But you have reported this lady missing, and until we locate her...'

I interrupted him. 'Actually, to be strictly accurate, I didn't.'

The smile faded, and once again the frown appeared. 'What?'

'I didn't report her missing. In fact, I was telling the young policeman that perhaps I was making a fuss about nothing. That Joyce might have gone home. A misunderstanding, you know.' I shrugged dismissively.

DI Phillips sat back in the chair and looked at me. 'You were running around like a maniac, shouting her name. You've accused the café staff here of lying.'

I cursed that young policeman. He'd put ideas in my head.. and in the DI's head. I could see them, floating there, waiting to cause me problems. Abruptly, I stood. 'It's all been a mistake. I haven't made any formal report and I think I would like to go now. Joyce will turn up at the airport. She knows the time of the flight.'

'Maybe she's gone to this hotel you take her to,' DI Phillips said.

I gave a start of surprise. The hotel, could she have gone there? Why hadn't I thought of that? What was wrong with me? Of course, that's where she was. Probably worried because I hadn't shown up. Damn, poor Joyce. I'll go there, she'll be waiting. I'll tell her about the episode in the ladies', and we'll laugh about it together.

'You're probably right.' I nodded at the detective dismissively. 'I'll go around there and see.'

To my consternation, DI Phillips stood. 'We'll come along with you, just to make sure.' He smiled. 'I've always wanted to have a look-see in that hotel.'

81

What could I say? It would have been churlish to have told the detective to piss off, not to mention a dangerous thing to say to a policeman. Especially in the circumstances. I just needed to keep it together until I found Joyce. Everything would be all right then.

It was only a ten-minute walk to the hotel from the station. The two detectives bracketed me as we walked. What did they think? That I was going to run away? Without Joyce?

Their company, especially that of the detective whose name I had immediately forgotten but whose presence in that deplorable jacket was slightly harder to forget, wasn't going to do much for my reputation in the hotel. But even as I had that thought, my step lightened. What did it matter? I was never going to be there again.

The doorman recognised me, as I knew he would, I always tipped generously. 'Afternoon, Bob,' I said.

'Good afternoon, Mr Mitchell,' he replied respectfully, his eyes glancing questioningly at the two men who walked beside me.

I shrugged, raised my eyebrows in an 'it takes all sorts' kind of way and moved into the foyer.

Joyce and I always had the same room when we stayed there,

and although I hadn't made a reservation for that day, that's where she would be. I just knew it. She had to be. Where else? If there was a little pickaxe chipping away at my certainty, I refused to feel or acknowledge it.

I kept my voice positive, cheerful even, as I approached the reception desk. The receptionist was one I had dealt with before, so I addressed her familiarly. 'Hi. Here I am, back again.'

Her response was five-star, as befitted the hotel. 'Welcome back, sir.' She smiled as if she really and truly meant it.

I nodded. Just a slight inclination of my head in acknowledgement of her recognition, not the nod of relief I wanted to give. It was all as I expected. Joyce would be waiting. I mentally gave myself a kick. Honestly, how could I have made such a stupid mistake?

'I assume we have our usual room. I'll settle up now if I may and we'll leave our key on our way down.' I slid my credit card across the desk.

'Certainly, Mr Mitchell,' she said, and I swear her eyes didn't look down to the card to read the name.

She did the usual clickity-click on the keyboard. Did a couple more clickity-clicks then yet a few more, a look of confusion growing with every clickity, becoming more pronounced on the final click. 'I'm sorry, I appear to have made an error. Did you say you wanted to settle up?'

I nodded sympathetically. After all, even in the best establishment, one is allowed to make a mistake.

She didn't move. She looked down at my credit card and back up at me. 'We don't appear to have you registered as a guest today, Mr Mitchell.'

I shook my head. Really, this was too much.

'We usually have room seven,' I said sharply.

'Yes, but your last visit was a week ago.' She hesitated. 'There is nothing outstanding on your account.'

I hit my forehead with the palm of my hand. 'Of course, it won't be in my name. How stupid of me. I do apologise. It will be in my girlfriend's name. She checked in before me. I didn't make a reservation, this time.' I was babbling, I heard myself and bit my tongue on further explanations that, in any case, were redundant in five-star hotels. 'Joyce Mitchell,' I said, and left it at that.

She gave a smile of acknowledgement and returned to her clickity-clicks. I noticed her nails were glossy red, perfectly manicured. A sparkling solitaire twinkled on her left hand, catching the light as her fingers flew across the keys. Clickity-click.

I could feel warm breath on my cheek and turned quickly, a smile on my lips, expecting to see Joyce's smile, Joyce's mouth, her eyes. Instead, I looked into the bleary, hard eyes of Detective Inspector Phillips and yelped in surprise. I had forgotten completely about him and his seedily dressed companion.

'Seems to be a problem,' he said, stating the blinding obvious.

'Just a slight mix-up,' I reassured him, nodding toward the receptionist, who just at that moment finished her finger dance and looked up.

I could tell before she opened her perfectly lipsticked mouth that the news wasn't good. 'I'm sorry, Mr Mitchell. We don't have a Joyce Mitchell staying in room seven.'

'It probably wasn't free this time. She must be in a different room.' I shrugged a shoulder, trying for elegant nonchalance, hoping the two men behind would see it as that. They, after all, couldn't see the confusion that flitted across my face, the anxiety that shot into my eyes. 'A different room,' I reiterated. Looking down I saw the white knuckles of my fingers, the red-white of my neatly manicured nails, blood struggling to negotiate the death-grip I had on the reception desk.

The receptionist didn't move. No more clickity-clicks. It was stand-off.

When she at last spoke, her voice was the polite but firm one reserved for troublesome guests, the ones who insisted there must be a room available, the ones who questioned the charges, who swore blind they hadn't had a drink from the mini-bar or watched adult movies. I'd heard it used before, in the Northumberland and elsewhere. But never, ever directed at me.

'We don't have a Joyce Mitchell staying in any room, Mr Mitchell. I am sorry.'

She didn't sound sorry. She sounded mean, cruel.

I could feel breath brushing my cheeks again, knew this time it wasn't Joyce. This time it came from both sides as the two men moved in, brushing my arm on each side, straitjacketing me. I could smell cheap aftershave wafting from Jacket-man, but it didn't hide the acrid smell of fear that wafted suddenly from my own body.

'There must be some mistake,' I said calmly. There must be, Joyce had to be there.

The first hint of exasperation crept into her voice. 'Mr Mitchell, I have looked. There is no Joyce Mitchell registered with us.'

Before I had a chance to open my mouth, DI Phillips opened his. 'Perhaps Ms Mitchell came and you didn't have a room.'

There was a flicker of relief in the receptionist's eyes as she turned from me to him. 'I didn't have any requests for a room that I had to turn down. I can check with my colleague. Or perhaps she came while I was at lunch.'

DI Phillips nodded, and we… all three of us… stood and waited as she walked to the far end of the reception area and spoke to the other two receptionists who manned the long desk. She didn't point at me, but after a few minutes, I could feel their eyes swivel towards me. I resisted the temptation to wave and gave a slight smile. I recognised them all from my frequent visits to the hotel. I knew they would recognise me. One of them would have spoken to Joyce earlier in the day and would know where she was.

My fingers still gripped the desk, four fingers above the wood, my thumbs underneath pressing against a carved ridge, pressing harder, feeling the pain intensify, relishing it, grabbing hold of the pain like a lifebuoy to keep me afloat. If I could feel pain, then everything was real. I wasn't dreaming. It wasn't a nightmare, and everything would be okay.

I kept repeating that to myself as I watched the three receptionists huddled together like three witches for what seemed like hours, while I stood corralled by my two guardians, their hot breath dampening my cheeks. They didn't say anything, and I had nothing to say.

With a final nod, our girl turned on her shiny black heels and made her way back to us, her face closed, eyes narrowed.

She stood with her hands resting lightly on the desk before me. There was no sparkle from the ring now. Cubic zirconium, I thought with a sneer, at the same time noting that one of the red nails was chipped. Definitely not top-drawer, I decided. The Northumberland had let its standards slip.

'I checked with my colleagues,' she said, 'but I'm afraid they are adamant. No Joyce Mitchell requested a room in the hotel today.'

82

I forced myself to give a the-joke-is-on-me kind of laugh. 'Obviously, our arrangements have become completely confused,' I said, then added dismissively, 'thank you for your assistance.'

I wanted to push away from the desk, to use the momentum of the push to start walking, and keep walking. But I couldn't with the two detectives glued like barnacles to my side.

Before I could figure out what to do, DI Phillips spoke again, addressing the receptionist. 'Can you give us a description of Joyce Mitchell, please?'

I was surprised at his request. Hadn't I described Joyce in great detail? Or had I? It worried me that I couldn't remember.

The receptionist shook her head and gave a little shrug of her shoulders. 'I've never met her, I'm afraid.'

My thoughts had been drifting but at this my head snapped up. 'What?' I bit out sharply. 'You checked us in just last week, you surely remember.'

Her lips tightened at my tone. 'I remember checking you in, certainly, but I don't recall anybody with you. Perhaps Ms Mitchell joined you later?'

No, Joyce had checked in with me. We'd met at Paul's as usual and strolled over together. She had stood beside me as we'd checked in. I told the receptionist this, she shook her head again.

'I'm sorry. I really don't remember seeing a woman with you. Ever.'

Ever?

I laughed then, the laugh petering out as I realised she was serious. 'For goodness' sake,' I snapped, 'Joyce and I have been here several times over the last few weeks.' I looked toward the other receptionists. 'Perhaps one of your colleagues is more observant.'

She didn't walk away this time; she lifted the phone and seconds later I heard the soft brrr of the phone ringing on the other end of the desk. To my relief, it was a receptionist who had checked Joyce and me in a couple of times. She put the phone down and walked toward us, nodded at her colleague and gave me a slight smile.

'Hello,' I said, allowing relief to show in my voice. 'I'm glad it's you. Perhaps you would be so kind as to give this gentleman' – I indicated DI Phillips with a casual wave of my hand – 'a description of the lady I usually stay here with.'

A lady of obvious intelligence, she thought before she spoke. 'I'm sorry, but I'm afraid I don't remember seeing you with a woman.' She didn't elaborate or explain. Just that blunt ignorant statement. Where the hell was the Northumberland getting its staff?

When the third receptionist was free, she came over. She was no better. How could all three be so unobservant? Joyce wasn't a head-turner but dammit to hell, we had been there several times recently. We had been the picture of romance, strolling in, hand in hand. We insisted on the same room each time, had joked about how it was our love-nest.

I reminded them of it, of comments we had made, of our insistence on the same damn room every time. And what did they do? Looked at me as if I was making it all up. 'This is ridiculous. You're all bloody useless. I'll be making formal complaints about you all. Joyce and I *were* here.' Pity softened the three faces. I wanted to reach across and slap it away. Pity me! Me! I wanted to tell *them* about my house in Elgin Crescent, my job with Sebastian et Sebastian, that I wasn't someone to be pitied... that I had it all.

I turned away from them and their unwanted sympathy. 'You'll have to make do with my description, I'm afraid, Detective Phillips. Anyway, I am sure Joyce will turn up at the airport. She'd never miss this holiday; it's been planned for months.'

DI Phillips's bulldog expression had set. Ignoring me, he looked at the receptionists. 'You mean to tell me that not one of you remembers seeing Joyce Mitchell? That's a bit odd, surely?'

'It's a busy hotel. We see a lot of people,' one of the three said in explanation, 'plus we would be more likely to remember the person paying the bill.'

I watched DI Phillips anally retentive brain's rusty cogs clunking around. 'I suppose that makes sense.'

'What now?' Jacket-man said, his voice bored.

DI Phillips frowned at him but said nothing.

I shook my head, tried for a humorous lilt to my voice. 'This is Joyce all over, she causes chaos wherever she goes. I'll meet her in the airport, and I bet she'll try and tell me that's what we had planned all along.' I gave one of those women-what-can-you-do-with-them smiles, throwing it over one shoulder and then the other, expecting it to be reciprocated by one or other of the two men. It wasn't, by either.

I had to get going. Taking a breath, I pushed back from the desk, pushing against them, catching them off-guard so they had stepped away before realising what had happened. 'I need to get going, gentlemen. Thank you for your help, and I'm sorry for putting you to so much trouble. I'll send you a postcard from Caracas.'

Because Joyce or no Joyce, I had to leave.

83

Neither man recognised a dismissal when they heard it, because they didn't move. Just stood there looking at me suspiciously before exchanging glances with one another in some wordless communication I wasn't party to.

I didn't care. I had to get away. Had to catch that flight.

Suddenly it hit me. What for? If Joyce wasn't with me, what was the point? What would I do in Venezuela alone? It would all fall apart if I stayed, but if I went alone, it would fall apart anyway. My world spun; I shouldn't have let go of the desk.

I stepped back and sagged against it with a grateful sigh. 'No,' I said, committing myself. 'I'm lying. Joyce is the most organised, the most stable person you could meet. Something must have happened to her. You have to find her.'

Typical for the bulldog mentality, DI Phillips picked up on one thing. The wrong thing. 'Why did you lie?'

'For God's sake, does it bloody matter? Try and focus on the important thing, would you? Joyce is missing.'

He shrugged, the two shoulders rising and falling in perfect tandem. 'So why lie? Why try to put us off?'

'Because... I don't know... I'm confused, stressed...'

'Let's sit,' he said, and looked around the foyer. 'Wait here.' He approached a young couple who occupied a corner cut off from the main part of the foyer, and spoke briefly, nodding to where DS Dobson and I stood.

The young man muttered something to his girlfriend and they both stood, gathering their coats and the multiple bags that hinted at how they had spent the morning, and headed towards the lift. They passed close to us and couldn't resist a curious glance in my direction.

I smiled and shrugged and was just about to thank them for their seats when DS Dobson brought my attention back to him.

'Come on,' he said, and indicated the newly vacated seats, waiting until I moved ahead of him, following close on my heel. I wanted to ask DI Phillips what he had told the young couple to make them vacate their seats so quickly. He must have read the question on my face. 'I told them your mistress has vanished, that the circumstances were suspicious, and we needed to question you. They were delighted to be of assistance.'

'I would never describe Joyce as my mistress,' I said haughtily.

DI Phillips gave a humourless laugh. 'Well, she wasn't your wife, and you were doing the horizontal with her. How would you describe her?'

My love, I wanted to say, but knew his lips would curl up in a sneer, so I said nothing. He couldn't even begin to understand what Joyce meant to me. I looked at him in his cheap raincoat and worn shoes, his poorly cut hair, and the tiny scab under his chin where he had obviously cut himself shaving that morning, and pitied him for a life that was so obviously lacking. No, he could never understand. And with that knowledge, I felt so much better.

My voice was stronger, in control. I sat back and crossed my legs. 'May we concentrate on the fact that Joyce is missing?'

'You say you don't know where she lives, so how do you know she hasn't gone home?'

How?

'After all,' he continued, 'you say you were going to Venezuela on a holiday. Wouldn't she have needed luggage?' His eyes narrowed. 'And where are your suitcases?'

Lies came easily to me, they always had. I'd had a lifetime of experience, after all. I could lie without the slightest hesitation, my eyes neither looking to the right or left because I never could remember which direction was supposed to be a giveaway. 'I left them with left luggage, Joyce's too. We weren't going to drag them around with us, obviously.'

The tangled webs were getting too thick. *Where could she be?* 'Can't you put out an APB on her? Isn't that what you should do?'

Jacket-man yawned, showing a set of yellow teeth, then sat forward and looked at me. 'How about a BOLO?' He sniggered and sat back.

I threw him a disgusted look and concentrated on the senior officer. 'Well? Whatever it's called, shouldn't you do it?'

DI Phillips shook his head and muttered something about television programmes. I didn't catch what he said. He took out his mobile and pressed one button. Who could he have on speed dial that would help? 'Milly,' he said quietly. 'I'm going to be late for dinner.' He listened for a few seconds before continuing, 'I know. Again. That's the way it is.' Without a goodbye, he disconnected.

With a jerk of his head that included me and Jacket-man, he stood abruptly and strode across the foyer. I remained seated, even after Jacket-man got up and slouched after him without the slightest glance to see if I was coming or not.

I debated staying where I was, but then realised they had my address. I didn't want them going there, not yet. It was way past the point of no return. The ball was rolling, and it was hang on, or get run over and squashed by the damn thing. I hung on, got up and walked to where the two men stood just inside the hotel door, waiting for me. They started walking just as I reached them, so I didn't have the chance to ask where we were going. I just followed on the invisible leash, ducking and dodging around people as we speed-walked back to Charing Cross station.

I hesitated by Paul's, looked at our seats with an incalculable longing that caught my breath, wanted to sit and wait, sure Joyce would return.

The leash pulled me, and I scampered after the two detectives who hadn't even slowed down. I slipped on the steps down to the station, grabbed onto the rail and held on for dear life. Luckily the two detectives had rounded the bend in front of me and weren't witness to my clumsiness. By the time I caught up, I had regained my equilibrium.

Without warning, DI Phillips stopped and extended one of his hands, palm up. People were walking around us, to and from the trains, up and down the stairs behind us. I wondered if they knew what was going on. Because I sure as hell didn't.

I looked at his hand, then did the only thing I could think of doing, the only thing that seemed to make sense. I reached out my hand, put mine in his and said, 'Well, goodbye. And thank you very much for trying to help me.'

He pulled his hand away with a, 'Tchah.' Then, after wiping his hand on his other arm, as if to rub off dog shit he had mistakenly picked up, he held his hand out again.

'The docket,' he said bluntly.

Docket?

His hand stayed there. I swear it didn't tremble or waver or haver or any-damn-thing. It just floated there, waiting for the docket to reclaim the cases that I had stupidly, stupidly, so fucking stupidly told him I had put in left luggage. A lie to hide the truth that Joyce and I had planned to leave everything behind and start afresh in Venezuela. We had no luggage. No luggage, no docket to reclaim them.

'The docket,' I said as if enlightenment had smacked me across the face. 'Joyce has it.'

The silence separated us from the unceasing movement of the self-obsessed entities that swirled around, in and out, up and down. Normally I would be one of them, but not today. Today I am the other. The one who doesn't belong, who is sidelined, over-looked, the outsider. Part of me relished it. If I had been the hat-wearing type, I would have tilted it over one eye, Cagney style. If I'd been a smoker, I would have spoken with the cigarette clenched between my lips, my eyes squinting to keep out the smoke that would have curled upward atmospherically. Or maybe I would have puffed it sneeringly at the ubiquitous 'No Smoking' warnings.

I dropped my chin and glanced upward from narrowed eyes.

Neither man looked impressed, in fact they were exchanging frankly puzzled glances, so I dropped the cigarette and threw the hat away. 'What now?' I asked, reclaiming my former persona without difficulty.

'Can you remember the docket number?' DI Phillips asked.

I pretended to think deeply, furrowing my brow, and letting my gaze drift out of focus. 'Maybe it was six... or was it sixty... or maybe sixty-six.'

Jacket-man shifted his feet. 'Maybe 106?'

I shrugged. I didn't know, I'd picked a number out of my head and went with it. They'd never get permission to search through all the luggage.

84

If I'd stymied them, it was only temporary. Brushing away the luggage as a dead end, they regrouped and switched tack.

'Okay,' DI Phillips said, and I could see trying to be calm was taking its toll. 'Let me get this straight.' He raised a large hand that by the look of it had never seen a manicure, nails ragged and dirty. He was a smoker too, his index finger as brown as his unfortunate shoes. Making a fist of his hand, he poked one finger out with each point he made. 'One' – he stuck that reprehensible index finger in my face, so close I could smell the trace of nicotine – 'you say this friend of yours, this Joyce Mitchell who nobody but you has seen, has gone missing. Two' – his middle finger sprung up, its nail topped with a half-moon of dirt – 'you don't have an address or phone number for this woman, have no idea where she lives.'

I raised my hand to interrupt. 'That's not precisely true, actually. I know where she lives.'

He kept the fingers where they were. 'Where?'

'I told you. Bristol.'

Jacket-man had been quiet for a while. He shouldered his way between us to face DI Phillips. 'For Christ's sake, let's just take the bugger down to the station and sort this out there.'

Whatever look DI Phillips gave him, he backed off and moved to one side, glaring at me as though this was all my fault.

DI Phillips waved his two fingers in front of my face again. '*Bristol* does not constitute an address, Mr Mitchell. Three' – another finger sprang to attention – 'your luggage is in left luggage and the missing woman conveniently happens to have the docket.'

I was tempted to say that if my luggage was really there, it would hardly be convenient for me. But thought better of it.

'Four,' he said, and now I was seeing his face through the thick bars of his fingers, his eyes squinting in an attempt to meet mine, 'the hotel staff, where you claim you've stayed with her several times, say they've never seen her. And five, you've lied a number of times. And that makes me very suspicious.'

And with that, DI Phillips rolled his fingers back into a fist. After a moment's delay, he shoved his fist into his coat pocket and turned away to talk to DS Dobson, who was standing looking increasingly bored.

I was tempted to run. Jump into a taxi and head to the airport. Maybe Joyce was there. I didn't know where else she could be. Why had she left? Because of Ann? Despite the fact that it had been Joyce's idea, had she left because I'd killed my wife for her?

I could have explained that I'd had a change of heart... but I couldn't, could I, because if I had, I'd have had to admit that Ann's death had been an accident, and that I was only going with Joyce from necessity. It wouldn't have been the best start for the rest of our lives.

So many lies... I wasn't sure what was the truth any more.

There might be no point in going without Joyce, but I couldn't stay either. I wasn't putting my children, Jane and Adam through all that would follow. My arrest, the court case, my imprisonment.

Even if I pleaded guilty. It would be too much for them to take. And too much would come out into the open. They'd find out about my parents. All the years of lies. No, I thought, looking around in sudden terror. I had to get away.

I'd made the first step when DI Phillips turned and pierced me to the spot with his gimlet eyes. 'Mr Mitchell,' he said quietly, walking over to stand next to me. 'We have nothing to charge you with. As far as we can see, no crime has been committed. DS Dobson here would like to charge you with wasting police time but I think we'll forget about that. I would advise you to get some help. You seem to be quite a disturbed man. I don't believe Joyce exists, or your luggage, or that you're going to' – he searched for the name of the country, shaking his head in frustration when it didn't come – 'wherever it was you fantasised about going to. You've a Walter Mitty syndrome, Mr Mitchell. Get help.'

Walter Mitty syndrome! I wasn't using fantasy to escape from a humdrum life... my life was exciting, my future full of possibilities. It was my week to be flabbergasted. I stood looking at the two policemen, my mouth opening and closing like a hungry goldfish and felt a rage sweep through me. Luckily it swept through; I was just about to tell them what I had done. But then it was gone, and I was reeling from its impact, reeling from my life falling to pieces around me.

DI Phillips looked concerned as I swayed. 'Is there someone can call for you?'

Shaking my head, I reached for the wall and anchored myself. 'I'm fine. Thank you. I'll go up and get a taxi.'

Turning away, I started back up the steps to street level, unbelievably relieved to be going. Halfway up, I heard a mobile phone ring behind me, heard DI Phillips call my name. My feet kept going even as I heard his footsteps pounding up the steps after me.

It was over. Someone had found Ann. Probably that irritating Rosario, sneaking back early to keep an eye on us. Or that overly solicitous Julie, believing we could never manage the house without her. One of the two. I turned to watch as the detective came up behind me. He looked at me but said nothing, matching his steps to mine as we climbed to the exit.

'I didn't kill her,' I said quietly, believing it was important to get that in as soon as possible. 'At least, I did plan to, but then she drowned. That was an accident. Honestly. I went in and she was already under the water. I didn't push her under.'

We had reached the top of the steps at this stage. I couldn't help looking at the table outside Paul's, the empty chairs. I stopped and turned to look at DI Phillips. His face was a mixture of puzzled shock. 'Joyce drowned?'

It was my turn to look puzzled. 'No, Joyce didn't drown. I don't know where she is.' My voice, even to my ears seemed petulant.

'So, who drowned?'

'My wife, Ann, of course. Who else would be in the bath?'

DS Dobson had puffed up beside us by now, his breathing ragged and wet. DI Phillips beckoned him closer. 'You better hear this, Dave,' he said, and reaching out, he gripped my arm. 'Mr Mitchell, I'd like you to repeat what you just told me but before you do, I need to read you your rights. Do you understand?'

'Yes, of course I understand.' And I did. I understood it was all over. Listening to my rights being read to me, outside the coffee shop where I had planned for my life to be so different, the irony was almost unbearable.

'Do you understand your rights as I have read them to you?'

'Yes, yes, yes. I understand.' I understood it was all over, all my dreams. The life that had seemed so damn perfect.

'Okay, can you repeat what you told me please, about your wife.'

'About her death being an accident, you mean?'

He nodded, briefly, put his hand up to silence Jacket-man, whose mouth opened to make some comment.

'Simply that. It was an accident; I didn't kill her. I'd planned to, okay, I'll concede that, but I didn't *actually* kill her. She drowned before I had the opportunity. Well,' I clarified, 'I'd changed my mind by then, really. Decided against taking such a dramatic step.'

The two men looked at each other. Finally, with a shake of his head, DI Phillips said, 'Are you telling us that your wife is dead in the bath, in your house?'

It was my turn to look puzzled. 'The call? I heard your phone ring. You came running after me.'

He looked almost sympathetic. 'The call was from my wife, Mr Mitchell. I came running after you because I saw you sway again. I was afraid you were going to fall. We haven't had any report of a dead body at your house.' He nodded at DS Dobson who reached into his jacket pocket and to my horror pulled out a set of handcuffs. Walking behind me, he roughly pulled my arms back and I heard the click as he closed the cuffs, felt the cold metal bite.

DI Phillips was on the phone again, presumably to get some transport because within minutes a police car siren was heard, the noise increasing until it pulled up in front of us. Jacket-man had a hold of my arm and he propelled me forward. Resisting, I turned to DI Phillips. 'Wait! What about Joyce? She is still missing.'

Just then, a flash of red at the corner of my eye caught my attention, and wrenching my arm from Jacket-man's grasp, I turned to look. The seat outside Paul's was, once again, occupied. It was her. Joyce. Just as she was when I'd first seen her, wearing that damn red coat, eating a flaky pastry, sipping on a coffee.

'It's her,' I said to DI Phillips, my voice laced with relief and regret. 'Look, it's Joyce.'

Both detectives look to where I nodded. Then they looked

back at me. 'Where?' DI Phillips said.

I laughed. 'Are you blind? There. On the chair. Outside Paul's.'

Jacket-man had a hold of my arm again and he tried to push me into the car. 'Please,' I beseeched DI Phillips. 'Can't I have a word with her? Please? I need to tell her what's happening. It won't take a minute.'

For the first time since we met, DI Phillips looked kindly on me, sympathy in his eyes and in the half-smile on his lips. Yes, I thought, he'll let me go over to Joyce. Give me time to explain. And she would wait for me. Joyce would wait and when I got out, we'd go and make that life together.

'There is no one there, Mr Mitchell. The chairs are empty. There is no woman there.'

I looked over. She was still there. And even as I looked, she turned and smiled at me. 'Are you mad?' I shouted. 'She's there, look, you fool.'

Then, as I watched, he went over and sat in the chair Joyce was sitting on. He sat and looked back at me, stood up, looked behind at the empty chair, looked back at me and waved at it as if he had magicked her away. I watched as he walked purposefully towards me and said firmly, 'You see, Mr Mitchell. There is no woman there.'

I looked back, wanting to see, as I always did, what wasn't there. Always trying to be something I wasn't. And it was over. I knew it. At last, I understood. There was no Joyce sitting there. There was no Joyce. There never had been. London dust and dead leaves swirled around the empty table and chairs.

This time, I was unresisting when DS Dobson pushed me into the car, more gently now, as if he understood the necessity. As if he knew I might break into tiny, miniscule pieces that would float and swirl to join the debris of the street and be swept away.

Or maybe, just maybe, he realised I'd already broken.

EPILOGUE

Everything happened so quickly after that. I was taken to the magistrates' court on Monday after my arrest, but my solicitor refused to allow me to speak and entered a plea on my behalf of *not guilty by reason of insanity*. I listened to him explaining his reasoning and was impressed. I'd have thought I was insane too, listening to him.

My case was sent to the Crown Court to be heard in some hazy future, and I was brought here to the hospital unit in Pentonville Prison. I've a room of my own. I'm grateful for that.

The Crown prosecution service are trying to argue I'm sane enough, citing the complex arrangements I'd made to ensure Ann was home alone with me. I imagined Rosario and Julie took great pleasure in telling anyone who would listen how insistent I was that they take days off.

It was one of my many regrets that neither of them, in the end, was the one to find my wife. It was the police, following my confession, who entered and discovered Ann laid out in the bath where I'd left her.

The Crown prosecution were trying to argue I was sane... but with the psychiatric report and the evidence of DI Phillips, who was insisting I was, as he succinctly put it, *barking mad*, my solicitor was convinced the Crown Court would find me not guilty.

'They'll make a Section 37 order which will confine you to a secure hospital unit.' The solicitor spoke slowly, as if afraid I wouldn't understand. 'Initially for six months, then there will be a further evaluation and the order will probably be renewed.'

He paused as if to see if I understood and I nodded to keep him happy.

'Unfortunately, there is no limit to the number of times a Section 37 can be renewed, so you may be here for some time.'

Some time, I guessed, was a euphemism for many years to come.

* * *

The psychiatrist I spoke to at length suggested that the traumatic discovery of my parents' death was partially to blame for what he referred to as my 'breakdown'. 'I think you are suffering from post-traumatic stress and adding your financial collapse to that mix...' He shook his head as if to say he didn't need to say more.

He didn't because I wasn't listening anyway.

I did what I was told, went to the sessions with the psychiatrist and psychologist and some *ists* I'd never heard of before and none of which made me any wiser.

Adam visited me this morning. He came into the visitors' room looking ghastly, pale, red-eyed. He sat opposite me and refused to meet my eyes. I waited for him to say something and when he didn't, I muttered a quiet, 'I'm sorry.'

'You're sorry?' He looked at me then and I saw a mix of emotions cross his face: anger, sorrow, frustration. 'So many fucking lies, Jake. All these years. I don't understand any of it!' His

fingers raked hair that had grown a bit too long. 'Ann... I don'
understand why... she could be a nightmare but...' He swallowec
and shook his head.

There was no point in telling him that I'd had a change o
heart, that I hadn't in the end tried to murder his sister. That hac
been an accident. It was too late. Anyway, he knew me for a liar
why would he believe anything I said? It was better to focus on the
positive. 'How are the kids?'

'They're fine. Happy. Jane is spoiling them.'

I didn't ask if they missed me or Ann – I knew what the answe
would be. I also didn't add insult to injury by saying something
good had come out of all I had done. 'And Jane?'

He pressed his lips together. 'She's devastated. Racked witl
guilt too. She said she knew there was something wrong when she
spoke to you that day and wonders if she could have done
something.'

I shook my head. 'Tell her there was nothing she could have
done.'

'Of course there was nothing she could do! You always dic
what you bloody well wanted.' His anger died as quickly as i
erupted. 'You could have told me, you know, about running away
from home. I'd never have judged you, the way you judged me.'

I was taken aback. 'I never judged—'

He held a hand up, stopping me. 'Yes. You did. The posh boy
who wouldn't understand.' He got to his feet. 'I'm not sure I'll be
back, but we'll make sure you're kept updated on how Fi and I
are, okay?'

He turned away before I had a chance to say anything.
watched him leave; his shoulders slumped from the weight of all
had laid on him. I wanted to run after him, beg his forgiveness, tel
him how much he had meant to me over the years... but it was al
too late.

Guilt held my hand as I trudged back to my room, the clunk of the lock loud in the silence as it was shut behind me.

'Was it that bad?'

I sat on the bed, pulled my knees up and wrapped my arms around them. 'Bad enough.'

'I told you what you should do.'

I lifted my head and looked at her through the foggy lens of tears. She was still wearing that damn red coat, but now it glistened and undulated although she was sitting absolutely still.

'Tell me again.' I listened this time... took note of what Joyce said... started to plan. I'd done such a good job for Ann; I was certain I could do the same for myself.

Especially with Joyce urging me on, whispering in my ear day and night, telling me it was the best way.

She'd been wrong about Ann, but she was right this time.

ACKNOWLEDGMENTS

I'd like to be able to say each of the books I've written has come into life fully formed, but that wouldn't be true. Instead, each has been a tumble of words that have been whipped into shape by a team: my incredibly patient and supportive editor, Emily Ruston, the copy editor, Cecily Blench, and proofreader, Shirley Khan. A huge thanks to you all.

Once the whipping into shape has been done, it's down to the marketing team to send the novel out into the world – and Nia Beynon and Claire Fenby, with the help of amazing graphics by Jenna Houston, do a fantastic job of making it fly – thank you all so much.

Writing would be a lonely business without the supportive and friendly wider writing community – readers, Facebook groups and Instagrammers.

Huge thanks to my fellow writers, Anita Waller, Judith Baker, Keri Beevis, and Diana Wilkinson. It's some journey we've been on together!

Special thanks to the writer Jenny O'Brien for her endless support and encouragement.

Thanks too to my Irish buddy, the writer Pam Lecky, and to my US friend, the writer Leslie Bratspis, for your valuable friendship.

I would also like to thank all the readers, bloggers and Instagrammers who read and review and who contact me with their comments, they all mean so much.

And a final thanks to those who underpin everything I do –

my husband, Robert, my large, ever-extending family, and my friends.

And not forgetting our cat, Fatty Arbuckle, who occasionally tries to help by plonking himself on the keyboard!

I love to hear from readers – you can contact me here:

Facebook: www.facebook.com/valeriekeoghnovels

Twitter: https://twitter.com/ValerieKeogh1

Instagram: www.instagram.com/valeriekeogh2

Bookbub: www.bookbub.com/authors/valerie-keogh

Valerie xx

MORE FROM VALERIE KEOGH

We hope you enjoyed reading *The Trophy Wife*. If you did, please leave a review.

If you'd like to gift a copy, this book is also available as an ebook, digital audio download and audiobook CD.

Sign up to Valerie Keogh's mailing list for news, competitions and updates on future books.

https://bit.ly/ValerieKeoghNews

Explore more compelling psychological thrillers from Valerie Keogh.

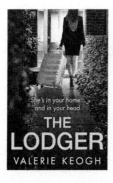 

ABOUT THE AUTHOR

Valerie Keogh is the internationally bestselling author of several psychological thrillers and crime series, most recently published by Bloodhound. She originally comes from Dublin but now lives in Wiltshire and worked as a nurse for many years.

THE

Murder

LIST

**THE MURDER LIST IS A NEWSLETTER
DEDICATED TO ALL THINGS CRIME AND
THRILLER FICTION!**

**SIGN UP TO MAKE SURE YOU'RE ON OUR
HIT LIST FOR GRIPPING PAGE-TURNERS
AND HEARTSTOPPING READS.**

**SIGN UP TO OUR
NEWSLETTER**

BIT.LY/THEMURDERLISTNEWS

Boldwood

Boldwood Books is an award-winning fiction publishing company seeking out the best stories from around the world.

Find out more at www.boldwoodbooks.com

Join our reader community for brilliant books, competitions and offers!

Follow us
@BoldwoodBooks
@BookandTonic

Sign up to our weekly deals newsletter

https://bit.ly/BoldwoodBNewsletter

Printed in Great Britain
by Amazon

56751855R00195